STO

SHORT STORIES

SCIENCE FICTION

S0-BXC-991

Hermit's Swing

Macmillan's
Best of Soviet Science Fiction

Hermit's Swing

VICTOR KOLUPAEV

Translated from the Russian by Helen Saltz Jacobson

Introduction by THEODORE STURGEON

MACMILLAN PUBLISHING CO., INC.
New York

COLLIER MACMILLAN PUBLISHERS
London

Copyright © 1980 by Macmillan Publishing Co., Inc.

Macmillan Publishing Co., Inc.
866 Third Avenue, New York, N.Y. 10022
Collier Macmillan Canada, Ltd.

Library of Congress Cataloging in Publication Data
Kolupaev, Victor Dmitrich, 1936–
   Hermit's swing.
   Translation of Kacheli Otschel'nika.
   CONTENTS: For love of earth—Mindpower—The biggest house.—[etc.]
   1. Science fiction, Russian—Translations into English. 2. Science fiction, English—Translations from Russian. 1. Title.
PZ.4K837He   [PG3482.7L8]   891.73'44   80-18824
ISBN 0-02-566350-X

10 9 8 7 6 5 4 3 2 1

Printed in the United States of America

Contents

Introduction

Fiction is two things: what is said, and how it's said.

Science fiction (this from Isaac Asimov) is three things: "What if —," "If only —," and "If this goes on —," often mixed in various proportions.

Victor Kolupaev's special gift lies in what is said about "What if —."

Science fiction is a hot tile in a greater mosaic called "fantasy." (The late Fletcher Pratt was once moved to remark, "*All* fiction is fantasy!")

Victor Kolupaev often, and sometimes startlingly, moves off the science fiction tile onto the overarching design, and there are stories here which will fill with anguish, if not fury, those hard-core, nuts-and-bolts science fiction addicts who insist that their chosen literature must follow the strict rules of chemistry and physics, and clear extrapolations thereof. For Kolupaev rejoices in the unexplained and the inexplicable and is quite happy injecting fantasy into his space opera. What prompts him to do this is, almost invariably, his great concern for that *inner* space in which dwells the humanity of human beings: love and yearning, the sweet burden of parenthood, self-sacrifice, courage, and loneliness.

What else, for example would prompt a science fiction writer even to entertain the notion that the crew of a spaceship, parsecs from Earth, would experience so poignant a longing for this "big blue marble" that the longing itself would instantaneously return them home?

What else would make a writer create a character who, in the most terrible instant of his life, creates for his three children a whole planet, complete with funny trees?

Along with his compassion, Victor Kolupaev has a funny bone, and like a surprisingly large percentage of his colleagues, the target of his ironies is the bumbling bureaucrat, the pompous administrator. What pleases us so very much about such satire, coming from Kolupaev or Lem or Savchenko, Kafka or Hinko Gottleib, is not at all that bumbling and pomposity appear to be an Eastern and Central European characteristic, but the revelation that they are as universal to humanity as the color of blood. We witness these traits constantly in academia, in big business, in big publishing. A personal reminiscence: I was running a bulldozer on a very high-priority construction job, and one day, driving my machine through a company street, I saw a gang of some twenty hand-laborers filling a trench. I slewed the 'dozer around and made one pass from end to end of the trench, filling it completely, while the shovel brigade applauded enthusiastically. I was then blistered from head to toe by their foreman, who complained bitterly that he now had to transport the gang to another site and go through the trouble of telling them what to do there, when they could have stayed on this one for two more days. I tried to explain to him that it was not hubris which made me backfill his trench; I really felt that the project should be done, and every bit helped. He didn't see the point, and never will. You can imagine, then, my pleasure with Kolupaev's yarn herein about an engineer who finds he can meet a quota for electronic devices by using mental power, purely by concentrating on the blueprints until the devices appear, and that he can meet the quota in two-thirds of the estimated fulfillment time. All hell breaks loose, as you will see. (I wonder if anyone has thought of pomposity as a possible channel for planetary brotherhood and understanding . . .)

Then there's the wild story of the man who collects smiles. Here Kolupaev treads through fantasy to surrealism. For all its hilarity, one must be touched by the collector's archetype, the most beautiful smile of all, given him by a girl who died when she was twenty.

More than touching is the brief tale of *The Biggest House*, a kind of miniature *Aniara*, one that will be with you for long after you have put the book down. And then there's the pretty girl who sells tomorrow's newspapers, and because of something she reads in one of them, makes a frightful choice.

The title story is a novelette, with plenty of fine extrapolative science fiction in it, as well as large portions of the author's humanism. Whether or not you can completely follow the complexities of his theory of time is moot. Maybe it doesn't matter. His strength is in what he says; how he says it may possibly obscure some of the fine points, but the race and flow of his narrative carry well, and the mystery and suspense are sustained, and the final revelation is satisfactory.

One must smile at a minor point. Twice in the story someone has to go and fix coffee and sandwiches. Who is told to go off and fix coffee and sandwiches? Elsa. Not Ezra, not Early, not Sven. Elsa.

In a future of parsecs and galaxies, ships hurtling faster than light, a science which can girdle a world with differential bands of time-rates, will it still be Elsa who has to go for coffee and sandwiches?

Theodore Sturgeon
San Diego 1980

For Love of Earth

1.

A dazzling blue light flared on the 3-D television wall for an instant, flickered, and, spreading out slowly, filled the room. Espas settled down a bit more comfortably in a deep, leather armchair and stretched his legs. He always enjoyed watching the latest news. Holographic images transported him to the four corners of the Earth, to the depths of oceans and into endless Space. He felt himself a participant in events that he could never really be a part of.

For several months Espas had been living in the mountains, in this secluded hotel on the shore of the sea. He never went more than a kilometer from it and averted his eyes from the glider field when he went for his walks. Espas avoided people, although he was generally a cheerful person, often even witty.

He wanted to know everything about Earth, and he would sit by the television wall for hours at a time, delighted that he could see everything.

This passionate love of Earth, its oceans, forests, trees, animals, and cities was almost a sickness with him, but he never thought much about it. If he did, he would just as soon not part with this sickness. Only when his eyes and brain tired from this abundance of information did he go down to the sea, lie on the hot, white sand for a while, scramble onto a small rock, and dive into foaming crests of waves. He would swim a good distance, occasionally floating on his back, and return only when he was thoroughly tired. Then he would lie down on the sand again, gaze at the sky with its white feathery clouds, and when the sun's rays had warmed his whole body, he would rise and walk back to the hotel.

On only two occasions had he forced himself into a glider, soared into the air, and flown to Elsa in Limik. He remembered where she lived, but both times he had stopped short of her door: something inside him had turned him away. He had returned to his hotel, Mountain Hideaway, and settled down in front of the television set.

Each evening he would go down to the bar on the first floor, sit in front of a huge old fireplace in which resinous logs were burning, and listen to the chatter of the other guests. The Mountain Hideaway attracted people who for various reasons wanted a few days respite from their daily affairs. Here, no one intruded in your personal life, no one asked why you had come to this hotel. One could spend days on end scrambling through the mountains or swimming in the sea. One could arrive unannounced and depart as abruptly without giving the management advance notice.

During the few months Espas had been here, he had made no friends. Now and then he would exchange a few pleasantries with other guests. He enjoyed his solitude, enjoyed the feeling of his oneness with Earth. The Earth filled his whole being with happiness.

This evening, as usual, he was sitting at the bar, close to the fireplace, watching the tongues of flame lick the logs. Several men were sitting near him. A burly bartender occasionally brought them goblets filled with hissing drinks.

Next to Espas and closer to the wide-open window sat a tall man of about forty with graying black hair. This in itself would not have made any impression on Espas were it not for one circumstance: often, too often to be attributed to chance, the stranger would glance at him.

Thus did the guests sit for about an hour, and Espas was about to go to his room to participate again in the events offered by the enormous television screen when suddenly the stranger shifted his chair closer to him and asked:

"You are Espas, aren't you?"

Espas did not reply at once. Something about the man's face

seemed familiar. Or was it one of those faces that one meets everywhere on Earth? The eyes looked at him almost guardedly, as if he expected a negative reply, and at the same time, almost mockingly, as if Espas's reply could in no way deceive him.

"Yes, I am Espas," he finally replied, and he rose slowly, hoping to nip the conversation in the bud.

"I'll drop in to see you," said the man. This was a statement, not a question, as if the man had no doubts about his intentions. "In about ten minutes," he added.

Espas nodded automatically. When the meaning of what had been said struck him, he felt uneasy and irritated about agreeing to do something he did not want to do. He had no intention of developing friendships here; it would distract him from his beloved television, his joy and solace.

Espas pushed his chair aside to pass and left the bar with a light step. He was tall, almost two meters, and well built. His walk was a bit strange, as if only the feet, and not the head and trunk, were moving forward. Yet there was a certain elegance in his walk. Two women followed him with their eyes, but he did not notice.

As soon as he entered the room, he turned on the television set and thought, "Let the stranger start a conversation if he wants to."

The newsreel on the television set featured a fishing scene on the Litvund bank, and many large fish, which he could not identify, flapped at Espas's feet. Then the announcer introduced the chairman of the Commission on Remote Space Travel who advised his listeners that a competition to fill crew openings on the *Prometheus-7* expedition was now in progress. Espas smiled; he wouldn't venture into Space for anything. Without Earth he couldn't live a single day. And this expedition would take many, many years.

An old newsreel was shown next. The clips were the last stills of *Prometheus-6*. The shots were so poor that it was impossible to make out the faces of the crew.

But Espas's attention was diverted for a few seconds by a

knock at the door, and he missed the commentator's remarks about the expedition. Communications with the ship had broken off: no signals were coming through now.

It had to be the stranger. Espas led him into the room without a word or an invitation to sit down. But he made himself comfortable anyway. Espas was grateful that he hadn't occupied his favorite chair, although it stood closer to the door. Espas settled into it and stretched his legs. The newsreel was over. Now something from a series, "Journeys through Siberia and Canada" was on the tube.

Without rising from his chair, the stranger leaned over and turned off the tele-wall.

"My name is Roid," he said.

Espas nodded.

"How many months have you been in this hole?" asked Roid.

"Mountain Hideaway," Espas corrected him. "Almost six months."

"It's still a hole," said the stranger as he waved his hand disparagingly. His face, with its stubborn, symmetrical features was half-turned toward Espas. Something familiar about it continued to elude him. Espas was about to broach the subject, but Roid had anticipated his question. "You're trying to recall where you had seen me?"

"Yes," replied Espas. "You have the kind of face one runs into very often."

"I'll grant you that. Although we spent almost two years together. . . . But I can well believe that you've forgotten me. . . . Do you remember anything at all?"

Espas smiled. "Whatever I need to remember."

"H'm, only what you need to remember? And more than that? You're trying to forget, or have you really forgotten?"

For the past six months Espas hadn't given any thought to the matter. He had simply emerged from the darkness, as it were, and now enjoyed life, not his own personal life, but the life of Earth itself.

"I don't need anything," he said firmly.

"All right," said Roid, smiling. "Let's take things in order. How would you like to find yourself on the *Prometheus* expedition?"

"Ha, that's a good one! What the hell are you, a recruiting sergeant? You mean to tell me people aren't signing up?"

"Actually there is a competition for places in this expedition. A thousand applicants for each place. And that's after a general commission culled out plenty. So, you're not interested?"

"No, thanks. It's great for me right here on Earth."

"O.K. Next, you haven't forgotten Elsa, have you?"

"No." Espas's mouth tightened. He didn't want anyone to discuss her. He was still too confused, even here.

"Have you seen her?"

"No, I haven't," Espas replied, only because he sensed something behind these questions. Still, the conversation began to annoy him.

"I know why you haven't seen her. She'd throw you out. *This* Espas doesn't exist for her. You even tried to see her but got cold feet. Come on, you don't love Earth all that much. You're just afraid."

"Shut up!" Espas gripped the armrests of his chair and thrust his whole body forward. "Do you hear? Shut up!"

Roid fell silent, smiled to himself, and said,

"All of us love Earth. . . ."

For about five minutes no one spoke. Espas tried desperately to remember where he had seen this man. What did he want of him?

"What do you want of me?"

"I want you to remember everything and to return. You're badly needed, but you can return only if you want to."

"Return? To where?" Espas knew of no place he wanted to return to. He was very happy here. "Where should I return to?"

In reply Roid threw back a question: "Think hard, now. Think about the time before you came to this . . . this Mountain Hideaway six months ago. What can you remember about it?"

"Elsa," whispered Espas. "My God, how long ago that seems."

"And?"

"A desire to see Earth."

"What else?"

"Nothing more. I can't remember anything else."

"But you want to, don't you?"

"Yes, I do." Suddenly Espas began to understand why he had been avoiding people. Yes, avoiding! He couldn't even force himself to see Elsa. "I do. But I'm afraid. Something terrible must have happened. . . ."

"I don't think you can conceive of anything more terrible. . . ." Sensing that he had gained the upper hand, Roid spoke with him now as a father to a son—slightly authoritarian, but with respect and even a certain affection. "Pack your things. We're going on a trip."

"Where to?" asked Espas wearily.

"To see Kirill."

"To see Kirill? I don't know any Kirill. Is it far?"

"About three hours. You knew Kirill too."

"Did I?" Espas whispered in surprise.

"You did. You knew many people. We're all getting together."

"Why?"

"To clear our consciences."

"OK, I'm ready. I have nothing to take with me."

2.

They left the hotel and headed for the glider field. It had grown very dark. The sky was clear and full of stars. Roid halted, looked up, and gazed for a long time into the black void. Then he spoke.

"Have you ever wondered what it is that drives people into Space?"

"No, I can't understand them."

"A love of Earth. . . . Let's go."

They located a two-seater almost at once. Roid slid back the dome, lit up the control panel, and motioned to Espas to sit down. The glider soared into the sky, hovered briefly while Roid selected the route on a special map, and surged ahead.

"What are we going to do at Kirill's?"

"Talk. And you'll be doing the talking. I would do it myself, but he doesn't want to see me. He's scared of me. You'll have to do all the talking."

"About what? I don't even know the guy."

"About whatever you please. If he asks about me, you can tell him. I'm not keeping any secrets from any of you."

"Look, maybe you can tell me everything so I'll have a better idea of what I must do."

"I suppose that would help. I tried to do it once. But our darling Kruss almost had me put away for it. You know damn well that they'd believe him sooner than they would me. . . ."

Espas leaned back in his seat and closed his eyes, but he couldn't fall asleep. Something stirred in his memory, vague recollections of events, faces. Suddenly he sensed that he had once remembered *everything*, and rather recently, too—perhaps not many months ago. What was this elusive circumstance that he had tried to forget? Had wanted to forget. But he had not forgotten Elsa! In fact, he could remember everything about her—her face, her tender touch, her sweet caresses. He remembered how they had first met, how they had planned to marry. And then there was the parting—without tears, without resentment, but not without pain. It was as if they were parting forever and ever. . . . She had even seen him off! It was more than a parting. She had seen him off to somewhere. But to where? Damn it, Espas, what's the matter with your memory? Try and remember. Try! Where did she see you off to?

Not once in the past six months had he given this question any thought. . . . Roid knew about Elsa. And about him as well. In six months his memory had grown rusty and now his head ached from the effort to think and remember.

"Roid . . . who am I?"

"Oh, just a visitor from another stellar system," laughed Roid.

"Come on, I'm serious. Where were the two of us together?"

"In some distant galaxy."

"So, you don't want to tell me?"

"You wouldn't believe me anyway. Find out for yourself. And I'll try to help you. I have a vested interest in it too."

Dawn began to break. They cruised at an altitude of ten thousand meters. Now one could distinguish something through the fog's ash-gray haze. The taiga stretched out below them. Espas had never been in Siberia. He had always been drawn to warmer regions. Although it was warm in the cabin, he huddled up, shivering.

They landed somewhere on the banks of the Ob in a small village about one kilometer long. The glider was left on the shoulder of a country road leading into a coniferous forest. It was about eight o'clock in the morning. Grasshoppers chirred in the grass. A bird chirped: "Have you seen a bear? Have you seen a bear?" A cargo glider carrying tetrahedral tanks beneath its fuselage flew by soundlessly. Its pilot was a young girl, almost a kid, wearing a white kerchief and a gaily patterned dress. She shouted something, but Espas and Roid didn't catch it.

The village was clean and tidy; two-story cottages lined both sides of its only road. Half the houses faced the Ob, the others, the pine forest. There were few people in sight; mainly some kids toting fishing rods. Occasionally a glider would land in a field near the houses, a small soundless aircraft covered with a checker-board pattern; then, a figure would jump from this local-service glider and hurry off somewhere.

Espas and Roid walked to a small hotel and halted.

"You're going in alone to see Kirill," said Roid. "He lives at the end of the street, in the next to last cottage on the left side. I'll wait for you here."

"What am I supposed to say to him? Or ask him?"

"Anything you like. I've already told you. Just chat with him and take it from there."

"You said that I had known him at one time. So should I give him my real name?"

"If you want to."

"At least can I tell him that Roid sent me? And that you're here?"

"I told you, you can say anything you wish."

"Why can't you talk to him?"

"He probably wouldn't want to see me."

"But didn't you speak with him on the commline?"

"Show me your left hand," Roid said, ignoring his question. "Where's your commdisk?"

Espas blushed. "I still . . . I probably lost it. Wait, no . . . I left it at Mountain Hideaway. But it doesn't work at all. It's broken."

"I presume that Kirill doesn't have his commdisk either," said Roid in a cool, harsh tone. "If you don't have any further questions, go!"

Espas walked along the path near the cottages. Roid disappeared into the hotel. When he reached the next to the last house, Espas halted and looked at it. A very ordinary house. A small fence and a latched gate. He opened the gate and walked along the path to the steps. There the path led to a small ridge. It continued past a tomato and cucumber patch, then past a bed of gladiolas and phlox. A tired-looking woman stepped through the doorway and gave Espas an inquiring look. He greeted her.

"Excuse me. Can you tell me if Kirill lives here?"

"He does," replied the woman. "Come in. My name is Anna."

"I'm Espas." The spontaneity of his response surprised him.

"No, no," the woman whispered, frightened. "No, you won't take him away. He doesn't want to go. And I won't let you!"

Espas regretted giving his name. If it had such an effect on Anna, there must be something to this puzzling mission.

"I'm not taking him anywhere," Espas assured her. "I only want to speak with him."

"Oh, please, I'm sorry. It's just that I'm . . . I worked on the night shift today. There was an accident on the farm. I'm a cyberneticist. I am so tired, tired of everything. Tired of waiting . . ."

"So may I see him?"

"Yes, of course. He went fishing with little Andrew. It's not far. Down the path. By the little bridge. . . . Shall I call them?"

"No, I'll go myself. How will I recognize him?"

"You mean you don't know him?" The woman was dumb-founded. "Well, of course, . . . he's wearing a white sweater, white, all white."

She waited until Espas disappeared over the ridge and then went inside.

The sandy bank sloped gently toward the river. Some fifty meters away Espas saw two people sitting on a wooden bridge—a man of about forty wearing a white sweater and a boy of about seven. They both sat on the boards with their bare feet dangling above the water. Judging from their floats, they weren't having much luck.

Espas walked toward the water and called out loudly, "Kirill!"

The man looked around, clicked his tongue, and said softly, "Well, that's that." Then, aloud, "Hello there!"

"Kirill, I'd like to speak with you." Espas shifted hesitantly from one foot to the other.

Andrew tugged his father's sleeve, "Papa, they're biting."

"Hold my rod," said Kirill, rising reluctantly. He shuffled along the bridge and stepped onto the sand. "Well, what did you want to talk to me about?"

Espas shrugged his shoulders. "Just wanted to have a talk with you. They say that you and I worked together somewhere. Is that true?"

"Could be. The world is a pretty big place. How about you, don't you remember?"

"Nope, I don't remember anything."

"Neither do I. Maybe we met somewhere. Let's sit down on that log. Get a load off your feet." They sat down. "You'll have to forgive me for not inviting you to come to the house. But Anna just came from work and she's very tired."

"Why aren't you wearing your commdisk?" Espas asked suddenly.

"Oh, that. . . . I probably left it home. Who needs it, no one calls me anyway. I spend my time fishing with my son, or we go mushroom hunting in the pine forest. . . . The weather is great."

Kirill yawned. "Well, that's the way it goes."

"Something strange happened to me," said Espas. "I lived at Mountain Hideaway for six months. You know, the place people escape to for a little peace and quiet. Yesterday I began to wonder what I was doing before that. I couldn't remember a thing. Even yesterday I wasn't particularly anxious to remember, but today I feel very different about it. I want to remember, but I can't. I have the feeling that any minute my memory will awaken from a big sleep. But it needs more than a jolt to do that. Would you help me?"

Kirill fell silent, bent over, and found a stone in the sand. He was about to toss it into the water but changed his mind. Still holding the stone, he remained seated on the log.

"I don't know how I can help you. Memory is a tricky thing. Maybe it's better for you not to remember anything. . . . Well, I guess that's about it. We've had a chat. I suppose I'll go now."

"Yes, we've had our chat." Espas rose and, without saying good-bye, began walking along the bank toward the hotel.

"Espas, wait!" Kirill shouted suddenly. "Who sent you here?"

Espas halted. "Well, I'll be damned," he said to himself. He hadn't mentioned his name to Kirill. Did that mean he knew him?

"Roid."

Kirill moved closer.

"Roid? Is he here? Did he return too?"

"So, you know him? Where do you know him from?"

"We went to school together."

"And me? You called me by my name."

"Did I? Well, there is a fellow by the name of Espas who lives in these parts. You look like him. So, I guess it just slipped out. Anyway, what about Roid?"

"Roid plans to get us all together."

"Well, well. I'm going to stay here a little longer with my son." Kirill turned and headed for the bridge.

Espas followed him with his eyes and thought, "It's clear that Kirill knows everything. At any rate, a helluva lot. But for some reason he isn't talking. Looks like he's scared. Roid won't talk because I won't believe him. All right, I'll have to figure it out by myself. Then, there's Elsa. . . ."

Roid met him in the hotel lobby. He asked no questions, but gave Espas a searching look. Espas started the conversation himself.

"There's no doubt that Kirill knows me. In any case he called me by name, although I hadn't introduced myself. But when he realized what he'd done, he talked his way out of it. He said you were an old schoolmate. He was surprised that you were here. . . . You won't tell me everything because I might not believe you. And he won't, because he's scared. That's clear. OK, I'll figure it out without you. I'm going to fly to Elsa right now. I'll find out everything there."

"She'll throw you out. Believe me, you don't exist as far as she's concerned. It's pointless to harass her. Without us you won't be able to figure out a thing."

3.

"Andy," said Kirill to his son. "You stay here and fish. I have to go some place now."

"Will you be back soon?" asked the boy.

"I don't know yet, but I'll try to get back as soon as possible."

Kirill climbed onto the ridge and hurried home. Anna was sitting in the living room, frightened and stunned.

"What's going to happen now, Kirill?" she asked. "Did you tell him everything?"

"I didn't tell him anything. . . . It's enough to drive one mad. Anna, I can't go on living this way. I'm going to catch up with them."

"All this time I've been expecting this: I've been afraid this would happen."

"You wouldn't want to be the wife of a coward, would you? And what about Andy? Someday he'll ask why I'm here. He's not a stupid kid. How will he feel knowing he's the son of a coward?"

"But you love us, darling! You love everything! The whole Earth!"

"Forgive me, Anna." He went over to his wife and embraced her. "Forgive me, Anna."

He left the house and strode boldly toward the hotel. When he saw two men leaving it, he ran and caught up with them.

"Roid!" he shouted. "I'm coming with you!"

Roid and Espas looked around and halted. Kirill was so happy to see Roid that he gave him a friendly punch in the shoulder.

"Captain, Sir!" he shouted. "Damn it, I'm coming with you!"

Roid received him rather coolly but extended his hand. "I was counting on you, Kirill. Really counting on you."

Espas looked at them in surprise and felt rather agitated. They knew each other and probably everything about each other. But where did he fit into all this?

"Espas," Kirill turned to him. "Of course I know you! Although I had begun to forget everything little by little. I don't know how long it would have taken me to forget absolutely everything."

"If you wanted to badly enough, you could have," said Roid. "We're going to fly to see Kruss now. We still have to look for the rest of them."

"Kruss?" Kirill frowned. "I don't remember any Kruss. Did we have a Kruss with us?"

"We did," said Roid. "Kruss, the computer specialist. He almost had me put away in a mental institution. But now the three of us together will have a chat with him."

"He's a bastard all right," said Kirill. "By the way, Vsyevolod dropped by to see me once. I think he was planning to return."

"Do you know where we can find him?" asked Roid.

"Yes. He told me. The Time and Space Institute near Gravipolis. He's the supervisor of a special-problem laboratory. Even on the expedition he had started looking for a theoretical basis . . . especially since he was trained as a theoretical physicist. Shall we go there now?"

"Let's go," agreed Roid.

"Have you had breakfast yet?" asked Kirill.

"No," replied Espas. "We even skipped supper last night."

"With a frame like yours, you sure need some good grub. How about stopping at my place for a bite?"

"No," said Roid. "We'll grab a snack at the hotel bar so we don't lose any time."

They sat down at a table while Espas selected some food at the automatic food dispensers.

"First of all," said Kirill, "None of us has our regular commdisks. I don't think any of us even tried to register for them. But we have our personal disks. We can communicate with each other. We won't be flying together all the time. How many are left there, Roid?"

"One. . . ."

"Only one? For shame. . . . Most likely each of us thought he was the last one. But everyone left."

"Why can't we register for regular disks?" asked Espas.

"Because Roid, Kirill, Espas, Kruss, Vsyevolod, and Santa received them long ago and their numbers have been given to others by now. No one will give us new ones."

All three rose and left the bar. It was now about nine o'clock in the morning. Mosquitos whined, landing on Roid and Espas; they weren't interested in Kirill.

"It's my secret microgenerator that keeps them away," laughed Kirill.

"We need a three-passenger glider," said Roid. "How fast can we get one?"

"You can get a long-distance glider within an hour," replied Kirill. "You have a two-passenger one, don't you? We can manage to get the three of us into it. One of us can stretch out in the baggage compartment. Nice and soft there. You guys haven't slept yet, have you? So, who gets it?"

"Espas can have it," said Roid.

Espas welcomed the idea of a nap and agreed. They squeezed into the glider, which was still parked on the shoulder of the road. Roid took the controls again.

"We'll arrive in the evening," said Kirill. "Vsyevolod won't be at work then. I suggest that we wire ahead so we don't have to start looking for him when we get there."

Roid sent a wire on the glider's special transmitter.

Meanwhile, Espas didn't have the slightest idea of what was going on. Of course, as soon as he was prepared to believe, they would tell him everything. But he himself must try to remember something. Take Roid for example. Espas was now convinced that he had known him at one time. And Roid's manner of speaking? A somewhat authoritarian voice. His bearing? Slightly aloof, calm, almost without emotion. Kirill had called him "Captain." Who is usually addressed that way? The captain of a bathyscaphe, the leader of an expedition, the captain of a spaceship. Was he, Espas, ever at the bottom of the ocean, in Space or on any other expedition? No, he couldn't recall participating in any of these adventures. But even Kirill didn't remember everything! Hadn't he forgotten about Kruss, who, Roid said, had also been with us? If Kruss had been with us, perhaps he, too, remembered nothing. Most likely Roid had told Kruss everything and Kruss tried to have him committed to a mental institution.

"I spoke to the manager of Mountain Hideaway," said Roid, interrupting Espas's thoughts. "They'll forward your commdisk to Vsyevolod in Gravipolis. Both Kirill and I are wearing ours now. We can contact each other whenever we wish."

Espas dozed off. He dreamed of a black void strewn with shining dots. He had a strong salty aftertaste in his mouth. A human face, illuminated by a short beam of light, bent over him. It was a woman. Some sort of obstacle separated them. Then he began to slip back into the void again.

"Espas, wake up! It's me, Verona. Espas, wake up!"

He woke up. Between the dark backs of the two seats ahead of him shone the lights of the instrument panel. Bright stars sparkled through the transparent dome above his head. He sensed that something familiar was happening out there.

"Verona," he whispered.

"He's up," remarked Roid. "What? What did you say?"

"Verona," repeated Espas.

"Verona!" shouted the normally calm Roid excitedly. "Do you remember Verona?"

"I just saw her."

"Verona remained there alone! Do you understand? Verona was with us. She remained there alone. Finally something's come back to your memory! She saved your life. What else did you remember?"

"She looked at me and said, 'Wake up, Espas. I'm Verona. Wake up, Espas!' And then only a black void. And white dots, like fireflies. And that's all."

"What was she wearing?"

"I don't know. Our faces couldn't touch; something came between us. I didn't see anything more."

"It was your space suit, Espas. A special protective space suit. We encountered some kind of cosmic body. Then you and Verona went to take a look at it. For some reason, there was an explosion, and you were badly bruised. Three cracked ribs and some head injuries. Am I right?"

"Yes, you are. So, does that mean I was in Space? It could have happened somewhere in the asteroid belt. I thought I'd never been in Space."

"It happened a little further out," smiled Roid.

"But where did Verona remain? Not on Jupiter?"

"No, no. . . . It's great that you've begun to remember. Now it won't be long before you believe us."

"I believe you right now! I'm fully convinced."

"Wait until we see Vsyevolod. We're over Gravipolis now. The dispatcher wired that Vsyevolod would wait for us at his villa, somewhere on the shore of the Hudson. The glider is under ground control now, so we'll be there in five minutes."

The glider began to descend and soon landed on a small, brightly illuminated field surrounded by pines. Roid slid back the dome. The three men jumped to the ground. Espas stretched his legs; the baggage compartment hadn't been that comfortable after all.

A man emerged from the darkness. He was slightly shorter than Espas but much broader across the shoulders. One sensed great strength in his arms. He ran toward them at an odd angle, waving his hands comically.

"Hi there, everybody!" he shouted. "Oh ho! It's Roid! And Kirill! And this, of course, is little Espas! Hey, friends, just wait until you taste my coffee! Let's hurry. I'm alone now. A friend had stopped by, but I managed to get rid of him so we wouldn't be disturbed. Oh, Espas, here's the bracelet with your commdisk." He handed Espas a shiny object. "I was wondering why it had been sent to me. Shades of Treasure Island, like the mark from the pirates. Well, let's go, guys. I'm sure glad to see old buddies."

They sped toward the villa, and as they passed a lamppost, Espas glanced at the inscription engraved on the bracelet's inner surface: "Espas. *Prometheus-6.*"

4.

Burly Vsyevolod managed to fill half the room, one wall of which was lined with shelves of many varieties of cacti. The coffee was good and hot and served with cookies and halvah.

"Sit down, friends. Make yourselves comfortable." Vsyevolod bustled around his guests. "Four chairs, four guys, and a four-sided table. Quite a coincidence, eh?" He laughed heartily.

"Vsyevolod," said Roid, "The three of us have decided to return."

"I haven't promised anything yet," Espas protested.

"Never mind, you're a decent sort, you'll return. So, Vsyevolod, as I was saying, we've decided to return. Now we want to ask you, Will you come with us?"

"Listen fellows, I'd take off with you right this minute! My

space suit is lying over there in the corner. What a question!
We'll finish our coffee and get going. So, drink up. If you knew
who brewed it, you'd go nuts."

"Vsyevolod, we're dead serious," said Kirill. "And you're treat-
ing it like a big joke. It's not that simple."

"Enough said! It's all settled. What's there to discuss? Let's
finish our coffee and take off. Tell me, when did you leave? Espas
and Kirill had left when I was still there. I know. When did you
decide, Roid?"

"Two weeks ago. Everyone had hidden, like rats. I barely managed to find Espas. He's so tall, it was easy to spot him. I had
known from before where Kirill lived. . . . The only one left there
was Verona."

"Verona, Verona . . . I forgot something. Ah, yes, now I remember. First I tried my luck at the Academy. I told them I had an
idea, but to them it sounded as wild as spending weekends on the
moon. . . . They didn't even laugh at it. They threw me out. I
rushed around here and there and finally settled down here, at
the Time and Space Institute. They're crazy about my ideas here.
. . . At the beginning I couldn't figure out why the devil I was
thinking about her. She was on my mind and that was it. I
couldn't even work, couldn't do my mathematics. I was a complete flop. I'd look at a sheet of paper and see everything but
math. They said I had begun to rave. Then, one day I walked
into the house, and there she was. 'Listen, Sevka,' she said to me,
'I know you love me. You even went on the expedition because I
was on it. A week after my husband saw me off he found himself
someone else. . . . So, now I'm your wife. Let's clear out of here.' "

"Who is she?" Kirill couldn't restrain himself and laughed.
Sevka had told his story very comically.

"What do you mean . . . who is she? You didn't know? Zhenka!"

"Oh, you liar, you!" came a voice from the doorway. 'Oh, does
he love to exaggerate! So, *I* came to you. . . . Is that the way it
was?"

"Zhenka!" shouted Roid.

"Zhenka, I sent you next door . . . only for five minutes . . . so I could have a little chat with the guys. Then I would have called you back."

"Well, all right. Everyone knows how you love to talk. Roid, of course you haven't come here just to visit, have you? And you are Kirill. And, is this . . . Espas? Am I right?"

"You are," confirmed Kirill. "But I barely remember you. Very, very vaguely."

"We all know that feeling," said Vsyevolod. "At first I remembered almost nothing, as if I'd just come out of a shell. Then I began to wonder about the past? At that point Zhenka came and a few things began to fall into place. And I began to remember. When I decided to return, almost everything came back to me. I thought this was some sort of secondary phenomenon, but then I figured it was more than that. Something compelled us to come here and forget where we'd come from. It's as if we had disturbed some people and they didn't want us to visit them. First there was an attempt to frighten us. Remember Espas's accident? Mere child's play. Then they found a method. An infallible one."

"Verona stayed behind," interjected Roid.

"From what I've heard and seen these past few days . . ." began Espas.

"It hasn't been days," interjected Roid again.

". . . I've come to the conclusion that all of us were members of an expedition that was launched on *Prometheus-6* two and a half years ago."

"Well," said Roid, "so you believe it? You still haven't remembered much, but you believe it, don't you?"

"It doesn't all come together yet. But you're not trying to put something over on me, are you?"

"That's why I didn't tell you everything at once. You would have sent me to the nuthouse."

"Probably. . . . But what about the ship. . . . Did it return too?"

"No, Espas," replied Roid. "It did not. The ship is continuing its journey. Verona remained alone on *Prometheus-6*. All alone! Do you understand?"

"Then how the hell did we get down here?"

"We still don't know the physics and mechanics of the phenomenon. But some reasons for it are quite clear. First, everyone
yearned for Earth. All of us wanted so desperately to find ourselves back here again. And secondly, we feared we would never
see Earth again. . . . Those two are quite enough."

"But Verona stayed!"

"Verona and I were left. We tossed a coin to decide who would
leave the ship. I won. I was convinced that you weren't returning
to *Prometheus-6*. So I had to assemble all of you and convince
you to go back."

"Bullshit! Zhenka and I already had our bags packed. Right,
Zhen?"

"That's true," she said.

"So, there are five of us. Kruss is the sixth. Who knows where
the rest are?" asked Roid.

"I know where Santa is," said Zhenka. "But it's pointless to call
her here. She's getting married."

"To whom?"

"I don't know. But she's a good gal . . . always wears her
commdisk bracelet." Zhenka flipped over the disk on her own
bracelet. It didn't glow. She repeated the call several times. No
one answered.

"We can try to contact Robin," she suggested. "We haven't seen
him at all. But he called us once. Said he was going to devote his
time to submarines. 'An irrevocable decision,' he said. But should
anything happen to us, he would come to our aid immediately."

"Call him, Zhenka," said Roid.

Zhenka touched the dull disk again. Seconds later, Robin's anxious face appeared.

"What happened, Zhenka?"

"Robin, five of us have gathered here—myself, Vsyevolod, Roid,
Kirill, and Espas. Roid wants to speak with you. All right?"

"Put him on," replied Robin, without the slightest enthusiasm.

"The five of us have decided to return. Verona is the only one
left on *Prometheus-6*. We're doing this voluntarily. It's impossible
to live this way, haunted by guilty consciences, knowing that we

are cowards. We love this Earth. But it's our very love for it that drives us to unknown worlds. I guess it's easier for me than for the rest of you. I don't have a single relative left on Earth. But I love it anyway. I'm here now and I've come here for you and the others. The flight must continue."

"Roid, it's not simply a matter of continuing our expedition. An expedition should produce results, something new and unknown. Well, we all encountered such a phenomenon. No other single discovery ever made can compare to it. People must be told about it. I went to the Council on Intergalactic Problems three times. And three times no one believed that I was Robin, that I was a member of the *Prometheus-6* expedition. You've got to convince them to believe you. Maybe they'll send out another expedition. They are making preparations for a *Prometheus-7*. But you must prove to them that everything that happened to us actually did. Do that and I'll agree to return."

"I had also thought of approaching the Council," said Kirill. "But I decided immediately that they wouldn't believe me. . . ."

"Listen, my friends, they can't believe we're all lying," boomed Vsyevolod. "Let's go bow down before the Council chairman and bang our heads against the nice, shiny parquet floor and maybe we can get something to filter through to that brain of his."

"All right, we're leaving today. Robin, are you down in a bathyscaphe now?"

"No, I didn't go into submarine work, after all. In three hours I'll be at the base of Kilimanjaro. Where are you bound for now?"

"I would like to meet Kruss again. We'll all go together to see him. He doesn't wear his disk bracelet any more. He doesn't consider himself a member of our expedition. We'll meet you at the Council at 1200 World Time."

"OK, I'll wait for you." Robin turned off the disk.

"I think he's a little annoyed with us," said Kirill.

"Nothing puzzling about that," said Espas, expressing his opinion on the matter for the first time. "At least he tried to do something without fear of being disgraced. He has a right to be angry . . . at me, anyway."

"Finish your coffee and let's go," said Vsyevolod. "We'll show that Council, all right!"

"We have a two-passenger glider," said Roid. "We need another one . . . a three-seater."

"Aren't you counting Kruss?" asked Espas.

"He doesn't exactly live in a desert," said Roid. "He got himself a job as custodian at the Space Museum. He's in charge of an exhibit called *"Prometheus-6."* He shines our things that were donated to the museum and tells visitors about what great, strong, and courageous people went off into Space on *Prometheus-6*, including one Kruss, the ship's computer specialist. I can imagine what he says about him."

"I want to have a chat with him too," said Vsyevolod. "I'll call for a glider right away."

5.

The Space Museum was located in a Paris suburb. It was an enormous glass building situated on a natural elevation. On the broad, stone steps leading to the building young couples lounged, children romped, and groups of tourists and individual visitors climbed toward the entrance. Roid, Kirill, Vsyevolod, Zhenka, and Espas entered the lobby and joined a group that was on its way to view the *Prometheus-6* exhibit.

As Roid had suspected, Kruss led the tour. And one could see that he had become rather well versed in the delivery of eloquent lectures. The astronauts were described in the most glowing terms, and Kruss himself certainly did not occupy a back seat among the heroes.

The tourists studied the displays—the inner settings of the cabins and the ship's compartments—with interest. Suddenly Espas noticed a plaque with the inscription:: "Espas. Navigator." He entered the cabin and looked around in surprise at its fittings, even daring to touch some of the objects.

At first the group of astronauts lingered at the rear of the tourists. Then Roid and the others moved forward to the first rows until they were almost face-to-face with Kruss.

Kruss recognized them. For an instant the blood had drained from his face and his delivery had floundered. Still he managed to complete the tour. When the tourists had gone he alone remained with the crew of *Prometheus-6*.

"Kruss," said Roid. "There's no point pretending you don't know us. We've decided to return to *Prometheus*."

"My name is Anthony," replied Kruss. "It's amazing how you resemble the crew of *Prometheus*. If you'd like, I'll show you the display of their three-dimensional photographs."

"*We* are the crew of *Prometheus*," Roid interrupted, but Kruss began to speak again:

"People say that even I resemble one of them. Kruss . . . is that who you said I resembled? An amazing coincidence. What are we standing here for? Come, I'll take you to the director of the museum. An amazing coincidence."

"Kruss, we're going back. And that's it. Are you coming with us? Each of us had his or her own reason for returning to Earth. But no one felt any better for having come back, only shame and guilt for abandoning our responsibilities. To regain our self-respect, we must return."

"That's all very interesting," replied Kruss. "But who will believe that you are the *Prometheus* crew when the ship is somewhere in Space, twenty parsecs from Earth? No one!"

"We're on our way to the Council on Intergalactic Problems. We have a lot of facts to present to them. They'll believe us."

"Will you admit your cowardice?"

"Yes, we shall. Moreover, we'll overcome it. You know, Kruss, you were the first one to leave the ship."

"You're wrong! It wasn't me! It was Espas! Try to remember. And before him, many wanted . . ."

"So, you're Anthony, eh?" asked Vsyevolod. "Basking in the rays of your own glory? You'll spend your whole life feeding on it, extolling yourself, admiring yourself. Because you think no one will learn the truth? Because *Prometheus* is destined to return before your death? Think about it, Kruss. There's still time."

"No! You won't dare go to the Council!"

"We're leaving," said Roid. "We don't have much time." They left.

"I remember him," said Espas. "In fact, everything's beginning to come back to me."

"I remember him too," said Kirill.

6.

Everyone gathered for dinner at two o'clock. In the small, cozy dining room stood eight tables with four places at each one. People usually broke up into groups, sometimes moving to different tables several times during the dinner hour for a change of company. Near one wall stood twelve automatic food dispensers, offering the crew dishes of their choice.

Roid was a vegetarian; he said it kept his mind clear. Vsyevolod loved his meat, often consuming five steaks at a single meal. Espas, on Zhenka's instructions, was observing a special diet, although he felt rather well now.

Dinner was always a cheerful time. Besides, one could exchange ideas in a relaxed atmosphere, argue, and simmer down with a cool drink or a cup of coffee.

But recently the mood had shifted. There was a lot less joking and laughter. Less informality. An exaggerated politeness. Now, quite the reverse of the early days of their journey, there was constant talk of Earth: "My little Andrew . . .," "Once my brother and I . . .," "My wife said to me . . ." Everyone would cluster around the speaker and drink in every word. Questions that would have been considered absurd at another time or place were asked. This condition was diagnosed as nostalgia by Zhenka, the expedition's physician.

They had been in flight for two years. Their yearning for Earth and loved ones left behind grew stronger and stronger. The ship moved faster than the speed of light. They knew that the people they discussed had long since matured, aged, or passed on. For the past twenty-two months they had had no contact with Earth. It would be two more years before they reached their goal—Blue Star, where, on one of its planets, they expected to find life, possibly intelligent life.

Captain Roid introduced changes in the ship's daily routine. Physical exercise was increased and the crew met together more often. But it was all in vain. Their yearning for Earth assumed a strange form. With increasing frequency the crew requested Captain Roid's permission for a jaunt outside the ship, and for hours they each drifted about alone in the void although they pretended to prefer the company of their shipmates.

One day Robin, not having breathed a word about it before and not addressing anyone in particular, said aloud with mixed joy and sadness, "If you only knew what a beautiful granddaughter was just born to me. . . ."

He didn't notice the surprised looks around him.

"Hey, why don't I hear any congratulations?" he said softly, looking at everyone.

Roid went over to him and shook his hand.

"Congratulations, Grandpa!" He said it so simply and naturally, as if there were nothing contradictory or untruthful in Robin's announcement. The others followed Roid's example while Robin sat there happily accepting congratulations from his crewmates.

Roid went to his quarters immediately and summoned Zhenka a few minutes later. The following day all hands underwent a medical checkup. Everyone realized that this had been inspired by Robin's eccentric behavior. But he alone did not understand that. Zhenka subjected him to a psychiatric examination using all the tools available to her aboard ship. His mental health was pronounced excellent. But the "granddaughter" obsession persisted.

The second peculiar incident involved Tracy, the ship's cyberneticist. He happened to remark that *Prometheus-7* was being prepared for an expedition and he named the date of departure. That there would be a *Prometheus-7*, followed by a *Prometheus-8* and so on was general knowledge. But knowing the precise date of departure of *Prometheus-7* was another matter entirely.

He had dropped the information in passing, apparently inadvertently.

The following day Zhenka told Santa that once again she had failed to see her daughter.

Then Kirill informed Roid that his son Andy had broken his leg. And he asked to be excused from his regular watch in the control room. Roid agreed to take over Kirill's shift. Then something incomprehensible happened. Kirill put on his space suit and left the ship for an airing; but one day passed and he still had not returned. His oxygen supply was only enough for twenty-four hours. Roid, Verona, and Conti, the third pilot, scoured Space in planetary ships but found no trace of him.

Toward the end of the second day an ecstatic Kirill returned to the ship and announced, "Everything's OK. The doctors say it will heal without leaving a scar."

An examination of his oxygen tank indicated that only an hour's supply had been consumed.

Roid summoned Kirill to his quarters. Then he called in Robin, Tracy, and Santa. Vsyevolod, Conti, and ship engineer Emmi came voluntarily. Then he summoned the rest of the crew.

The interrogations yielded the most incredible information: Seven members of the ship's crew had each made several visits to Earth.

Actually, it had all started with Robin when he had stepped out of the ship and into Space. These solitary space walks were absolutely essential for him: Here his thoughts were his own and no one distracted him from this activity. Lately his thoughts, like those of his crewmates, were centered on Earth, on his family whom he would never see again. He was filled with such a powerful, overwhelming desire to see his family that he scarcely registered surprise at finding himself standing in the middle of his own study in his own home. But the absurdity of the situation—the fact that he was attired in a space suit—sobered him up somewhat. He decided to take advantage of this unexpected visit, leaving clarification of the causes of this phenomenon for another time. First he had to get out of the space suit. Then, he cautiously opened the door leading to the staircase and heard crying.

An infant was crying. He heard the voices of two women and recognized them as belonging to his wife and daughter. From their conversation he learned that a granddaughter had been born. He didn't dare show himself. Returning to his study, he donned his space suit, and . . . once more found himself drifting in a void, no more than a kilometer from the ship. Reaching it, he passed through the air lock. At dinner he could no longer restrain himself from blurting out the news of his granddaughter's birth. From that time on he began to visit his home regularly.

Tracy, Santa, Kirill, and all the others who left the ship periodically for space walks had similar experiences. Kirill even lived at home for two days. Although his wife couldn't make any sense of his explanations, she simply accepted the sudden appearance of Kirill, who supposedly had departed forever, as proof that he could come home. She didn't want to let him leave.

The mood aboard ship shifted, as if a heavy weight had been dropped from people's shoulders. Those who had visited Earth pressed each other for details. Those who hadn't began at once to plan such trips. Only Roid and Verona declined to visit Earth—Roid, because he had neither family nor friends there, and Verona, because she knew she could never force herself to return to the ship once she had visited Earth.

Vsyevolod and Roid tried to investigate this phenomenon, but they didn't know how to approach it. Besides, it seemed almost too incredible to accept. The simplest assumption was that it consisted of a wave guide, a very narrow one in three-dimensional space through which people could pass from Space to Earth and back. When people disappeared, the gravitational field analyzers recorded a small surge, and when they returned, the same surge occurred, but the polarity was reversed.

No one knew when this phenomenon began or when it would cease. A schedule permitting brief visits was arranged, but nothing was to be taken from the ship or brought back to it.

For several days everything proceeded normally, except that the crewmates grew impatient waiting for their individual turns. Then one day, Kruss did not return. Another day passed, a week, and still no Kruss. Tracy followed suit without dropping the slightest hint of his intentions. Then, in succession, Espas, Kirill, Zhenka, Conti and Emmi left. For a while after that, the situation stabilized: No one left the ship and no one returned.

Suddenly, one day, Vsyevolod, Robin, and Santa disappeared.

Prometheus-6 continued its journey through Space. Its crew consisted now of only two people—Verona and Roid. They continued to work, and Roid patiently awaited the day when Verona, too, would abandon the ship. Although he didn't feel Earth's powerful attraction as the others did and could not justify their actions, he still hoped for their return.

About three months after Roid and Verona had been alone on the ship, they overtook *Prometheus-1*. Roid's call to the ship went unanswered. For eighteen hours they ran a parallel course, and Roid managed to get a good look at it. Although it had gone off its charted course, it appeared completely intact. The ship was deserted.

By that time Roid had concluded that his crew would never return voluntarily, therefore someone had to seek them out and convince them to come back. He and Verona cast lots and he won. Verona remained alone on the ship.

Roid found Kruss very quickly, but Kruss insisted it was a case of mistaken identity. With Kirill, too, Roid felt his mission was hopeless. He found no trace of the rest of the crew, and he was afraid to risk approaching the Council. Espas was spotted quite by chance: he stood out in any crowd. Then he and Espas had flown to see Kirill. . . .

7.

The chairman of the Council on Intergalactic Problems had known all the members of the Prometheus expedition personally. It wasn't his fault that he had refused to believe Robin on the three occasions Robin had presented himself to the Council. Now, besides him and the other astronauts seated at the round table were physicists, psychologists, and other scientists.

"Well," said the chairman when Roid had finished his story,

"this amazing phenomenon will be investigated. It's a strange thing. . . . We all considered the 'time paradox' indisputable. That means we are dealing with something else here. We are pleased that you were able to summon up the courage to come to us. I can understand your feelings. I can understand how desperately you longed to return to Earth. And here you had to overcome a formidable psychological barrier in order to present to us a complete account of what had happened. There was shame and the fear that you would not be understood. In a certain sense you were alienated from Earth. It's good that you are back with us again. What are your plans?"

"The six of us are returning to *Prometheus*. Verona can't hold out much longer by herself. We've excluded Kruss from the expedition. Of course you may not agree with us. But here is what we would like to do. There are still four of the crew somewhere on Earth. It's possible that they have been trying to reach each other and contact the Council. They must be helped to find each other and to return to the ship."

"Your wishes will be taken into consideration. We shall locate Santa, Tracy, Conti, and Emmi."

"And one more request, Mr. Chairman. May we ask you not to make our cowardly action public, at least for the time being?"

"You needn't worry about that."

"Then we are going to leave. At 0800 we shall put on our space suits and take off at one-minute intervals."

"Very good. The appropriate apparatus will be ready by that time. We hope that your flight will yield us at least some information. I want to thank Vsyevolod and Robin for the research they conducted. Everything you have left here for us—materials and other information—we shall use for *Prometheus-7*. The program for its expedition will be changed. *Prometheus-7* will concentrate on the investigation of the phenomenon you encountered. Your mission remains the same. On the return trip you may abandon the ship and return to Earth. We shall await your return with impatience."

At three o'clock in the afternoon they left the Council building. Vsyevolod flew to his villa near Gravipolis; Kirill, to the banks of

the Ob; and Espas, to the Adriatic Sea. A meeting was being
arranged for Zhenka and her daughter. Robin flew to the British
Isles, and Roid to the Apennines.

8.

Roid was the first to approach the ship, and for a minute he
waited anxiously for Espas. But Espas appeared right on schedule. They were immediately in radio contact with each other.
Five minutes later all six approached the ship together.

"I wonder how Verona is doing." thought Roid to himself.

When they were close enough to the ship to distinguish its
details, they suddenly sighted five people in space suits flying
toward them. The ether was filled with excited cries:

"Roid, you all returned?"

"Who's talking?"

"Santa!"

"Tracy!"

"Conti!"

"Emmi!"

"Verona!"

Within minutes everyone had gathered in the ship's lounge and
exchanged greetings. Verona was almost in tears.

"How did you all get here?" asked Roid.

"The four of them turned up last week," replied Verona.

All had seen Earth again, all except Verona. . . .

"Verona," said Roid, "tomorrow we're sending you down for a
week. You will see Earth."

But the following day they missed the region where wave
guides formed. Verona did not see Earth, but she took it very
well. Her crewmates hardly knew what to say to her. Then Roid
went over to her and kissed her.

"This kiss is from your mother," he said.

For this he had flown to the Apennines.

Prometheus sped on toward Blue Star.

Mind Power

"Nani," said the chairman of the Council, "the director of the Institute is on his way. Also some people from the Committee on Intragalactic Problems. Get me two specialists on mid-twentieth-century affairs. Send them over immediately."

Nani, a section head at the Time Institute, didn't ask questions. Something pretty serious must have happened if the director and specialists had been summoned. Who in his section should he send over? he wondered. Santis, perhaps? Yes, that would be the man . . . Aleksandr Tikhonovich Samoilov (Santis to his colleagues). And his friend Erd.

"Nani," continued the chairman, "remember, no verbal communication with Santis or Erd unless absolutely necessary. What's of utmost importance here is a silent meeting of the minds."

Nani nodded. Three more people entered the room, all strangers to Nani. The chairman started to rise from his seat but the director stopped him.

"Let's leave the introductions for later. First we'll finish our business. The problem is as follows: We have a city and an organization in that city. We have the names of both. The organization has a plan, and that plan must be fulfilled. More specifically, it's the plan of one section of the organization that must be fulfilled by a target date."

"Do you know what it means to intrude into another time period? Do you realize what's involved? After all, we are still in the experimental stage," declared a member of the Committee.

"We do know," said the chairman. Someone with expert knowledge of twentieth-century electronics must be sent there. At this end we'll station someone familiar with the equipment."

Santis and Erd appeared in the doorway.

"We'll get this thing started right now," said the chairman.

"That's why I decided to come to the meeting myself. A ship called *Challenge*, launched from the Earth one hundred years ago, had an accident in a remote stellar system . . ."

Shoving his hands into the pockets of his lightweight overcoat, Samoilov went to work. He hadn't any idea how his position as a senior engineer at the plant had been arranged. He walked up to the third floor of the engineering building.

"Aha! The new man is here!" was the first response to his quiet greeting.

The slightly bewildered Samoilov was showered with questions: "Where did you work before? Where did you get your training . . . what school?"

"Good morning, Aleksandr Tikhonovich!" the section chief bowed gallantly. "I am Vereshchagin . . . Vereshchagin, Yuri Yurevich."

Samoilov muttered something unintelligible in reply.

The chief of the laboratory to which Aleksandr had been assigned slapped him on the back, while the rest of the workers clustered around the new man and introduced themselves. Aleksandr nodded shyly.

Gradually everyone moved away from Samoilov, but the noise didn't abate. Out of the blue, technician Svidersky began to tell a weepy tale of woe from his own incredibly sad and unlucky life. His outpourings were rather crudely interrupted by chief engineer Vyrubakin, who declared that "Pakhtakor" would come out among the top ten in the computer chess tournament. This prediction was hotly contested by Svidersky, and others quickly took sides. Minutes later the entire section was involved in the dispute.

Samoilov didn't know what he should do; he hadn't the vaguest idea of what they were talking about. He went to the window and looked down. At the building's entrance several people, yelling at the top of their lungs, were chasing after an employee who was late for work. Shielding his face with his hat, the man dodged his pursuers.

When he had torn himself away from this absorbing specta-
cle, Aleksandr noticed that the entire section was now working on
a legendary chess problem. The temptation was too great; the
new man was soon tackling the challenge with the rest of them.

Before long, Strizhev, a brainy, efficient chap, solved the problem brilliantly and conversation shifted to local topics: the
weather, nature, hunting, and fishing. Outbursts of hearty laughter frequently interrupted the group's light and relaxed chatter.

Soldering irons smoked vigorously with molten rosin. Blue, red,
and green eyes of voltmeters, oscilloscopes, and generators
winked cheerfully at each other. Clouds of tobacco smoke veiled
the ceiling. Section chief Vereshchagin paced the far corner of
the room mournfully. How he longed to participate in the lively
conversation of his subordinates: he knew a helluva lot of good
stories. But his position prevented him from joining them.
Finally, Vereshchagin weakened and went over to the design section to chat awhile.

The morning passed quickly.

After lunch, the soldering irons, which had grown cold, and the
instruments were turned on again. Samoilov straightened up the
table assigned to him and looked around. Some engineers were
leafing through technical journals, others were tinkering with
models, but all without noticeable enthusiasm. Samoilov couldn't
understand the lull in activity.

"We don't have any experimental models," explained Vereshchagin. From the expression on Vereshchagin's face, the new man
realized that this periodic disruption of work was nothing new
and there was no end in sight to the pattern.

"We sit here all day, frittering the time away! When we get
close to the deadline, we'll be spending our nights here. We
planned and planned and still haven't gotten anywhere."

Samoilov sat down at his table and began to look through some
papers. "What the hell is my job here?" he sighed sadly. "No one
explained anything to me. All they said was 'only your presence
there is necessary.' I wonder what would happen if I . . .?"

"Hey guys," a voice rang out, "I think I'm going nuts. I can't figure it out. The dials on the amplifier are swinging like crazy. Somebody come over and take a look!" appealed engineer Gutarin, leaping from his chair.

This startling event immediately aroused the entire section. Questions and advice flowed freely. Samoilov also joined the group clustered around Gutarin's table and, looking over someone's shoulder, peered at the screen of the oscilloscope.

On the table lay a tray with some soldered condensers, resistors, and transistors, and next to it, a diagram. Samoilov glanced at the schematic. It was rather simple. Pondering it, he thought such an amplifier should not behave that way.

"It stopped! The excitation stopped!" shouted Gutarin joyfully. "And I didn't do a thing. It stopped by itself."

"Why the hell did you get so hysterical?" asked his colleagues, filing back to their tables reluctantly.

"H'm," thought Samoilov, "that feedback might have been a little too strong."

"There it goes again!" shrieked Gutarin. "Who the hell is practicing witchcraft here? Come on, you bastard, confess!"

"It's me," whispered Samoilov. "Now watch this. I shall say 'The amplifier is excited.' Well, is it? And now it's going to stop. Right?" Samoilov's face took on a haggard look. His suddenly acquired supernatural gift frightened him.

Instantly, Samoilov's table was surrounded by technicians, engineers, and project chiefs nervously discussing this incredible phenomenon.

Vereshchagin asked cautiously, "What else can you do?"

"I don't know. I never tried."

"What do you feel when you do this?"

"Nothing special. A little mental exertion. I simply picture the amplifier functioning normally."

"Could you lift a safe?" asked an engineer timidly.

"I'm afraid not," replied Aleksandr haltingly. "I can't imagine it."

"Well, well, what do you know!" said engineer Palitsin as he began flexing his muscles. He walked over to the safe, lifted it a little, turned it in the air, and returned it to its place.

"What the hell are you doing!" yelled another engineer. "The liquor's in there!"

"And you said it was all gone," fumed Gutarin.

Stunned, everyone gaped, glancing back and forth from Samoilov to Victor Palitsin.

"You won't be able to lift it again," said Aleksandr calmly.

"I could lift two of them," replied Victor with dignity.

But the safe would not budge. He turned red and sweated from the effort.

"Forget it. You won't be able to lift it anyway. It was I that did it . . . with mindpower."

"But you just said you couldn't lift it mentally," said Lyubochka, astonished. "So how do you explain it?"

"I can't lift it mentally," agreed Samoilov, "but I can picture very clearly not lifting it."

"But that's supernatural . . . mystical. There has to be some sort of explanation," said Sergushin.

Samoilov shrugged his shoulders in bewilderment.

"Come on, show us something else!" the others urged him.

"My trigger won't release," announced engineer Kulebyakin joyously. "Maybe we can try it? Eh?"

Samoilov examined the rig, silently studying the main diagram for a while. He noted to himself that it wouldn't hurt to change the parameters of the differential series and the ratings of the memory capacitance, and he said aloud:

"It's OK now."

Kulebyakin flipped the switch. The trigger worked normally now.

"Terrific! Say, will it stay this way?" asked Kulebyakin cautiously.

"Honestly, I really can't say. I don't know anything."

Crowding around Samoilov, the entire section followed him around from table to table until quitting time, watching delightedly how generators began generating, triggers triggering, and amplifiers amplifying. Everyone was highly excited.

Just before the shift ended, Aleksandr's boss called him aside and warned him to take good care of himself and to be very careful crossing the street. Samoilov promised to heed his advice.

A crowd of kids stopped him in front of his dormitory and demanded that he show them some tricks. "How did they find out?" wondered Aleksandr in surprise. But he couldn't refuse them. Since he was rather ignorant of this ancient art, his initial attempts elicited only faint contemptuous smiles from his young audience. But then his imagination warmed up and the kids roared with laughter. The madcaps among them ran around him shouting:

"The circus is here! Hooray! The circus is here!"

The astonished tenants of the house across the street gaped from their windows. After launching a multicolored kite, which lulled all the kids' suspicions, Samoilov made a hasty exit.

In his dorm room he met Kulebyakin and Gutarin, who were on their way to the dining room, and he decided to join them. Then came an insistent knock at the door. Aleksandr opened it. On the stairwell stood a delegation of tenants from the next building.

The chairman of the building committee coughed and cleared his throat. "We're actually here on business. Aleksandr Tikhonovich, could you help us install some posts?"

"Posts? What kind of posts?" Aleksandr was surprised and curious.

"We have nothing to hang our wash on in the yard."

"And we need tables and benches," interjected the chairman of the building's sports committee. "We're having a domino contest, but there's no place to play."

"H'm . . . OK, let's go. . . ." replied Samoilov, wondering how the word had spread so quickly. Intelligence here was certainly on the ball.

An enormous crowd watched the installation of the clothesline posts. Samoilov sweated. First the holes were too shallow, then the posts were too wide. Most of the advice was offered by the women. In the beginning the men approached the site warily for fear of being called upon to do some digging; growing bolder, they began to help the women give advice.

Samoilov, with the connivance of mindpower, was putting the finishing touches on the last post when Gutarin burst through the human barrier, grabbed Aleksandr by the sleeve, and dragged him to the dining hall.

"Why the devil are you wasting your talents on that crap? Posts! God almighty!"

"Who's going to put up the clothesline?" came voices from the yard.

"He's trying to get out of work!" yelled someone.

"What the hell did you get involved with them for?" Gutarin laced into Samoilov. "Do you think that's what your precious mindpower is for? We'll figure out something a lot more interesting."

"Hey, hold on," Samoilov stopped him. "What did you say?"

Gutarin stopped short, surprised.

"What's my mindpower for?" shouted Samoilov.

Only then did the pieces fall into place.

"Finally," sighed Nani tiredly. "I was about ready to give up hope." His gray hair was matted and it drooped over his forehead like icicles. His eyes were sunken and hundreds of wrinkles appeared on his forehead. He needed sleep desperately, but had refused to give in. His thoughts flowed smoothly and calmly but strayed occasionally.

"Those two sent only a single communique from *Challenge*. It was received by the robot space ranger. The robot makes the rounds of one hundred and fifty thousand stars in one working cycle, bringing emergency patrol service and recording electromagnetic signals if they contain information. On a planet of one of those stars, two pilots are waiting to be rescued. The robot did not record the code of the stars or planets, which means that they lacked radio beacons. The robot had brought only a message. . . . But from where? If only a human receiver had been there instead. Robots aren't programmed to cope with such elusive and highly improbable processes and events. Who could have known that?"

"Nani, why didn't you tell Santis anything about his mission . . . About the purpose or how he should tackle it?" asked Erd, sensing that Nani wasn't sleeping.

"Because everything must proceed as naturally as possible. It mustn't appear forced. Besides, he's a terrible actor. He had to enter this situation without making the slightest ripple. Then later he can pull all the stops out without raising suspicions. A strange phenomenon will have astonished them, and nothing more. Its consequences will appear to follow logically."

Nani was deep in thought again. "Dozens of interceptors are combing space now in the vicinity of thousands of planets. Although it seems pretty hopeless, we might as well try. . . . Suppose we're lucky. . . . No one believes that these probes will turn up anything because there won't be a second message from *Challenge*. There isn't sufficient energy to launch a huge object like an emergency transmitter to the ship. And a portable transmitter was not installed on the ship because some design department didn't have time to do it. It didn't fulfill its plan. Yet the search for the ship goes on. Perhaps to clear someone's conscience? But whose? The people who lived one hundred years ago? They're gone. To clear our conscience? But we're not to blame for anything. There's one chance in a thousand. And Santis must raise the possibility a thousandfold."

When Samoilov walked into his section the next morning, the tense silence was shattered by a barrage of questions. He couldn't make out a single sentence in the noisy confusion. His boss tried unsuccessfully to make his way to Samoilov through the crowd.

The crowd put the pressure on Samoilov, demanding a display of his powers. Smiling hesitantly, he went over to the wall and drove a nail into it without striking a blow. The crowd quieted down for an instant and then grew even more demanding. He had to drive in another nail. Ten minutes later the outline of a flower, the kind kindergarteners usually draw, adorned the wall. The startled spectators calmed down somewhat. Vereshchagin could now make his way to Samoilov rather easily.

"Samoilov, aren't you tired?" he asked with concern.

"A little. Really, not very."

"I have a job for you. I must speak with you." Evidently the boss had done a lot of thinking during the night. "Our work plan has gone to pot," he complained.

"What needs to be done?"

"We must have twenty-five models finished this month. Your job is to help turn them out in the model shop."

"What's the quota for the plan?" asked Samoilov in a choked voice.

"Fifty," sobbed Vereshchagin, drying the corners of his eyes with a handkerchief. "If only you could do twenty-five," he added.

"No," replied Samoilov firmly.

"What do you mean—you can't!?"

"Make it fifty."

"Twenty-five."

"Fifty, and that's it. Take it or leave it," Samoilov concluded abruptly.

"Well, all right," agreed Vereshchagin wearily. "Let it be. Just so there's no hard feelings between us, I agree to fifty."

So Vereshchagin, head of the electronics section, went to look for the head of the model shop, Pendrin Immanuil Gavrilovich. He looked everywhere, in every section, every room, every corner. But Pendrin was difficult to locate. Samoilov had heard about the strange head of the model shop and now he was finally convinced that the stories about Immanuil Gavrilovich's talent for invisibility had a solid foundation. Breathless from their fruitless search, Vereshchagin and Samoilov returned to the tool shop. Cheerful toolmakers were fulfilling the plan by producing potato scrapers. A few components of future portable transmitters lay forlornly in the cubicles of metal shelving.

"You'll have to do it yourself," said Vereshchagin to Samoilov, vexed. "Well, my boy, you might as well begin. The chief drafts-man will be here in a minute to help you."

"Good luck!" echoed the heads of two laboratories. "Go to it!"

"OK, right away," replied Samoilov, trying to figure out the drawings.

Somov, the chief draftsman, arrived in a few minutes. He grabbed the drawings and muttered, "It's a lot of rubbish. This is wrong, and that should be like so."

The drafting pen flew over the drawings. Samoilov followed the chief draftsman closely, trying to understand the altered sketches.

Two hours later two experimental models, a mindpower production, stood on the carpenter's bench. They weren't exactly deluxe examples, nor did they have anything in common with the drawings. Samoilov looked with surprise at the sad results of his labor. So did his bosses. The toolmakers made some malicious remarks. Only the chief draftsman, stroking the models affectionately, sighed tenderly:

"Ah! A wonder to behold! But how in the world did you manage to squeeze everything into those dimensions? We'll pattern all our new drawings on these models."

"Would you say that these models are up to standard?" asked Vereshchagin, wide-eyed.

"It's a miracle! An absolute miracle! The surface could stand a little leveling. And maybe this could be altered slightly."

Suddenly, Pendrin Immanuil Gavrilovich, head of the model shop, materialized from the stuffy, dusty air. He nodded to the group and shouted, "I told you! The model shop would never let you down!" Then he vanished without a trace.

Samoilov and Somov corrected the drawings. The other engineers, now solidly ringing the shop's workers, blocked the light, chain-smoked, and offered extraordinarily worthwhile advice. By lunch break, two metal models had been constructed to perfection.

"Meets universal standards!" announced Somov, walking to the entrance.

"You did a great job! No question about it. But it took much too long," said Vereshchagin sadly.

"Naturally, it was the first time."

"Tomorrow you'll have to make half of the models. Then we'll have them assembled and tune them. Oh, by the way, you'll be assembling them too."

Right after lunch, the workers from other departments began a pilgrimage to the model shop. Everyone wanted to see Samoilov. Then, of course, he had to satisfy them with a mindpower nail-driving demonstration. Being a considerate fellow, he covered the entire wall with his art.

In twenty minutes the pilgrims returned to their workplaces; the time was up for the unauthorized postlunch break. Then the electronics department received an emergency order—to get ready to tune up the test models.

After lunch, productivity rose markedly. Now and then the head of the model shop would materialize, only to vanish again. Suddenly, the modelmakers abandoned their workbenches, selected grandstand seats, and with mixed surprise and indignation, gazed at Samoilov's work. They were angry because no one had taught them such superb and productive methods.

And Samoilov kept turning out the stuff. One quick glance at the sketch of a component triggered a mental image of it, and where his knowledge of a component was obviously deficient, he used his intuition.

No sooner did he picture a detail than he applied mindpower, the dosage strength depending on the component's complexity; and low and behold, a finished component appeared on the table. Samoilov neither sat at the workbench nor wore an expression of intense concentration. He would run near the workbench, glance at the drawings, sculpt and plane something invisible, pause for a second, mumble, shake his head disappointedly, then laugh heartily. To put it mildly, his behavior was startling and puzzling. By evening, five more assembled models adorned the workbench.

The management of the electronics section carefully transferred the experimental models to their department. Samoilov tried to help them but was politely pushed aside. After all, the management could not entrust the most crucial part of the job to anyone.

By the end of the second shift, Samoilov had finished assembling, and now seven models were ready for tuning.

It had grown noticeably colder outside. Aleksandr pulled up the collar of his coat and put his hands in the pockets. Gradually his head cleared. "I wonder," he thought, "who is to blame for the plan going to pot? Vereshchagin said that everything had been planned properly. Then it got bogged down: the draftsmen didn't get the drawings from the laboratories on time, and the labs couldn't finish the drawings on time because the models were delayed in the model shop. The model shop was late because the designers took a long time correcting the drawings. The designers . . . Well, it was just a vicious cycle. Then there was the matter of getting parts—transistors, knobs, fasteners. The problems piled up, snowballed. . . . What the hell was all the coordinated planning for? Why the scientific organization of labor?"

Almost all the windows in the dormitory and in the building opposite it were dark. No one was shouting, "The circus is here! The circus is here!" No one was demanding tricks and post-holes. The night was still.

Everyone in his room was asleep except Gutarin. A night light burned on a small table.

Gutarin asked, "Are you hungry?"

"A little," replied Aleksandr, his stomach rumbling.

"Then let's go."

"Where to?"

"To Agrafena Ivanovna, the dorm manager. I've got a bottle. For some reason she feels sorry for you. She invited you. . . . So let's go there, OK?"

Agrafena Ivanovna's room was at the end of the hall.

"Come in, boys. Come on in. Here, in the kitchen. The old man is in the other room. He swings a broom around all day, comes home and sleeps." The old woman began to bustle about. "Everything's good and hot. Sit down."

"H'm, strange," thought Aleksandr. "Why is she going to all this trouble? Maybe she wants me to do something for her?"

"I simply feel sorry for you," said Agrafena Ivanovna, divining his thoughts. "Simply sorry. You're a wiry fellow, but not made of iron. So you mustn't overstrain yourself. I've heard all about you. I saw you put the posts in yesterday. And at work, too. From the very beginning you've been working day and night. There are plenty who will take advantage of you. And you'll let them?"

"I can't help it, Agrafena Ivanovna," replied Aleksandr. "I must do it."

"Then go ahead and do it," she said mockingly. "Do you have children?"

"No."

The dorm manager was an efficient old woman. She set the table briskly, sliced some bread, put a pot of tea on, in passing shoved a basin of lime into the corner, straightened her shawl, and performed a dozen other chores while carrying on a conversation.

"H'm," thought Samoilov. "It would be nice to do something special for her. Perhaps whitewash the walls? Nothing to it."

While packing away roast duck and tomatoes, and washing it down with dry wine, Samoilov mentally whitewashed the walls and even managed to carry on a conversation with Gutarin and his hostess.

Agrafena Ivanovna left the kitchen and gasped: The walls of the other room were covered with splendid still-life renderings of wild game, vegetables, and wine. Each still life was unique, and each was executed in true Rembrandt style. When Samoilov saw what he had done, he wanted to erase it, but Agrafena Ivanovna stopped him. It was beautiful. And one could always paint over it.

When their plates were empty, the old woman pushed them out the door with a word of advice, "Be sure to soak your feet or take a shower. You'll sleep better."

Aleksandr fell asleep instantly.

In the morning the tuning went forward at a furious pace. The administrators of the electronics section rushed ahead. Any day, the director of the plant would display interest in this unusual spurt of activity toward the end of the accounting quarter, and the scientists would display curiosity about this extraordinary phenomenon.

Vereshchagin did not spare himself. After all, accountability for a job is always more difficult than doing the job.

In the department everyone stopped smoking—temporarily. Everyone forgot about "Pakhtakor"'s standing in the tournament —temporarily. Everything was forgotten . . . everything but tuning.

A full-scale offensive was mounted. Onward! Onward!

Work continued around the clock; the workers took turns sleeping on two empty workbenches. They ate on the run. Go! Go! Go! Storm the bastions! Through a dense veil of fatigue and frayed nerves, the workers noticed the sparkle, the joy of battle in each other's eyes. Action! Movement! Normally all schedules and programs plunge ahead, caught in the wave of the onrushing assault at the end of the year. But never at the end of the third quarter. This was a unique and unnatural phenomenon.

Imagine that a part of an army has begun to storm the enemy's bastions before its basic forces are prepared to go into battle. The enemy will route the small band of daredevils and start to attack along the entire front.

An all-out assault must be properly timed. It doesn't occur to anyone to storm a plan at the very beginning of the year.

Nani and Erd took turns relieving each other on duty; they executed Santis's mental orders, transporting into the past whatever he demanded. It was damn hard work. No one could replace them because it would be very difficult to find even one person whose thoughts were on the same wavelength as Nani's and Erd's. And time was precious now.

When Santis, back in the design section, dropped from exhaustion and slept for half an hour, Erd asked, "Nani, why do you think the plan fell apart at the seams?"

Nani laughed. "I'm afraid there are no simple explanations. I'm sure they had all kinds of meetings and conferences. They also tried to answer the question, Why? I don't believe that anyone deliberately wrecked the plan. It happened by itself.

"You can't set up a plan with one hundred percent guarantees for the perfect execution of all its components. That would no longer be a plan. Therefore, alternate possibilities, plus time, people, and money are held in reserve. But these reserves must be minimal. If they are too inflated, then you can't call it a plan. Even in our time it's a difficult process. And in those days computers were rarely used to develop plans, especially in such small organizations. It's very difficult to consider all the possible factors, for example, illness of key personnel, intellectual abilities of workers, employee relationships, and finally, weather. Or suddenly it turns out that the management lacks any authority and cannot help its subordinates at crucial times; the head of the laboratory lacks organizational ability, and the chief engineer is a specialist in a completely unrelated field, although he is a very intelligent person. Conflicting emotions take over. Someone isn't at his work station. The chief engineer spends his evenings composing music and comes to work exhausted from insufficient sleep. Besides, he's not particularly interested in his job, and he can't live without music. Thousands, millions of little tragedies have occurred because a person isn't doing the kind of work he or she wants to do. Yet in most cases, not even one's family or closest friends or the victim himself suspects it.

But all is not so bleak. We have successes, too. In general, as in a volume of gas, everything approaches an average, normal level. But there are and always will be deviations . . . in both directions . . . up and down. And we acquired one that deviated to the down side of the curve. If this were the rule, it would be terrible. You and I wouldn't be here, dear comrades."

Persistent rumors circulated throughout the sections, laboratories, and offices: The electronics section intended to complete the plan on schedule, in three whole quarters. This was treason! A knife in the back!

The director of the plant quickly summoned Vereshchagin to his office.

With the speed of a pianist, the director's hands flew over documents, files, and directives. His pale, sharp-featured face with its high forehead bent stubbornly over the desk seemed to issue a

challenge to primordial forces. Broad, shaggy brows meshed the
bridge of his nose.

"Well . . . What's on your mind?" said the director.

Vereshchagin shrugged his shoulders embarrassedly. "I'm dying
for some sleep."

"So sleep! H'm, tell me, what's going on in your department?"

"We're working. . . . But I sure need some sleep. So does everyone else in the department."

"Well now," Volkov's high, metallic, staccato voice sounded as
if the words were riveted together, "joking aside . . . we'll leave
that till later, what's going on? Ten days ago you were practically
praying to God to help you meet the half-year plan on schedule.
Right?!"

"Right," said Vereshchagin, barely moving his tongue, then
covering his mouth, he yawned.

"There are rumors that your department is trying to finish the
plan in three quarters. Are they true?"

"They are."

"What the hell are you trying to do?! What's the rush?"

"Oh, I wish I could sleep," said Vereshchagin, and he yawned
again and began to fold up slowly over the desk. The director
grew furious. Vereshchagin came to and murmured, "We'll make
it. . . . Except that everyone wants to sleep, especially in the
morning. . . . Then the feeling passes. . . . Black coffee does it."

"And who in the hell gave you the order to fulfill the plan?!"
raged the director. "Who? Who, I ask you?!"

Instantly, Vereshchagin was wide awake.

"We've been going according to the schedule and program,
Pyotr Vladimirovich."

"According to the plan," Volkov mimicked him sarcastically.
"You fellows think you're smart, don't you? You don't understand
a damn thing! Birdbrains!"

The director clasped his head in his hands and, with the look
of a cornered eagle, stared vacantly ahead of him.

"The letter to the ministry is on the way, and those jerks, for no
reason at all, decided to complete the plan on time." He was talk-

ing to himself; then, suddenly rousing himself, he fixed his gaze on Vereshchagin.

"You damn well know that we don't have enough space, we're short on lathes and personnel, and supplies are arriving slowly. At this point it's easier to explain to the ministry our failure to fulfill the plan than the opposite. What will I say to the ministry? Conditions are the same throughout the plant, and yet one out of four departments fulfills the plan. Do you understand what you have done?! You've made mincemeat of us!"

The director fell silent again and stared blankly at the desk. Vereshchagin struggled to stay awake, digesting his boss's speech with difficulty. "And, by the way," began the director, this Samoilov really . . .

"Here it comes," thought Vereshchagin. "It's begun. It's goodbye Samoilov. He'll be removed." And hanging his head, Vereshchagin said, "Really, Pyotr Vladimirovich."

"How did it all begin?" asked Volkov sternly.

"With him." Vereshchagin was on the verge of tears.

"Get him over here right away . . . Samoilov . . . from the electronics section," the director issued the order to his secretary.

About ten minutes later Samoilov appeared. He was very pale and thin. His hair, uncombed for days, stuck out in all directions. His suit was wrinkled and stained with rosin.

Gradually the room filled with senior and junior administrators: the chief engineer, the head of the patent office, the head of the technical department, the personnel inspector, the supply chief, the heads of sections, the heads of laboratories, and supervisors.

Once again Samoilov began driving nails. He was showered with requests to drive one into the wall, the ceiling, the floor, the windowsill, the door, the doorjamb. And drive he did . . . every which way: parallel, perpendicular, zigzag. He drove them in singly and by the dozen . . . skillfully, beautifully . . . with such talent! All sensed that this was no mere hack. This was a true artist. A great artist! A steady, restrained flow of ooh's and ah's filled the director's office. Everyone stood, except Vereshchagin, who was sound asleep with his cheek against the desk. He slept peacefully, comfortably, happily, evidently lost in pleasant dreams.

"Well done, Samoilov," the supply head said warmly. "You're a terrific guy! A fool, but a terrific guy! You ought to join the circus. You'll be a sensation! Or join me in Supply . . . or join Ferrous Metals . . . for one hundred and thirty rubles. How about it? You're a terrific guy!"

"Hey, can we patent this?" asked the chief engineer. "Has patent clearance for this phenomenon been checked? It's absolutely got to be patented."

"Oh, you certainly are a crafty fellow. You knew and didn't say a word," someone said to Samoilov.

"Well, we've talked enough," the director's stentorian voice rang out. "Sit down and let's get started."

This was the shortest meeting of the enlarged techcouncil in the plant's entire history. In only four hours it was over. The day's agenda was expressed in rather general and vague terms: "The possibility of granting senior engineer Comrade A.T. Samoilov the right to fulfill the work plan for the first three quarters of this year in one quarter."

The director, the first to take the floor, regretted that such an unpleasant situation had developed. A letter had already been written to the ministry about the reduction in output. Everything was progressing smoothly, calmly, and suddenly, damn it, one department has met its quota! Almost. "Everything has gone down the drain!" he shouted. "Now, hear this: Like it or not, either the quota for the entire plan must be met or . . . you know what I'm driving at. . . ."

"But," Volkov concluded his speech, "one fact does please me no end. As a director I cannot make mistakes. Otherwise our plant, with the finest engineers in this city, would never find its way out of the abyss of backward organizations. I have always intuitively adhered to the laissez faire approach to administration. I admire the greatness and power of Man! And so, what I have always strived for in my own activity has found brilliant confirmation in the electronics section . . . meeting a quota with sheer mindpower! I am always in favor of it."

The shop committee chairman very opportunely reminded everyone about union dues. The editor requested a flash photo for the wall newspaper. . . . Samoilov and Vereshchagin were sound asleep. It would have been stupid of the editor not to have taken advantage of such a perfect moment.

Toward three o'clock, when an affirmative decision on the day's agenda had been arrived at by an overwhelming vote with one abstention (snoring Vereshchagin), a glass of water was poured over Samoilov and he was urged to return to his post. The faces around him were kind, affectionate, and slightly tense. With water dripping from his clothes, Samoilov did not reject their suggestion but frankly admitted that he didn't know how or where to begin. Nor had they the slightest idea.

The brilliant undertaking was about to die unborn. The enlarged techcouncil became agitated. Suddenly one bright head suggested calling in inventor Kobylin, known for his ten applications for invention rights and a single patented invention.

At once Kobylin seized the bull by the horns. "How many days do you need, Samoilov, to meet the quota for three quarters?"

"Not less than a month," Samoilov sighed heavily, and then he explained why. He would have to immerse himself in all the drawings. Then he must generate a mental image of all the components, connections, circuits, and chemical reactions. For him this was completely new, especially the chemical reactions.

For some five minutes Kobylin studied Samoilov intently and declared, "You'll never get anywhere that way! It won't work!"

Everyone nodded in agreement: "No-o-o, it won't work."

Kobylin sank deep into thought, very complex thought. The director's office grew noticeably warmer. The inventor's mental energy was transformed into thermal energy, threatening, should it continue, the entire universe with thermal destruction. Entropy is entropy! When the temperature became almost unbearable, Kobylin cast a serene look around the room, and everyone knew that the problem had been solved.

Like all brilliant ideas, this one was brilliant in its simplicity.

"We must have a broad outlook," began the inventor. "But Samoilov's thinking is limited, amateurish, one-sided. To make any piece of rubbish he first immerses himself in sketches. I-merses, mind you! That takes time. Assembly of equipment with mindpower also requires time! So does installation! And tuning! It's a real waste of time! Technologically unsound and unproductive! Let's not waste our energy imagining how to produce the equipment itself; rather, let us imagine what needs to be done to get the equipment produced on time, according to the plan. Components are lacking? That means that Comrade Volkov did not reprimand Baluyev, the supply head, in good time. Use mindpower, reprimand him mentally. Personnel shortage? The personnel section . . . The circuit doesn't align properly? The developer . . ."

"He's right," declared Samoilov, nodding in the inventor's direction. "We can try it."

"Oh, that's a good one! Baluyev will get a reprimand," guffawed the chief of the patent bureau.

"And two makes company," countered the supply head, pointing at the chief of the model shop, who had suddenly materialized out of thin air. "I'll bet Immanuil Gavrilovich gets one too."

"The model shop won't let you down!" its chief assured everyone, having missed the preceding conversation. Again he vanished into subspace.

"Will a reprimand really be given?" The chief of the design department paled.

"So, you feel a little guilty, too!" guffawed the patent chief.

"Yes, there can be a reprimand! Anyone opposed to it? Abstentions?" asked the director. "Or is anyone afraid? Guilty?"

There was dead silence, except for the whistling and snoring coming from Vereshchagin.

Aleksandr Tikhonovich Samoilov—Santis—locked the massive wooden door of the testing laboratory. He opened the hatch of the soundproof chamber and tossed into it a thick stack of programs, schedules, quarterly accounting statements, reports, announcements, and directives; then he dove in and screwed the hatch securely from the inside. To effectively concentrate mindpower, absolute silence was necessary. It was warm and dry in the chamber. Santis laid out on the table the documents he had brought with him, lit a cigarette, relaxed for about a minute without thinking about anything, doused the cigarette, and began to focus his thoughts on the first item on the list. Eight hours to go until the end of the third quarter. . . .

The director's office was filled with administrators. The air was filled with meaningless conversations, nervous laughter, shuffling feet, attempts at humorous anecdotes. . . . The suspense was agonizing. Almost all operations at the plant had been halted; there was no longer any point in working.

Only the electronics section was functioning. Only two untuned models were left. Anyone who was still awake gathered around Gutarin and Palitsin. The tuning would be finished any minute. Chief engineer Vyrubakin announced in a most dignified manner that "Pakhtakor" would rank among the top ten. He was immediately insulted by the lack of response. Technician Svidersky told a sad story from his own life, setting his listeners laughing until the tears flowed. Lyubochka typed up the last protocol and flitted among the workbenches. The lab grew livelier and livelier.

"Finished!" yelled Palitsin. "It can be sealed now."

"Mine too! That's it, guys," announced Gutarin joyously, his joints cracking as he stretched his limbs. "OK, so when do you marry me off?"

"Soon, my boy, soon," Strizhev reassured him.

"How about a drink to celebrate finishing up the job?" suggested Sergushin, rubbing his sleepy eyes.

"Only one?" said the lab's second shift supervisor as he suddenly woke up. "Is that all?"

"It's enough! So, gather 'round!"

"But Vereshchagin and Samoilov still haven't come back," complained Lyubochka, pouting fretfully.

"They're probably getting hell," replied heavyweight Palitsin.

"Like hell they are! A bonus . . . that's what they're getting. You'll see," snapped technician Svidersky.

"How about taking off?"

"First let's go to the store, then to the dorm," ordered Sergushin. "Samoilov and Vereshchagin will undoubtedly go there."

A minute later the lab was dark.

An ominous silence reigned in the director's office. Some three hours had passed since Samoilov had locked himself in the testing laboratory. No one knew what was happening in the chamber. That didn't sound too encouraging. On the one hand it was fine if the plan was fulfilled—a bonus! On the other hand, suppose there's a reprimand or something worse?

A shaken draftswoman burst into the office.

"Sdobnikov has disappeared!" she cried out.

"What do you mean . . . disappeared?" several people asked, turning pale.

"He disappeared. . . . He and Zakharov had gone out for a minute, and when they returned Sdobnikov disappeared. . . . He vanished—and that was it!"

"Such things don't happen!"

"They do, they do! Sdobnikov has disappeared!"

"Nonsense . . . you mean to say the earth simply swallowed . . ." Before the respondent could finish the sentence, he vanished . . . without a crackle, without a sound, without one warm parting word.

The crowd in the plant director's office began to get worried. Frightened voices asked one another: "Where is he? What could have happened to him?" Tension and fear mounted. This was an extraordinary occurrence; until now only Immanuil Gavrilovich Pendrin could vanish into thin air.

Suddenly the chief engineer leaped from his seat, raced down the stairs, flew outside, grabbed the broom from the startled caretaker's hands, calmed down, and immediately began to sweep the sidewalk enthusiastically, but with caution, without raising unnecessary dust. Here one sensed the hand of an artist. The caretaker was delighted with his unexpected replacement and went inside to see how his potatoes were doing.

The director squeezed the rim of his worktable so hard his joints ached. This minute another of his executives had vanished before his eyes. This was awful! The supply chief sobbed violently. It wasn't out of fright, but out of love of art. As elucidated later, he was now the leader of a drama group and was teaching its members the art of projecting oneself into a role.

"It's him! He's the one!" a bloodcurdling shriek sliced through the room. "It's Samoilov! We must stop him!"

Everyone jumped up at once, overturning the long conference table. Vereshchagin nearly fell off his chair and woke up. He looked around him in astonishment. On his right cheek glowed an enormous bedsore imprinted with designs.

"Stop him!" everyone shouted. "He'll do us all in."

Some thirty or forty people rushed to the door, squeezing one another into the corridor, and raced down the stairs to the door of the testing laboratory.

"Break it down! Storm it!" resounded the battle cry.

A relentless roar came from the ranks of the attacking battle-tempered warriors. Each group, like its predecessor, vanished without a trace. Finally someone brought a crowbar and wedged it between the door and the wall; the door fell down. To capture the chamber straight off was much harder. The attackers began to lose heart. So few of them were left: the personnel inspector, the chief of the patent office, the bookkeeper, Vereshchagin, and a few others. Holding their breath, they looked at each other for a few seconds. No one had disappeared.

"Is everyone here?" someone asked timidly.

"He's probably dead. We didn't make it in time."

"Has he been there long?" asked Vereshchagin, having finally figured out what was going on.

"Four hours."

"He must have suffocated. He probably chain-smoked the whole time," said Vereshchagin. "We must save him. Cut through with a torch!"

Several people hurried to find a welder. Someone called the first-aid squad.

"He should be put in jail for pulling such tricks," said the patent office chief.

"We certainly are to blame; we asked for it."

"Who knew it would come to this? Suppose the plan isn't fulfilled? Then what? Who'll have to answer for it?"

"But who is there to answer to now?"

Suddenly, out of nowhere, the model shop chief materialized.

Pendrin winked mischievously, "Well, how are things going? Is the commotion over?"

"Pendrin! You son-of-a-gun! You're alive! Any idea where the rest of our people are?" muttered the patent chief.

"I don't, but I can guess."

"Where the devil are they?"

"Oh, they're alive all right. I saw them rushing through the substratosphere . . . Volkov to the ministry, and the others in various directions."

"And what about you?"

"If I had known that something was going to happen here, I would have sat out the siege in the substratosphere. Well, so long for a while! To play it safe I'll stay there a little longer," and with that Immanuil Gavrilovich vanished. . . .

The ragged edge of the fused hole where the hatch had been had barely cooled when Vereshchagin leaped into the chamber.

Samoilov lay next to the desk, his arms flung apart, in a soaked, unbuttoned shirt. He had stopped breathing. In any case Vereshchagin could hear nothing, no matter how carefully he listened. The desk was strewn with signed and confirmed quarterly reports, folders with technical records and testing protocols. On the floor stood mock-ups and test models of various types.

The third-quarter plan was fulfilled. On top of all the papers lay an order from the ministry granting quarterly bonuses to the plant's employees. . . .

The doctors diagnosed Samoilov's condition as extreme nervous exhaustion. He came to in a week. His room was bright and quiet. From somewhere in the distance slow, strange music drifted into his room. Samoilov sighed and fell sound asleep.

His health improved rapidly. Visitors were not permitted, and letters were not allowed to contain any mention of production activities at the plant.

Finally the day arrived when he was permitted visitors. The first one was Agrafena Ivanovna, the dorm manager. Then came Vereshchagin, two lab supervisors, chief engineer Vyrubakin, technician Svidersky, Strizhev, Palitsin, Gutarin, and Lyubochka. The room grew noisy and lively.

"Sashenka, dear boy, those accursed people have overworked you," the old woman wailed.

"I also spent a week in the hospital," said Vereshchagin enthusiastically. "You know the bedsore on my cheek refused to heal. They even gave me shots."

"And our Gutarin is getting married!"

"And I captured first place in the city with barbells."

Santis felt good. He looked from one face to the next . . . joyously, silently.

"Can you still drive nails into the wall? A delegation of scientists has been trying to get to you all week," said Lyubochka.

"No, I can't. I tried, but nothing happened," replied Santis, and he added cheerfully, "The secret is lost! Say, why were you people always asking me to drive nails? I could have done something a lot more interesting."

"And you certainly did," replied technician Svidersky, and everyone agreed with him.

"It's a good thing you've lost the secret," interjected Agrafena Ivanovna. "You'll learn to use a hammer."

"Well, and how are things going at the plant?" asked Santis.

"Fine," replied Vereshchagin. "Volkov was transferred to the Ministry of Agriculture. It turns out that he was trained to be a veterinarian. And the chief engineer is working as a caretaker, not as an ordinary one of course, but as a team leader. The slate has been wiped clean in our department! . . . A few more have been shuffled around, in all, around forty people. Everyone was given the kind of work they sincerely desired. We have a lot of new staff. Pendrin sat out the siege. So he's still the chief of the model shop, but he's always afraid of something."

After every sentence uttered by Vereshchagin the two laboratory supervisors nodded and said in chorus: "Right . . . That's also true . . . Right . . ."

"And you, you know, will not be promoted to chief engineer. I requested it, but they said your probationary period isn't over yet."

Visiting time was over. The visitors' departure was as noisy as their arrival.

Samoilov nodded to all of them; he did not yet have the strength to raise his hand.

Several hours after Samoilov's return, a second message was sent from *Challenge*. Then a third. The robot space ranger had received them. A rescue party was now on its way.

The Biggest House

The little girl woke up but neither stirred nor opened her eyes. Her tiny fists clutched the sheet. The dead silence in her sleep had awakened her. Cautiously she opened her eyes and saw Mama's face.

Morning was still on its way as dawn began to glow in the eastern sky. A faint breeze gently ruffled Mama's hair.

"What's the matter, honey?"

The girl snuggled up to Mama and embraced her.

"It's so nice at home. . . ."

"Sure it is, honey. Now go back to sleep. It's still early."

"I don't want to sleep. I don't have real dreams. It's always so quiet and nothing's there."

"Do you want me to sit with you a little while?"

"Please, Mama. And sing me a song. Remember the one you sang to me when Papa was fixing the reflectors, and the rope got stuck, and he couldn't get back to us? The song about the biggest house."

"I'll sing you another one. About the forest and sun."

"Don't you remember the house song?"

Shaking her head slightly, Mama stroked the child's dark hair on the pillow. She hadn't forgotten the song; she didn't know it. And she knew hardly anything about her little daughter. And who did? Of course it made Mama feel terribly guilty.

"Close your eyes, dear. I'll sing very, very softly. Don't think about anything. Just listen."

Mama began to sing. Her voice was low and so full of love. She probably liked this song. The child tucked her hands behind her head and looked up into Mama's eyes without blinking or stirring. Mama sang and studied her daughter. Suddenly she realized that the child didn't see her, that she was looking through her, that in spirit she was far, far away. . . .

Tick, tick, tick, tick . . . Barely audible but so familiar that life without it would be frightening. Without it, there would be only dead silence. This welcome sound meant that all life-support systems aboard the spaceship were working properly. The little girl sat in a deep chair next to her papa's, playing with a homemade doll. Mama had made it for her from scraps of old dresses.

Her father glanced darkly from time to time at the dials of instruments and entered columns of figures into a computer, changed programs, and formulated new ones after receiving answers. Only one-third of the scanner screen was open, and the dim dots of stars were visible. Toward one of them raced the ship.

"Our house is out there," announced the little girl suddenly, pointing to the center of the screen.

"Yes, dear, our house is there."

The child was used to pointing to the center of the screen; her mama and papa had taught her that. But today her finger unknowingly pointed to another star now occupying the center of the screen. Papa didn't tell her that the ship was out of control. She needn't know. Anyway she wouldn't understand.

"Elfa, aren't you bored sitting here all day?"

"No, Pop . . . I'm learning how to be a captain of a big ship."

"Oh, no, my darling daughter," thought her father, "I shall do whatever I can to see that you never leave Earth once you get back there."

Meanwhile Mama was asleep . . . for four hours. The next four they would all spend together. Then Papa would sleep his four, and Elfa, too. While they slept Mama would take her turn trying to figure out how to get the ship back to Earth.

The door opened and there stood Mama. How pretty she looked, all dressed up! She was always changing her outfits or putting together something different or altering her clothes. Mama's hair fell to her shoulders and a narrow golden mass curved softly across her forehead. Right now Mama looked like an enchantress in a fairy tale.

"Are you the good fairy?" the little girl cried out.

"She certainly is," Papa chimed in cheerfully. "Isn't she?"

"Oh, yes, Papa!"

"If I am," said Mama, "then open your eyes."

The captain and his daughter opened their eyes and found apples in their hands.

Elfa squealed in delight. But Papa whispered something. He even seemed a little angry.

"You didn't sleep . . . again?"

"Oh, no, I did. I went to the greenhouse afterward." She looked at him anxiously. "Any luck?"

"Nothing yet."

Mama probably liked to sing. It was almost dawn and she was still stroking the little girl's head with her long, loving fingers and singing. She sang about funny little animals and streams so deep and clear you could see the bottom. Suddenly the child propped herself up on her elbow.

"Mama, you said our house would have a blue ceiling . . . and black . . ."

Mama was about to say, "Did I really say that?" but caught herself in time.

"Of course, dear. We'll have a blue ceiling. At night, when it's dark, it will be black."

"With fireflies?"

"Fireflies? Of course with fireflies."

"And will curly white puffs float on the blue ceiling?"

"Oh, yes," agreed Mama, thinking that this could be arranged.

"And sometimes the ceiling will split in two?"

"Everything will be just as you want it."

"Do we really have the very biggest house?"

"Well, not quite. There are bigger ones. Do you want to live in the largest house?"

"You said I would live in the biggest house."

"It's better to live in small houses . . . like ours, with woods, grass, and a little river, and a bluff above the river. In the woods . . ."

"Yes, I suppose it's better that way. But you said . . ."

"Sleep, dear. It's still very early and just beginning to get light. In the morning we'll go to the farm. Have you ever seen cows being milked?"

The child wasn't listening. Suddenly she sat up on the bed. The nightgown slid from her thin shoulders, but she didn't notice it or try to pull it back. "I'm leaving. I want to. Will you let me go, Mama?"

"Yes, I will. But first we'll have some milk. . . . So you weren't happy here with me, were you?"

"Oh, no, Mama, I liked it a lot. But I want to go. I want to see other houses. I hope I'm not making you feel bad, Mama."

The girl dressed and together they drank milk. Then Elfa, walking carefully on the dewy sand, reached the garden gate and waved to Mama, "Good-bye!"

When Elfa was out of sight, the woman turned a small disk on her bracelet. The disk flashed and then glowed dully.

"Edhead," said the woman.

A man's face appeared on the screen.

"Anything wrong?" he asked.

"She. . . she left," replied the woman.

The little girl walked along the country road, occasionally lifting her head to watch the stars disappear on this summer morning.

Lately the captain rarely appeared in the control room and Elfa saw less and less of him. When he would appear, smeared and soiled with metallic dust, she would hop onto his knees before he even had a chance to wash. He would play with her, then set her down gently, wash up quickly, and disappear. Now Elfa spent most of her time with her mother.

One day a series of strange events began. First Papa moved her sofa to the small library, and Mama said she would be sleeping there. For an instant, Elfa imagined herself alone in the darkness and she began to cry. This was the first time Papa had ever looked at her so sternly, but then he calmed down. That first night seemed endless to her, but instruments planted in the sofa indicated that she had cried only fifteen minutes before falling sound asleep.

On another day, Papa and Mama sat her down in a chair at a small round table in the lounge and told her that she was almost a grown-up now. (She was all of six years old.) To test her maturity they decided to confine her to the library for a week. For seven whole days she would not see them. Mama wavered, but Papa was firm. "No less than a week!" he said.

"Do I have to do it?" pleaded Elfa.

"It's for your own good, darling. So that someday you will see our home," Mama added.

"Can I have my dolls with me?"

"Of course," said Papa. "You can take anything you want with you. We just want to find out how brave you are."

She was locked in the library the next day. At first she wasn't at all frightened; it was even interesting. Then she began to get a little bored. Toward evening she burst into tears, but no one came to her. At that moment Papa was checking something in the small workshop in the ship's auxiliary quarters. Mama was at the computer but was watching her distraught daughter on a video screen next to the computer's control panel. The harder the child cried, the greater the number of wrinkles appearing on Mama's face, but Mama continued with her calculations.

Occasionally the captain would phone Mama and ask, "Well, how are you doing? Holding up OK?"

"I'm doing my best," she would reply cheerfully.

"For her sake, both of you must stick it out."

A week later Elfa left the library. Papa carried her in his arms while Mama kept saying, "Now everything will be fine. I know it will."

After that week's confinement Elfa really seemed to grow up. Mama taught her to wash dishes, prepare simple meals, and hand-launder her little dresses. She taught her to read and write.

Once Elfa and Papa left the ship, in space suits, of course. For a long time they floated in space, alternately moving away from the ship and toward it.

"Are you afraid to stay out here alone?" Papa asked.

"Oh, no, Papa," replied Elfa bravely.

At ten o'clock in the morning Elfa approached the glider station. Having walked several kilometers she was a little tired. But she had certainly enjoyed tramping through fields and woods, conversing with people she met and asking them where she could find the biggest house—her house. If they told her they knew where such a house stood, she would question them further. But alas, none of the houses were of the kind Mama had described to her. She didn't despair because everything to her was so cheerful and wondrous: the dazzling, yellow sun in the blue sky and the flowers everywhere with their unfamiliar, beautiful names. She had only to wish for Mama and Papa for them to appear at her side.

Only two gliders were left at the station. One was being loaded with large crates, and the second was ready to take off. Boldly she approached the second glider and motioned to the pilot to open the door.

"Elfa!" the pilot exclaimed in surprise. "What are you doing here?"

"Pop, I want to go with you."

"With me? All right. I can take you. But this was an unscheduled stop and I'm not coming back. I'll have to send you back with someone else."

"I'll stay with you, Papa."

"With me? Are you very sure you want to?"

"Well, not very, but your glider is so pretty."

"OK, hop in."

He lifted Elfa gently into the cabin and slammed the door. The glider soared into the sky.

When the girl pressed her face against the window to gaze in childish delight at the sights he had pointed out to her, the pilot carefully flipped the disk on the bracelet on his left hand. The disk glittered.

"Edhead," called the pilot.

A man's face appeared on the small lusterless screen.

"She's here with me in the cabin," said the pilot. "Glider type *Ladybird*, number 19-19. I'm headed for the taiga settlement on Aldan."

The face on the screen smiled. "Well, it looks like you'll have to take her there. We'll notify the settlers. By the way, what does she call you?"

"Papa."

"Did she ask you about the biggest house?"

"Not yet. . . . So you never did find it?"

"No," the chief educator shook his head. "She didn't know where it was. Who knows if it ever existed. Probably some sort of childish fixation. Too bad she's so obsessed with the idea. . . . Meanwhile, let her wander about. Thanks for calling."

Elfa gazed down in wonder at the green dots of forests, straw-colored fields, blue ribbons of rivers, and the mirrors of lakes.

"Is it a carpet?" she asked.

"Where? Oh, that? Yes, it does look a lot like a carpet. Do you like it?"

"Yes, I do. That's how it is where I used to live."

When the glider landed in the taiga settlement, the geologists clustered around it. They had been forewarned of Elfa's arrival.

"Hello, Mama," said Elfa to a short woman wearing a blue jump suit. The woman had lively dark eyes, a suntanned face, and dark hair.

Mama wore a blue jump suit then too. She always wore it under her space suit. Papa wore a blue one too. During those last days, they both spent lots of time with her. Papa played with Elfa, often setting her inside a small, one-passenger rocket and explaining the functions of various levers, buttons, and colored lights. She knew how everything worked by simply memorizing all the details with her still uncluttered child's mind. At any rate, she could pilot the rocket. On several occasions she blasted off from the ship, moved off a few dozen kilometers, made U-turns, decelerated, braked, and returned again to the ship. Of course, dual controls on the ship guided the operations.

Papa was unusually affectionate toward her. Mama seemed to be holding back tears all the time . . . as if she were expecting something awful to happen.

Then one day, Papa said, "Today!"

Again they sat her down in the chair in the library. They sat opposite her, real close so they could hold her hands in theirs.

"Elfa," said Papa, "you're a big girl now. Remember Mama told you about the biggest house?"

"She sang me a song about it."

"Yes, she sang about it. It's your house. You must live in it. You'll fly there in the small rocket, in the one you've flown in so many times."

The little girl clapped her hands in delight. Oh, how she wanted to see that house!

"You'll be flying alone. You'll be flying a very long time. You're not afraid of being alone, are you?"

"Oh, no!" answered Elfa bravely.

"Good girl! You won't be lonely. I've made a funny little man for you. He can walk and even talk . . . although not very well. You'll take him with you."

"What about you? Why can't you come with me?"

"Because there's only room for one in the rocket. Besides, we must do our work. Isn't that right?" he turned to Mama.

She could not reply and only squeezed the child's hand.

"But you'll come later, won't you?"

"Of course. We'll try. But until we come, you'll have another Mama and Papa at home. You will even choose them yourself."

"Will they be as nice as you?"

"Elfa, you will choose them yourself."

The girl nodded hesitantly.

"You know how to do everything you need to do. When you reach Earth someone will meet you . . . absolutely!"

A few minutes later she was seated in the rocket and the funny little robot man was next to her. A doll rested on her knees. In front of her were the controls: knobs and switches, capped to prevent Elfa from brushing against them accidentally.

Everything needed for the lengthy journey was foreseen: food, water, air, books handwritten by Mama, pencils and paper, even a small expander to exercise arm muscles, and a stationary exercise bicycle fastened to the floor. All this in only four cubic meters of space.

"Are you sure she has enough of everything?" Mama asked the captain for the tenth time.

"She has enough for a year and a half. But she'll be met before that . . . in four hundred days."

"She won't . . ."

"Don't worry. She won't pass near the Sun. I calculated it many times and you checked it."

"Yes, I did."

Beneath Elfa's seat lay a small box with documents and microfilm. This was their report on the expedition . . . the expedition they had undertaken together. They had done everything in their power to maneuver the ship back to Earth, but were unsuccessful. They could not return, but she, Elfa, must see Earth.

Papa spent almost a year rebuilding this small rocket, the last of three the ship once had. Nothing had been overlooked.

Mama could barely restrain herself. She knew she would collapse in tears when the rocket blasted off. Never again would she see her daughter.

"It's time," said Papa. His movements were now stiff and unnatural. "Elfa, you're flying to your home. It's your house. The biggest house in the whole world . . . in the whole universe. . . ."

"Elfa," whispered Mama.

"Does it have a blue ceiling?" asked Elfa.

"Oh, yes, yes!" shouted Mama. "And white clouds, like curls, float on its blue ceiling! At night it's . . . black . . . and fireflies . . ."

"Elfa, good-bye, my dear little daughter," said Papa. "Be brave."

"Elfa . . ." Mama's voice broke.

Elfa settled down in her seat.

"Blast off," commanded Papa, pressing a button on the control panel.

A streak of lightning jetted from the side of the ship and headed toward the Sun.

Mama was dry-eyed; she didn't have the strength to cry. But Papa cried.

"Now we'll have our dinner," said the woman in the blue jump suit. "Right here, under the open sky, by a campfire. You've never sat by a campfire, have you?"

"No," replied Elfa.

"Later we'll go up the mountain and meet a bear."

"A real one?!" asked the girl, her eyes shining with impatience.

"Yes, a real one."

"Let's go right now, Mama."

"No, dear. First you must rest a bit."

The entire geological party stood around her and smiled.

"Is it true that when you fly in a glider you see a carpet down below?" she asked them.

"It is," replied the pilot. "Even when you walk it's there. Look at this carpet of red bilberries. Pretty, isn't it?"

"Oh, yes," replied Elfa, squatting down and carefully stroking the tough tiny leaves. "Is it true that the sky is like a blue ceiling? Remember, Mama, you told me about the biggest house?"

"Yes, I do," replied the woman in the blue jump suit, playing it safe. She knew almost nothing about the child. And who did know anything about her? Perhaps Edhead, the chief educator on Earth, did.

"Please take me aboard! Please take me aboard!" These were the signals several ships in Pluton's vicinity had heard one day. A man's calm voice kept repeating: "Please take me aboard!"

One of the ships had changed course and received the small rocket of mysterious origin. To the crew's surprise, its passenger was a small child, and not a man. The male voice was a recorded tape.

"Papa, I want to go home," she said tiredly to the graying captain of the freighter that had picked her up.

"Where is your house, little girl?"

"Oh, I have the biggest house."

Later when she arrived on Earth Edhead spoke with her. The child was remarkably advanced for her seven and one-half years. Her knowledge was vast and she could do many things. On the flight to Earth she had quickly grasped everything the freighter's crew had explained to her. But she had two eccentricities. To everyone's amazement she would suddenly call some strange man "Papa" or a strange woman "Mama." And the other puzzling thing was that she persisted in asking people to show her her house. "The biggest house," she called it.

The Education Council conducted an investigation about her real parents. No, they had never had a large house. In fact, there wasn't even a house. Directly after graduating from the Astronautical Institute they had left Earth on an expedition into the remote reaches of Space.

"You'll see, sir," declared Elfa as she left Edhead, "I'll find my house." He didn't try to hold her back. He did the one thing he could; and now everyone on Earth knew that Elfa was looking for her house. All were obliged to help the child, to play the role of surrogate mother or father.

"Is it true that the roof of a house can rumble and shudder? And that it can even flash streaks of light?" asked Elfa.

"Oh, no," replied someone. Roofs are very strong these days."

"Right, it is possible," the glider pilot broke in. "When a thunderstorm comes you'll see for yourself."

"Is it scary?"

"A little, but very beautiful."

"Is it true that the walls of a house move away when you get closer and closer to them?"

"What nonsense . . ." whispered one man, but he was quickly hushed.

"It's true, Elfa," said the pilot. "See that wall beyond the mountain? We're going to fly toward it, and as we get closer it will move further away. No matter how much we chase it, it will keep moving away from us."

"Oh, Mama, isn't that what you told me about the biggest house, my house?" said Elfa to the woman in blue.

"*This* is your home. The whole Earth is your home. It's the biggest house in the world, in the entire universe."

"Yes, Mama, that's what you told me. . . ."

In the evening when they walked down the mountain to the campfire, the sky had already darkened. The woman asked, "Elfa dear, you're not leaving me, are you? You'll stay with your Mama?"

"Mama," replied the little girl, "don't worry, I'll come back. First I want to see my house. I want to see all of it."

In the morning Elfa boarded the glider again. When it reached the mountain, she shouted to the pilot, "Look, Papa, the walls of my house are moving apart!"

The Newsstand

1.

The fog was so thick you couldn't see a damn thing twenty steps ahead, that is, nothing but the street lights and the faint yellowish glow coming from the headlights of cars. Minus fifty degrees Celsius! There were no sounds except the piercing whining of tires and occasional crunching made by footsteps on the snow. And bitter, bitter cold . . . everywhere! In Ust-Mansk, its suburbs, and for thousands of kilometers around the city.

I dashed out of the hotel to the electromechanical plant where the conference was starting at noon. No one could pass me because I ran so fast to keep from freezing to death in my lightweight shoes and coat. My breath froze instantly on my face, and my nose was so numb I wanted to stick it under my arm. If it weren't so damn cold, I could look at my native city which I hadn't seen in so long; wander through its new sections; drop in to visit old friends, have a glass of wine, and go to the park with them. There, as in our younger days, we would roll down the hill, lose our caps and find them full of snow, laugh and throw snowballs, and horse around. How I longed to do all these things . . . because I hadn't seen Ust-Mansk in ten years, and before that I had lived there for twenty years.

Although the conference wasn't supposed to begin for another hour and a half, I wanted to be the first one there. Then, after I had thawed out, I could stand in the lobby and watch the human icebergs enveloped in clouds of steam stagger in, stamp their feet, and rub each others' cheeks.

"You can never get today's paper at this stand," said an irritated voice from the depths of a bundled figure that almost knocked me off my feet. "Sorry."

I jumped aside and saw before me a glass and plastic newsstand covered with laces of sparkling frost. It glowed brightly from within and looked like something out of a fairy tale, except that here undoubtedly sat some old woman selling newspapers. It probably was no more than ten degrees warmer in there. Maybe minus forty, give or take a few. Br-r! How does she just sit there? Could be she's already frozen to death!

I decided to buy a paper so I wouldn't have to waste time listening to some of the boring reports. The little window opened immediately in response to my frantic knock.

"Granny!" I shouted. "Five of today's *Pravdas* and one local paper."

"I'm not Granny. I'm Katya-Katyusha," replied a young lady's voice.

"Katya-Katyusha? OK, Katya-Katyusha! Now, how about the papers, Katya-Katyusha?" My numb lips had a hard time reproducing the Katyusha part, but I deliberately repeated it several times.

"I don't carry today's papers."

"So I hear. But what do I need yesterday's for? I've already read them."

"I don't carry yesterday's either."

"Then what the devil do you sit here for?"

"I only sell tomorrow's papers," replied the girl as her face, wreathed by a warm knitted cap, poked through the window.

"Good Lord! Your face is completely frozen! You've got to restore the circulation! Do you have far to go?"

"Just to the Electromechanical Club. . . ."

"You won't make it with that face. Look, why not come inside for a few minutes and warm up?"

"Is it OK?"

"Of course. Please come in."

I pushed the little door, but probably too weakly: it wouldn't budge. Meanwhile I hopped around, slapping my cheeks, elbows, and knees. I'd already lost all sensation in my toes.

"Harder!" shouted the girl.

I pushed with all my might and squeezed through, accompanied by clouds of steam forming instantly inside the booth, a space so small that one person could barely fit in it. Hesitating, I halted, bent over like a question mark.

"Sit down," the girl said as she pointed to a pile of papers.

I sat down and quickly shoved my feet toward two portable heaters.

Inside the booth it was bright, warm, and dry, and very clean and cozy.

"Your frozen cheeks will turn black and the girls won't like you," she said, laughing. "You must rub them to get the blood going through them."

I pulled off my gloves with my teeth and tried to straighten my fingers. I couldn't.

"You're in bad shape," said the girl, removing her mittens. She pressed her warm palms gently against my cheeks. I didn't object. She asked: "Are you from out of town or are you one of those dudes who deliberately flaunt winter and then spend years in hospitals?"

"I'm from out of town, Katya-Katyusha. I'm on my way to a conference . . . on the propagation of radio waves."

"Ah, yes . . . I've already read about it in the papers." Her warm hands stroked my cheeks several more times. "You're doing much better now."

"Thanks, Katya. I might as well introduce myself." I extended my partly thawed hand. "Dmitry Yegorov."

She also offered her hand and laughed so cheerfully that I had to join in.

"So, you were really badly treated at the conference?"

At this point the meaning of her words didn't sink in.

"And I was wondering which newspaper to leave, but they all were the same. So, you are *the* Dmitry Yegerov, the eternal dreamer?"

"Katya, you've got it all wrong. On the contrary, I'm a very down-to-earth guy. Can you picture radio waves penetrating the earth?"

She shook her head.

"Well then, I'll explain it briefly. I'm looking for useful minerals and water by using radio waves . . . without drilling or soil tests. There's nothing dreamy about that. Sound interesting to you?" I asked.

"It does," she replied. "Tell me more. But don't forget, your conference begins at noon."

I told her how our expedition worked in the Vasyugansk marshlands north of the Tomsk Oblast this past summer; how the midges and mosquitos ate us up; how our equipment had a tough time in the swamps; how the members of the party became irritable and withdrawn, and Goshka, our leader, began belting out songs. He was told to shut up, make himself scarce or else, but he kept on singing and spitting out the blood-sucking flies that managed to penetrate everywhere, and he called us a bunch of sissies. His name-calling didn't bother us; his singing did. Finally, someone sobbing in desperation broke into uncontrollable laughter. That did it: the rest of us couldn't restrain ourselves. We laughed so hard we were practically rolling on the ground.

"Want more of my singing?" growled Goshka. "You're just a bunch of sissies."

The mosquitos kept feeding on us and the equipment didn't work. But we started to get very angry at ourselves and our helplessness. We toughened up and refused to crawl out of the taiga although headquarters called us back three times. But our equipment still didn't work right, which came as no surprise to anyone. There are various kinds of equipment: electrical, magnetic, and radiation instruments, and gravi-prospecting apparatus. But we wanted to use something completely different, a new approach. We wanted to see through the earth, like through clear glass. The expedition failed.

"Still, it's an interesting approach," I finished my story, "and necessary. . . ."

I thought I caught a momentary spark of envy in her eyes. Perhaps she felt that I had, after all, done something, aimed at something, fallen and picked myself up again to pursue my goal, while she, on the other hand, had been spending God knows how many

years in this hole, selling newspapers and postcards, counting out
change through her tiny window into the plams of customers
invisible to her, and without an effort to better herself.

I straightened up and said, "Katya-Katyusha, how would you
like to join our expedition?"

"As a cook?" she asked seriously.

"Why as a cook?" I spluttered. "Well, then as what?"

"Oh, for example . . ."

"Fine, I'll go."

"Really?"

"Really. You wouldn't take me anyway. You're kidding.
Besides, selling papers is interesting too."

"I bet it is," I said sarcastically. "You'll just spend your whole
life sitting here."

She wasn't insulted. Her big brown eyes flashed at me without
a hint of envy, but they were full of irony, mocking me.

By now I was well thawed out but didn't feel like leaving. Not
a single customer had come to the window in all that time. Probably no one wanted to stop for a paper in this bitter cold.

I stole a glance at Katya. She was short, with dark curls peeking out from under her cap. Her eyes were black, and her puffed
cheeks looked as if she had blown them out ever so lightly. She
wore high-heeled leather boots, but I noticed a pair of felt boots
in the corner behind her chair. A lightweight winter coat with a
small collar was half-open, showing a fuzzy blue scarf.

"So, you're rushing into battle again?" Katya laughed. "You
want to prove you're right?"

"True," I replied.

"It's no use. You'll be called a wide-eyed dreamer again."

"Oh, Katya-Katyusha," I said disappointedly, "how can you say
that? You can't know that for sure. We don't even know yet
who . . ."

Before I could finish the sentence she shoved a newspaper into
my hand and said, "Go ahead. Read."

I quickly scanned the first page. Nothing of particular interest

there. The usual stuff: forest heroes, milkmaids, new undertak-
ings, competitions.

"On page three," prompted Katya.

I opened the paper and read: "The All-Union Conference on
the Propagation of Radio Waves is ending now in Ust-Mansk."

Katya giggled softly up her sleeve. The look of surprise on my
face was too much for her. "On the twenty-fourth of December at
twelve noon the All-Union Conference opened at the Electromechanical Plant's Palace of Culture . . ."

"What's today's date?" I asked hoarsely, terrified that I might
have lost a whole day.

"The twenty-fourth," replied Katya very seriously.

"Then why do you speak of the opening in the past tense? It's
not supposed to start for another hour!"

"But this is tomorrow's paper."

I turned the page. The dateline was 25 December.

"I'm confused. . . . What did you say today was?"

"The twenty-fourth. What else!"

"Look, Katya, you'll have to excuse me. My head isn't all there
right now. Probably froze my brains."

"There's not a thing wrong with you! This is tomorrow's paper!
I always sell tomorrow's. But they don't sell very well. Everybody
wants today's. And this stand doesn't get delivery of today's."

"Impossible!"

Nevertheless the article was written about our conference and
my report was called "harebrained."

"It's strange," I said. "Now I know what's going to happen to
me in the next few hours. Suppose I want to change things
around and not go to the conference at all?"

"It won't do a bit of good," said Katya. "There's no reason for
you to do that. After all, that paper isn't only yours, is it?"

"No, it isn't." For an instant I imagined Goshka's enraged face
and shuddered. "Looks like nothing can be changed. Unless
maybe some minor details that weren't in the newspaper. You
certainly are a shrewd one, Katya, selling tomorrow's papers.
Very interesting!"

"So, you won't take me on the expedition?" asked Katya in a mocking voice.

"Listen, Katya," I said, ignoring her question, "when do you close the stand?"

"At eight."

"I'll pick you up at seven-thirty. OK?"

"All right. But what will we do? You mustn't stay outside too long. You'll freeze to death."

"We'll think of something. I've got to run, Katya-Katyusha. I'm planning to do whatever I can to get them to call me a wide-eyed dreamer. That's just what I want them to say!"

"Good luck," she nodded. "I'll wait for you."

I stood rooted in the doorway, not knowing what to say. She was laughing at me again!

"Hurry, hurry! You're letting the cold in. I'll wait for you!"

2.

I dashed out into the frigid air and, shrouded in a column of water vapor, rushed along the avenue—past the university dorms, past a statue of Kirov standing with raised hand, past the Polytechnical Institute.

The spacious but tasteless lobby of the Palace of Culture with its candelabras, chandeliers, and leather couches was already rather crowded. I checked my purely symbolic coat at the cloakroom, ran up to the second floor and stared down from the balcony, hoping to find a familiar face in the crowd.

Luck was with me; within ten minutes I was chatting with an old classmate. The usual cross-questioning followed: Where? When? What are you doing? Married? Kids? How many? Your thesis? Semyon Fyoderov? Of course I remember! The frost? Here it's like that all the time these days.

I didn't meet any other friends and my classmate left me soon. He was one of the conference organizers, so I understood. Managing this conference was a pretty demanding affair.

Precisely at twelve noon the chairman's gong rang out. An eminent academician gave the introductory speech. Then came the announcement of the work schedules for the sections and subsections, committees and commissions.

I forgot to take one of Katya's newspapers with me. Why, I don't know. I was probably in too much of a hurry. So now I had to suffer through a lot of lengthy reports.

During the break everyone made a beeline for the bar, for beer and sandwiches.

Then the work of the sections began, and to my surprise forty people showed up in my section. And I thought that all the radiophysicists would head for the sections on the ionosphere, plasma, and the like, which are more closely related to astronautics.

Half the papers were given by doctoral candidates who needed to pile up six published works. After all, any report, even the most insignificant, is counted as a published paper. And the candidates themselves tried to rattle them off as fast as possible, then sigh with relief and humbly return to their seats. Questions and comments about such papers are rare.

The more serious papers followed. Some were simply brilliant. My turn came after five o'clock. I spoke calmly and confidently without interruption to an attentive audience, so attentive that I even felt that tomorrow's article about a wild dreamer would never appear. At first the questions were very simple, and I was already counting on emerging alive, but that was only the introduction, the light reconnaissance. Half an hour later my paper was torn to shreds. Particularly rough were the pundits from Ust-Mansk Polytech. As ill luck would have it, a journalist suddenly entered the room and took a couple of flash photos of me.

For some reason I wasn't particularly upset. Of course Goshka would really lace into me. We'd probably get a third of what we needed for the summer expedition. But I had done my best. I tried to change the report in tomorrow's paper. I tried my darnedest, but in vain. Now I knew that everything would appear in the press exactly as I had already read, which meant that the girl in the glass booth really sold tomorrow's papers!

3.

I picked her up at seven-forty. I couldn't get away before then. Twenty minutes inside the stand before closing time was enough to warm me up a bit.

"Well, how did it go?" Katya's eyes sparkled roguishly.

"You were right. My paper went badly. 'Harebrained,' they called it. This whole business is very strange. Where the devil do you get tomorrow's papers from?"

"From the printer's."

"And not even one eyebrow is raised in Ust-Mansk over your selling tomorrow's papers?"

Her face seemed to droop a little. "Hardly anyone notices that it's tomorrow's paper. Most customers think it's today's."

"Now wait a minute. Do you mean that *you* know it's tomorrow's paper, and for everybody else it's a regular newspaper—today's?"

"And for you, too, it's tomorrow's," Katya corrected me.

"OK, for me, too. And the others?"

"The others think it's today's."

"Do you often get customers who think it's tomorrow's?"

"Not very."

"But still . . . what about me?"

"You're the first," she smiled and wrinkled her nose. "I knew immediately that you would notice it."

It was time to close the newsstand. Katya changed into her felt boots, turned out the light, and closed the booth. We were lucky: in a minute we got a cab. It was impossible to stroll outdoors in such frigid weather, especially for me. I invited her to the home of an old friend from the Institute, and she agreed to go with me.

My friend lived in a two-room apartment. His wife had just returned from work and immediately began to fry potatoes. Three kids, ranging from six to nine years old, struck up a conversation with us about Tom Sawyer.

And out came a bottle of wine, the usual custom for such visits. We finished it off, of course. Around eleven o'clock we left. I

escorted Katya to her dormitory and even lingered in the lobby
for a while. Although we chatted for about another hour, I did
not repeat my invitation to her to join our expedition. Even I
would be delighted to be in the business of selling tomorrow's
newspapers.

Since I never let anything puzzling me go unpursued to the
bitter end, I asked Katya, "What's the point in selling tomorrow's
papers if no one is aware of it?"

"Ah, but I am," she replied.

"But still you can't do anything!"

"Who can tell?" she replied enigmatically. "When tomorrow's
papers are delivered here, no two are alike. Of course, it's only in
minor items that they differ, like the weather, maybe slightly
warmer or colder; or someone's illness or recovery; someone's joy
or sorrow. Yes, they're a little different when they get here, but I
choose one. And that is the one I sell."

Suddenly she pulled my head down to hers, kissed me on the
lips, and ran off, shouting, "Tomorrow at nine!"

I stood there for a while, bewildered but happy.

4.

The following morning I rose about seven. My roommate was
still asleep, and his masterly snoring probably resounded
throughout the entire universe. It had kept me awake all night,
but now, wide-awake, I couldn't stand his roulades one minute
longer. I dressed and went to the lunch counter for some hot sau-
sages. Then I returned to my room, grabbed my briefcase and
coat, and went to the lobby. I stayed there for about an hour. I
was supposed to visit Katya at the stand at nine o'clock, and it
was only eight now.

At eighty-thirty I couldn't hold out any longer and dashed
headlong into the frosty morning. It wasn't the slightest bit
warmer than yesterday, and after that bitter lesson I knew
enough to run, not walk.

As yesterday, the booth glittered as if covered with diamonds.

I knocked at the little window and shouted, "Katya-Katyusha, I'm freezing to death!"

She didn't answer, so I pushed the door and burst into the booth.

Katya was sitting there, clutching a stack of freshly printed papers to her chest.

"Am I on time? Am I late?"

"I don't know. Maybe." Her voice was barely audible.

I was somewhat surprised and disappointed. She was upset about something and apparently didn't feel like talking to me.

I asked, "Did something happen?"

"Yes," she said. "I must leave."

I didn't understand a thing.

"Forgive me, Dmitry. At ten o'clock a fire broke out . . . will break out at the Children's Home on Vershinin Street. I must run and warn them."

I glanced at my watch . . . more than an hour left. I knew it was only about a ten-minute walk to the Children's Home.

"Where's the nearest phone? All we have to do is call them."

"At the Radioelectronic Institute. But they might not believe me on the phone. I must go there."

"We'll make it in time," I said. "When did you read about it?"

"Just now, when you were knocking at the window."

"Let's hurry," I said.

"Don't come with me. I must go alone."

"Nonsense. Any details in the story?"

"Yes," she replied hesitantly as if she were holding something back.

"The kids got out all right?"

"All of them. One almost didn't."

I leaped from the booth. Katya followed me out, closed up the stand, and put the key in my pocket. The excitement sent my blood racing through me, so I didn't feel the cold as intensely as I had five minutes earlier.

She grabbed my hand and we began to run. We covered the

first hundred meters or so in silence; then she turned her head and gave me a searching look. I tried to smile but my lips were too numb.

"I'd go with you even as a cook," she said.

"So, let's go! Make up your mind!" My choice of words was great, but aloud they sounded rather unconvincing.

"Oh, it would be nice," she replied.

"So, let's go." I stopped her for an instant. "Why wait for summer? We'll leave in three days, when the conference ends. OK?"

She wrinkled her little nose in her funny way, nodded, and pulled me forward again. We ran along Kirov Avenue. We took a shortcut by the October movie theater and came out on Vershinin Street, directly opposite the Children's Home. Lights shone through the new, two-storied brick building, and there was nothing to suggest impending catastrophe. I suddenly wondered if Katya wasn't pulling my leg, or if she was testing me for some reason. But my doubts were banished instantly by the determination with which she pushed open the gate of the short fence. The gate swung open immediately with a scraping sound. But we had problems at the front door. Either the bell was out of order or no one had heard it. And only when we had the sense to circle the house did we realize that the front entrance was undoubtedly blocked by all sorts of junk and that we would have to use the rear entrance.

The rear door was open, but the light was off—an economy measure. Holding on to each other, we made our way into the hallway. It was well lit here. We could make out the front entrance at the opposite end, although it was barely visible through the junk piled chest-high against the door. To the left was the kitchen; pleasant odors drifted from it. In the room adjoining the kitchen, a sort of dining room, sat the children: shaggy heads and crew cuts, pigtails and short bobs. Two child-care workers carrying trays circulated among the tables. To the right was a bedroom. I had no idea, of course, of what was on the second floor.

Katya went right up to the door of the room where the children were sitting and indicated to the two women workers that she wanted to speak with them.

"May I speak with you for a minute?"

The women looked at her in surprise, and one of them, setting her tray down on a little table, went to the door.

"Hello," said Katya, beckoning the woman to step into the hallway.

"Hello," said the woman, following Katya.

"Don't ask me how I found out," began Katya. "It wouldn't make sense if I told you. . . . But, around ten o'clock this morning, a fire will break out in this building."

"Oh, God!" The woman clasped her hands to her breast.

"The children must get dressed quickly, and arrangements must be made with your neighbors to take them in."

"Oh, my God!" the woman repeated and called out to the other one, "Maria Pavlovna!"

The children watched this scene with interest and began to get noisy and playful.

"Maria Pavlovna . . . a fire," she began to wail.

"What happened?" asked Maria Pavlovna sternly. "Who are you?"

"I work at the newspaper stand, and he's an engineer. Please, listen to me. At ten o'clock a fire will start here. You must get the children out at once!"

"Outside, in weather like this?!" Maria Pavlovna was shocked at the suggestion.

"You had better get started," I broke in. "Do you have a telephone?"

"Yes," replied Maria Pavlovna, pointing to it. The telephone was behind me.

"While he calls the fire department you dress the children," said Katya in a very controlled voice. She tried to sound convincing.

The first woman, moaning with fright, ran to the second floor. The cook emerged from the kitchen and joined us. The caretaker, wearing a muffler wrapped almost up to his forehead, came inside and tapped a wooden shovel on the floor.

I dialed the number. When someone responded at the other end I said, "Get a fire engine to the Children's Home on Vershinin Street right away."

"When did it start?" he asked in a very businesslike tone, and he shouted to one of his colleagues, "Take out number seven! Then he asked me, "What's burning there?"

"Nothing yet. But the fire will start at ten."

"Pranksters again," said an irritated voice, and he hung up.

I dialed the number once more, but the conversation ended the same way. They didn't believe me.

Three women came down from the second floor. One was the director of the Children's Home.

"Our fire prevention system is in order," she informed us. "Did you come to inspect it?"

Katya had to explain everything again, but the director simply dragged us to the wall and forced us to read the "Instructions for Evacuating Children during a Fire." The instructions were first-rate, but the pity of it was that they could not be carried out in this building under any circumstances.

"Do you at least have a fire extinguisher?" I asked, glancing at my watch. It was almost ten.

"We do," replied the director. "That is, we did have one. They used to hang right here," she said, pointing to three dark spots on the wall. "One came down and almost killed poor little Tanechka Solntseva. We had to put it in the shed."

Time was running out. We had to do something quickly.

"Why the devil aren't the fire extinguishers on this wall?" I roared.

Immediately the director backed off. Who knows, maybe we really were fire department inspectors.

"Anikeich!" she shouted. "Get the fire extinguishers, and make it snappy!"

The caretaker dashed outside but returned immediately because he didn't have the keys. The women fussed about nervously, trying to find the keys. Finally Anikeich discovered them on himself and dashed outside again.

"Dress the children!" ordered Katya.

The women obeyed in a half-hearted way. The children were taken from the table and led through the hall. But all this was done very hesitantly, as if they expected the false alarm to be called off.

There were fifty children. I learned later that an additional one hundred twenty were on the second floor. I began to drag away the junk blocking the front entrance. I tossed sleds into the bedroom and rolled barrels containing the remains of sauerkraut into the kitchen. Someone tried to help me, but I ordered him out, shouting to all adults to dress the kids faster and get them outside.

Katya called the fire department again, and this time they believed her. I had cleared away half the junk and now I had only to get through to the door to throw the rest of the stuff outside. Out went some rakes, shovels, old mats, and buckets with gutted bottoms.

The cook extinguished the stove with water. We began to unplug the electric heaters, but they had been connected in the most inaccessible places, so it was almost impossible to reach the plugs. One of the women ran to the movie theater to arrange shelter for the children in the lobby. The director of the Home still didn't believe us. The Lord only knew what she might do to us should these preparations turn out to be unnecessary!

The rear door opened and the caretaker burst into the hall with two fire extinguishers. He sneezed several times while trying to tell us something. He finally managed to get it out.

"We're on fire!" he shouted, swearing and banging the extinguishers against the floor. But they were of no use at this point because the stuff that had burst into the hall along with the caretaker wasn't steam; it was smoke. My eyes smarted. The caretaker rushed over to help me. By the time we had cleared away the junk blocking the front door, the wooden partition was burning.

The fire engine arrived in twenty minutes. The children had already been transferred to the movie theater. The chief of the fire department stayed to investigate the cause of the fire. The child-care workers were still slightly hysterical. But I was flying through the city in an ambulance, holding Katya's cold, damp palm in my hand. Katya had tried to hold back the wooden partition between two rooms until the last of the children could be led to safety. They were taken through the emergency exit, then down the metal staircase from the second floor into the yard. All were led out, but Katya could not jump aside in time, and the burning wooden partition had collapsed and pinned her against the floor. Only a minute before, she had shoved a half-dressed little girl into my arms and shouted to me to stand outside by the window so the children could be passed through it to me.

I didn't even have minor burns. I wasn't allowed to look at her face; it was covered with something white.

5.

I sat in the clinic corridor, bewildered and exhausted. The doctors said they were doing everything to save her.

It was suggested three times that I leave because there was nothing I could do to help and only irritated the doctors with my questions.

When I was politely chased out the fourth time and continued to give excuses for staying, one of the young physicians said suddenly, "Let him help if he wants to. The news won't break in the papers before tomorrow; tonight it will be on the radio, but it may be too late. Where do you live?"

"I'm from out of town."

"H'm, that's a shame. So you don't have any friends here? . . ."

"I do, but very few."

"She needs a skin graft. We need volunteers, about fifty, maybe more."

"I'll get them for you!" I shouted and ran outside.

The conference was already in session.

I had sufficient presence of mind to play it cool and locate my old classmate from the Institute.

He heard me out and said, "It's hard to believe; she was in such a cheerful mood only yesterday." And he added, "I'm glad you told me. You did the right thing. Everything will be taken care of. We'll send your section down first."

Together we entered the room where the radiophysicist-soil scientists were working and I sat down in the nearest seat. My friend whispered something to the chairman of the section.

When the speaker finished his talk, the chairman made an announcement: "Comrades! An accident has occurred in the city. A skin graft is needed. I think we can recess for a while and go to the clinic together. It's not far, only two blocks. . . . A girl may die unless we help her."

The entire conference arrived at the clinic at scheduled intervals.

Around one o'clock I was permitted to visit Katya. Before me lay a white pillow, a white sheet over a body, and a mound of bandages instead of a face. Only tiny black eyes with seared lashes and barely delineated lips were visible. I sat down on the stool next to her bed. Katya looked at me without stirring or blinking. I didn't know what to say to her now. The words stuck in my throat. I would have liked to stroke her cheek and hair, but that was impossible. I simply nodded to her and tried to smile cheerfully. I don't know what she read in my smile, but her lips moved slightly; and from the shapes of the words I could make out what she said.

"My cheeks will turn black and you won't like . . ."

"I will, I will," I said. "Katya, I'll take you away with me from Ust-Mansk. In the summer we'll go to the Vasyugansk marshlands to feed the mosquitos."

I was told to leave her room. Katya had grown worse again.

"There's nothing you can do here to help," the doctor said. "Go back to your hotel. Call on Katya's employer and tell him what happened. Keep busy, do something. It will do you good. You can come back tomorrow morning."

I went outside and walked down the avenue.

6.

My brain was so numb not a single thought drifted through it. Even the cold didn't bother me. In this state I walked to Katya's newsstand, and then I remembered that her key was in my pocket. I opened the lock, entered, and turned on the light. My eye caught a newspaper open on the fourth page, and immediately I found a small item under "News Briefs." It said that a fire caused by faulty wiring had broken out yesterday at ten o'clock at the Children's Home on Vershinin Street and Katerina Smirnova, in her efforts to rescue the children, had died.

Katya Smirnova. I didn't even know that her last name was Smirnova. To me, she was simply Katya-Katyusha.

The item in the paper was untrue! She hadn't died trying to save the children. She was alive!

My eye fell on a crumpled page lying next to the newspaper, and suddenly I remembered . . . I remembered that this morning when I had stopped by to see Katya at the stand, she had crumpled the paper, glanced at the page that now lay before me, and only after that had she mentioned the impending fire. She knew what would happen to her, but went anyway.

I opened a crumpled newspaper. It was also yesterday's, and it had an item about the fire. But this one said that Dmitry Yegorov had died.

My head began to throb. Now it all made sense! Now I knew what she meant when she told me she selected one edition of the paper each morning from among a number of different copies. And today she had deliberately chosen her own death because I, too, was at the fire. It was I who was supposed to hold back the burning partition, but she sent me outside to do something anyone else could have done. I should have been lying there, pinned down by the burning wall.

I pulled another newspaper from the pile. . . . Dmitry Yegorov perished . . . A third paper . . . the same thing. I kept looking for one particular edition. There had to be a third version. There must be! Katya simply hadn't had the time to find it. She was in such a hurry. She was so happy that she had found the second version, that I would live . . .

Today *I* will choose tomorrow's paper.

I found what I wanted. This was the right edition. Hundreds of people did everything they could to save her life; hundreds of people tried to change the contents of a news item without knowing they were doing just that.

I decided that I would choose and sell this particular edition so that all would know that Katya was alive and would survive despite her terrible burns. Everyone who stopped to buy a paper would hear this from me loud and clear.

But it was so cold that no one wanted to pause, even briefly, to buy a paper. So I left the booth with a stack of papers and began distributing them to passersby.

"Read all about it! Read about Katya Smirnova," I shouted. "She's going to live! Read all about it! Katya will live! Think it, wish it with all your heart: Life for Katya!"

At first I thought that everyone would think I was crazy, but nothing of the sort happened. People took the papers, stopped, asked questions, and expressed their sympathy and hope that she would live.

"You must want it with all your heart," I said to everyone. "It is Katya who brings you the little and big joys day after day. Sure, you don't notice it because you don't know that it's all her doing. It is Katya who wants that fine weather for you, so you can go off into the woods and have a good time. And who do you think prevents catastrophes on our streets? Katya! Because of her, fellows find the girl of their dreams, and girls the guy they've always yearned for. True, she's helpless when it comes to some factory or plant, even small ones, fulfilling their quota. That's not so terrible. Others can do that. So, read the paper! Katya must live!"

"That girl is the Queen of Ust-Mansk," remarked someone.

People believed me, and now I knew: Katya would live because everyone wanted it so desperately.

I stopped at the main post office to drop off Katya's keys. Then I hurried to the conference, and the pundits from Ust-Mansk Polytechnical Institute said that I could work temporarily in their laboratories, that there really was something to my wild idea and they had already wired my Institute for an extension of my conference leave. They understood how vital my presence in the city was during this emergency.

I'm going to stay right here in Ust-Mansk until I can prove to them that it's possible to see through the Earth; until Katya recovers; until preparations for the expedition begin; until we can fly to the North together, to the marshlands, to the midges, to the mucky, rainy days and Goshka's miserable singing.

I ran to the clinic. The fog was so thick you couldn't see a damn thing twenty steps ahead. Minus fifty degrees Celsius. There were no sounds except the piercing whining of tires. And bitter, bitter cold . . . everywhere! In Ust-Mansk, its suburbs, and for thousands of kilometers around . . .

I ran to the clinic. I knew Katya was expecting me.

What Funny Trees!

At first there was nothing, then semiconsciousness. Although one thought was pulsing through his head, trying to awaken the other, sleeping portions of his brain, consciousness kept slipping from his grasp. This one thought was an order to come to. He clutched at this edge of consciousness like a drowning man clutching at a straw. For an instant a whistling sound and a crash broke through the shroud, but it was short-lived. Then a resounding silence. Now he was fully conscious.

He lay beneath a transparent dome, which lifted and slid open as soon as his consciousness returned. For another minute he lay there, feeling his muscles gaining strength, and his memory began to reconstruct past events until it was as complete as need be. Then he sprang down lightly. Now he remembered and knew everything. Somewhere along the line the restoration system had misfired. He shouldn't have experienced that unpleasant transition to life.

"What about the kids?" he thought. Their cabin was in adjoining quarters. He walked to the door of the control room and managed to scan all the signal lights. Everything was functioning normally except one green light, which seemed to be blinking apologetically. It was his dial gauge. Oh, well. He would look into it when they prepared for the return journey. Now he must see to the children.

As soon as he opened the door of the childrens' room, he realized that everything was in order, or rather, in disorder. A pillow fight was in progress accompanied by noise and screams. Apparently they had borne the transition splendidly.

"Papa," shouted Vina, "we had a pillow fight with Sandro. But he started it."

"Yes, I did, Papa," confessed Sandro. "But they were sulking, and I felt so good I thought I ought to cheer them up."

"Papa, are we there yet?" asked Oza. Being the eldest, she began to straighten up the room without waiting for her father to remind them.

"Yes," replied Father, "we've arrived and the ship has gone into orbit around this planet. And if you hurry you can catch a look at it on the scanner screen."

"Me first!" shouted Vina.

"I think," Father corrected her, "that you'll be last. It's going to take lots of time to straighten up your messy bed."

"I'll help her, Papa," said Sandro.

"Five minutes to clean up. Hurry now. But you must do a good job."

He left, pleased that the children had tolerated the transition so well. What was wrong with the apparatus? Why those whistling noises and crashing sounds? He thought about it while he walked to the control room and waited for the children.

He was very familiar with the ship's layout and so was at a loss to explain the origin of the thunderous sounds.

The door opened and the children burst into the control room. Aware that she was about to observe something interesting and instructive, Oza was serious and attentive. Sandro was determined and aggressive, ready to dash from the ship at the drop of a hat in order to be the first to touch the planet's surface. Vina burned with impatience, waiting excitedly to get her little hands on that new, interesting toy that everyone called Planet.

With the expression of a magician who is about to present the most dazzling trick in his repertoire, Father seated them in revolving chairs.

"Papa," hurry, hurry!" Vina shouted impatiently.

"Everything's ready," said Father. "Here's your planet for you!" He pressed a button. Sliding doors covering the screen parted and vanished. Presto . . . a transparent hemisphere appeared before them. It was so huge they had to look above their heads and below their feet to take in the entire image.

Vina squealed in delight. Sandro's whole body pressed forward. Oza sat rooted to her chair.

They stared at the foggy, immobile sphere, at the part now illuminated by the sun: blue streaks of oceans, light brown strips of deserts, mountain ranges, and dazzling polar caps peeking between the gaps in its spiraled cloud cover.

Yes, for this it was worth their long journey through hundreds of light-years. Father took photographs while the children stared wide-eyed at the miracle before them.

"Would you like me to go closer?" asked Father.

"I want to walk on it," declared Sandro with determination.

"We shall. After all, it took us a long time to get here."

"Papa, are we going to walk on it?" shouted Vina in delight.

"What do you think we brought our space suits for?" said Oza. "Of course we're going to walk on it. And run too."

"But we're so high above it now," said Sandro.

"We'll land and see all of it."

"What's its name?" asked Oza.

"I looked in the stellar atlas," replied Father. "It has a very strange name. It can't be translated into our language. And I don't understand its meaning either."

"We'll give it a name," proposed Sandro.

"No, son. This planet has it own name."

He sat down at the controls; the ship began to describe spirals around the planet as it moved in closer and closer. Soon they were flying just above the clouds through which rivers, lakes, forests, fields, and even cities could be seen. Real cities! True, somewhat strange ones . . . large and small ones wholly or partially in ruins, but some were completely intact.

"Papa," said Sandro, "Is there a civilization here?"

"Yes," replied Father. "Or there was one."

"If there is, we should be able to see it from here. How about hovering over one of them for a while?"

"All right," agreed Father.

The engines died down at an altitude of ten kilometers. Four pairs of eyes were glued to the screen.

There was no movement in the city. Their eyes were beginning to tire when Oza shouted, "Look, those spots . . . they're moving!"

"What spots?" Everyone was excited.

"Those, over there. They look like crosses."

"You're seeing things. They're not moving," said Sandro.

"No, she isn't," piped up Vina. "They are moving a little."

After watching them closely for several minutes, they concluded that the objects were moving, but so slowly that it was difficult to notice. Father compared their sizes to the buildings and decided they were of the same order.

"They couldn't be people," said Father. "They wouldn't fit into the buildings. Besides, they're not moving about on the planet's surface. See the shadows down there? So those objects are above the surface."

But where are the people?" Vina asked, bewildered. How anxious she was to see a real, live planet person.

"We'll drop down a little lower,' suggested Father.

The ship closed in at five hundred meters, in the thick of the flying crosses. Now the city's streets were clearly visible. . . . There was dead silence and absolutely no sign of activity. Oza noticed that here even the clouds didn't change their shapes.

"It looks like a dead world," said Father. "From a higher altitude it looked much prettier."

"Look, look!" shouted Vina. "Over there . . . a tree is growing. It's growing!"

"Yes," agreed Father, "I see it. But it looks like a dead tree."

"No, Papa! Not over there! Down there . . . right under us . . . a little bit to the left. Look, it's growing branches!"

"That dark bush over there?" asked Father.

"Yes, yes. But it's not a bush," said Sandro. "It looks more like a tree."

"What a strange tree," remarked Oza.

"Yeah, what funny trees here! They grow right before your eyes!"

And this tree was doing just that. Straight branches were coming from the tree at various angles, gradually curving and sloping downward. Then the entire tree sank and vanished.

"There's another one!" shouted Sandro.

"And another!"

"Papa, they're alive. Let's go down and see. Can we, Papa?"

"A little later," replied Father. "We can't land here, in the city. It would be better to find a more deserted place."

Something about these trees was rather disturbing to him. They grew not only where trees would normally grow, but even on pavement and rooftops.

As he steered the ship northward, they kept noticing the strange trees and the deserted, partially destroyed cities.

Again he heard those mysterious crashing and whistling sounds. He had a sickening feeling: Why had he taken the children here? He could have chosen a more suitable place for them: an old, established planet with all sorts of attractions including a tourist bureau, hotels, and guides. Next time they would visit another planet, and not such a strange, dead place as this.

They selected a spot on a green meadow; farther on, it turned into a slope sliced by a jagged trench that had probably been dug by some animals or eroded by water.

Father took an air sample, which turned out to be suitable for Earthlings. He decided to go out without a space suit, but he insisted that the children wear theirs. They strapped on their jet packs in case they had to escape rapidly from a dangerous situation. Although the children maintained their high spirits and curiosity, Father was somewhat worried. Something about this planet disturbed him.

They stepped onto the planet's surface. The space suits didn't hinder their movements: they jumped, turned somersaults, chased each other, and shouted with delight. The planet's strange quality was made even more striking by the dead silence, the absence of the barest puff of wind, and the total absence of any kind of movement.

Suddenly their father noticed a flying object. It came from a southerly direction and had an oblong shape. It dove in a steep arc toward the surface.

"Watch out!" shouted father.

The children stopped to watch the flying object.

"What is it?" asked Oza.

"A bird," suggested Vina.

"That's no bird," said Sandro. "It hasn't any wings."

Again Father heard a shrill whistle. The object struck the ground and began to tear into the soil, which began to stir and rise as if it were being pushed up from within. Suddenly the ground burst and shoots began to sprout—black shoots—in a variety of shapes. Before their eyes the shoots grew into a tall tree, like a beautiful fountain shooting skyward. Some shoots broke up and crumbled to the ground; others simply crawled out of the earth; still others reached a height of about ten meters. Not for a moment did the tree remain immobile: it played, lived, moved, grew, and died, branch by branch. This violent activity contrasted so sharply with the rest of this dead world that it excited and delighted the observers.

When the tree had fully matured, it began to shrink in size, break up, and disintegrate into tiny balls. Something flew past Father's shoulder and he managed to catch it. It was a fragment of this wondrous tree. It was hard as steel and warm, even hot, to touch. Father flipped it into the palm of his hand and put it in his jacket pocket.

"It's a tree! It's a tree!" shouted the children as they gathered the tiny balls into which the tree had disintegrated.

"Watch out, here comes another!" shouted Sandro.

All heads turned in the direction Sandro was pointing. Another oblong object, like the first one, was flying toward them.

"It's a seed!" said Father. "Yes, it's the seed of a strange kind of tree. See how it's pointed at the front end so it can penetrate the soil? And it rotates on its own axis. It enters the ground like a corkscrew and gives birth to a new tree." Father was very pleased with his explanation: everything fit neatly into his hypothesis. "See how it digs into the soil? Now watch the shoots come out!"

And Father, of course, was right. Again dark, living, moving stalks sprouted from the earth.

Suddenly several seeds came flying through the air together; then another, and still another! In swarms!

They approached slowly, mutely, and pierced the earth; in

many places the ground swelled and fragile stalks came through
and quickly grew into huge trees, and the trees into a forest. It
stretched from the northern horizon to the southern horizon in a
band several hundred meters wide. . . .

"Trees, trees! What funny trees!"

While some trees were only beginning to grow, others were
crumbling into fragments that fanned out slowly from the spot
where the seed had fallen. These fragments could also be considered seeds because they generated new, dwarflike trees several
centimeters high.

"Wow, isn't that something!" shouted the children. They had
never seen anything like it. Nor had anyone else. A wave of growing and dying trees rolled toward them. Now it reached a shallow
trench and passed over it.

"Papa," said Vina. "I want to go over there, right into the
middle of the forest."

"Me too," said Sandro.

"I'm a little bit scared," confessed Oza.

"No," said Father. "We're not going in there. We're not sure yet
what this is all about. Besides, it must be awfully hot there. Here,
feel this." Father caught a tree fragment flying slowly past him.
"See, it's warm. And there's a lot of them in there. You'll feel very
hot."

"But, Papa, we're wearing our space suits!" protested Sandro.

"You're wearing the lightweight ones now. Didn't you feel the
heat of that fragment?"

"Where do the seeds come from, Papa?" asked Vina.

"From there," Sandro pointed.

"Oh, I know that. But what do they come from? Do they grow
on trees?"

"Why not have a look," proposed Father. It was a good excuse
to get the children away from here. "Turn on your jet packs.
Head up and west."

They all rose together. The scene below was very picturesque.
They flew above this unique forest in the direction of the flying
seeds.

"There is some sort of pattern to all this," noted Father. "Their flight isn't a random one. They go where there are trenches, ditches, or whatever they're called. Maybe when it rains they fill with water and the seeds ripen there."

They flew about ten kilometers farther and noticed a graceful row of trunks ahead.

"I'll bet they fly somewhere from here," suggested Sandro.

"Why bet? Anyone can see that," said Vina.

"I don't like them," declared Oza.

"Oh, you should have stayed home!" said Sandro.

"Sandro, you mustn't talk like that!" Father scolded.

The tree trunks were smooth, without twigs or branches. The trees themselves bent over at a thirty-degree angle, appearing listless and gloomy. When their seeds left them, they did not stir but seemed to squat somewhat.

"Oh, this is dull," said Sandro. "The living forest was much more interesting."

"Look, seeds are coming this way too!" shouted Oza.

"Well, we've seen that already," grumbled Sandro. "While we were flying, those trees probably began throwing out seeds themselves. Let's go there. I want to have a look."

"Me too," declared Vina.

"I want to go back to the ship," said Oza wearily.

"Well, all right," said Father. "We'll fly back. We'll see what happened there with our forest, and then we'll return to the ship. We haven't eaten yet today. OK?"

"OK," said the children. By now they were rather tired.

They returned to the area where the wondrous, unique trees had multiplied into a splendid forest. They looked at the trees from an altitude of several dozen meters.

Only the forest was alive: everything else was motionless. Looking down, the visitors could clearly see star-shaped objects with shortened radii lying in a long, narrow trench. When a tree fragment fell into the trench, it grew too. Father also noticed that these trees were unusually hardy: they grew everywhere, in clayey or rocky soil. The strip of moving forest had already pushed foward to where the Earthlings had been standing a few minutes before, and it continued to push on.

"Back to the ship now, kids," Father ordered, "for breakfast and a nap. Then we'll continue our tour."

As they flew toward the ship, they noticed that the field was crossed by two more lines parallel to each other: two canals.

After they had boarded, Father sat down at the controls and took the ship up to an altitude of five kilometers. There it hovered.

Breakfast awaited them in the dining room. Excited by what they had seen, they chattered away and kept interrupting each other: "You should have seen that one tree . . ." "For some reason it didn't have leaves . . ." "And did you see? . . ."

"Those star trees looked a lot like people," said Vina.

"What?" Father began to choke. "What did you say?"

"They looked a lot like people."

"Yes, yes, they did," agreed Oza and Sandro.

"H'm, an interesting thought," said Father to himself. "All right, go to the lounge and rest while I work in the control room."

"Papa, will you be there long?" asked Vina.

"No, no, I'll be back very soon. I may go down below for a while. But don't you worry about it."

Again he heard that thunderous crash. Why would he hear it at this altitude?! When the echo died down, an absurd, silly, but frightening thought stole into his brain. No. It couldn't be!

He shut himself up in the control room, turned on the scanner screen, removed a film cassette from a movie camera, and started to insert it in the projector; then he changed his mind. Instead he left it in a very obvious place so that anyone entering the room would notice it at once. Then he strapped on his jet pack and set the timer for activating the ship's engines. Should anything happen to him, the engines would automatically start fifteen minutes from now and the ship would leave. He turned the automatic starter to the rhythm of his own brain waves in the event that emergency evacuation should be necessary before the timer was activated and before he was aboard. Then he entered the air lock. Fifteen minutes should suffice for what he had in mind. He headed below.

The closer he got to the planet's surface, the louder the whistling, whining, and thunderous sounds grew. When he had almost reached the surface, something strange happened . . . to time. . . .

Time began to accelerate at an incredible pace. Now, trees that bred in ten minutes, passed through the entire life cycle in a second or two.

He fell to the bottom of a trench, feeling as if he had been struck by a piece of shrapnel. His head was splitting from the whistling, whining, and deafening roar of explosions; from the piercing screeching of flying shrapnel. He tried to rise but could not; he raised himself slightly and then fell on his back.

"Thank God the children can't see this," he thought as his strength ebbed. He lay there, a hot wave surging through his chest. His gaze was turned toward the horizon where an immobile dot gleamed faintly. Then a new sound was added to the thundering and roaring around him: a steady hum grew louder and louder. Fighter bombers with swastikas on their wings appeared. Suddenly three bombers separated from the formation and soared upward.

"Sandro, Oza, Vina . . . They won't make it. . . ."

"Take off," he whispered.

"Vaska, what are you saying?" wheezed a soldier lying next to him. "Why should we get up? We haven't gotten the order yet. . ."

"Take off, Sandro, take off!" Unshaven, ashen, ghastly looking, he raised himself up on his elbows. Blood oozing from his chest welled up beneath his muddy overcoat.

He caught a glimpse of a shiny dot . . . the ship tearing into the heavens.

"Easy, Vas, easy now. Don't get up. We'll be attacking any minute."

Like a fountain, a strange, dark tree sprouted before him and dozens of its tiny shoots dug into his body.

The last thing he heard was, "Charge . . ."

The universe stood on end, flipped over, and vanished.

For him, the world from which he had come, or which he had simply invented for a few instants, and the world in which he had lived vanished forever.

And a wave of muddy, enraged soldiers yelling something spilled out of the trenches. . . .

Smile

1.

I grew sick and tired of philatelists and numismatists preaching about the great educational value of collecting stamps and coins and how these activities broadened the mind. The only thing that ever excited them was the acquisition of an extremely rare stamp or coin. I learned later that some people collected old-fashioned matchboxes. Pitying their useless labor and succumbing to an impulse or simply a desire to be contrary, I announced one day that I was going to collect smiles.

This elicited a great deal of good-natured laughter. Friends and acquaintances gradually forgot about my ridiculous outburst, and so did I.

Several years passed, and one day I ran into Ann at a graduation ball at the Polytechnical Institute. . . .

"Sashka," she addressed me simply, as usual, "how would you like a present?"

"I'd like that," I replied rather stupidly and carelessly.

"Would you like me to give you a smile?"

"A what?" I laughed idiotically. "A smile?"

"Yes, a smile," she said, and suddenly I saw the light. "You were collecting smiles, weren't you? . . . Don't tell me you've forgotten."

"I have," I replied, remembering that day very clearly. "You couldn't be serious!"

"Sashka, Sashka, you . . ."

I understood her before she could finish the sentence.

"No, Ann, no! I'm not blind. I see everything."

"Do you, really?" And she smiled.

How could I ever forget that smile? Bitter and sweet, happy and hopeless, all-knowing and perplexed.

"I love you too, Ann!" I shouted at the top of my lungs.

The music died on a rather vague note; everyone looked at us expectantly; all movement stopped abruptly, and we became the center of a silent universe.

"What do you mean—*too*?" said Ann. "I only wanted to give you a smile." And she laughed.

No one paid any further attention to us except Andrew. It would have been better if he hadn't; after all, he was in love with Ann.

"May your heart remain pure," were Ann's parting words.

Hunched over, I turned and stalked out of the jolly party. I knew she loved me but, torn by conflicting emotions, preferred not to display her feelings for me.

I was assigned to a job at the Time Institute in Ust-Mansk.

Six months later I learned that Ann was dead. Her illness began when she was ten years old and she lived until she was twenty, but her family and friends never once saw her crying or in low spirits.

Her smile was imprinted on my heart forever.

Shortly thereafter I noticed that I could elicit Ann's smile on the faces of friends or on anyone I wanted to. But I rarely did this because Ann's was a bittersweet smile.

2.

Later I met Olga, and she became my wife.

Here, too, everything had started with a smile.

It was the second smile that I could not forget. I noticed with surprise that everyone who smiled at me had Olga's smile: a happy smile; strong, inspiring, incredibly beautiful, and exuding confidence in one's self and one's friends.

On the streets of our city, in the taiga, in willow thickets near the river—everywhere—I saw that proud, open, inviting, yet slightly wary smile. This wariness was scarcely noticeable and was meant only for me, because she still didn't know anything about my innermost feelings.

There was something intangible, unusual, and exciting in Olga's smile that others could not catch or understand. A smile can't really be seen or heard; it can only be sensed or felt. It's an experience. How often we err in taking a fleeting movement of the lips and a curve of the barely perceptible wrinkles near the eyes as a smile.

Often, when working in the lab or walking down the street trying to recall Olga, I inadvertently elicited a smile from some girl passing by. Stunned, the girl would automatically stop, wondering why and to whom she was smiling. Sometimes I would get a rather cautious what's-wrong-with-you-look, although it seemed to me that I should have been the one asking the question.

"Oh, I collect smiles," was the first response that flew into my mind one day.

"What a nut!" came the reply, and I agreed.

Gradually I learned to catch various nuances in Olga's smile, and the boundaries between them were so elusive that trying to find them, I could not, at first, distinguish a smile of joyous anticipation from a smile of anticipated joy, a smile of physical anguish from a smile of mental anguish. And there are such smiles too.

To remember Olga's smiles required no special memory training; it was simply a matter of understanding Olga in all her simplicity and complexity, in all her harmony and disharmony, in her joy and grief, in her flashes of fleeting tenderness and irritability, in her songs and tears.

When she uttered those magic words, "I love you," I imagined for an instant that I knew all her smiles, and right then and there I was overwhelmed, dazzled, transported to cloud nine, dropped back to Earth and forgiven. . . . It was a lesson.

Still, I knew thousands of her smiles.

When she would come home from work exhausted from her pupils' mischievous antics or would cry over a cut finger, I mentally pictured her smiles, and immediately one of them would find its rightful place in her heart. And Olga smiled. She smiled and cried, cried and laughed, and she felt better.

Then she would say teasingly,

"Sashka, you certainly are a magician, aren't you?"

"Not me," I'd say. "You're the one."

"So, I guess both of us are," she would say.

At first my ability to elicit smiles from memory astonished my friends. Soon they grew accustomed to it. I myself couldn't explain this gift; it seemed to have developed without any effort on my part. I always felt that everyone should be endowed with it.

My collection included not only Olga's smiles, but those of my friends. For instance, there were Andrew's aloof, intent smiles, including the lean, lofty, absurd smile when he played fugues and preludes on the organ. His amazing smiles were as varied as his performance on the organ: smoothly flowing, now explosive, now sinking into a deep, mysterious whirlpool. It was useless to discuss the sensations his performance evoked in his listeners because any description, no matter how precise, would utterly destroy the absolute perfection of the smile and the music.

One day I could no longer restrain myself and I said to him, "Andy, when I hear your music I am suddenly overwhelmed by the most unusual sensation, a multidimensional layering of space and time. While you play I actually live several lives, all completely different. How do you explain it?"

He shrugged his shoulders. "I simply see Ann's smile."

3.

Andrew was not a professional musician. We both worked at the same research institute but with different machines, Time machines. Long ago, before we began to work here, someone dubbed them "mustangs," and the name stuck.

Almost every day, we sent our mustangs back in Time, observing—mind you, only observing and not interfering—scrupulously studying the facts, culling superfluous and minor information, bemoaning the knowledge of our own limitations when suddenly what was minor turns out to be important, and vice versa. We would argue until we were hoarse and bleary-eyed, trying to identify which segment of time that we were investigating had contributed to our own lives or to humanity in general.

What had the past given to us? Where was it taking us?

The future and the past do not exist apart from each other. Together with the present they form one tight little bundle; and within this bundle are all the contradictions and mistakes of the past, all the wishes and hopes for the future, all the joy and grief of centuries gone by. It contains the whole future and the whole past. The whole future, because it depends on the present. The whole past, because the future depends on it. But an instant of the present is so brief!

Humanity often makes mistakes that instantaneously become past mistakes, too late to correct. One can only try to moderate the consequences. But this wastes too much effort and, sometimes, human lives.

Our job at the Institute was to study the past, but we wanted to change it.

Afanasy Navagin, whose hobby was collecting wheezes, was obsessed with the idea of sending Spartacus a couple of machine guns. No one paid any attention to him, since any first-year student at the Institute knew the possible consequences of such an act.

Navagin visited clinics and hospitals frequently; when he returned to the lab afterward, someone would suddenly begin to wheeze. Afanasy also possessed the ability to reproduce . . . yes, reproduce wheezes. When the frightened engineer or lab assistant regained his or her equilibrium and began to look around plaintively, Navagin would guffaw and say over and over, "Anyone can do it. . . ."

"Yeah, some people can trigger smiles; others, dirty tricks," someone piped up.

But Afanasy was impenetrable; after all, he had a unique gift.

It once occurred to me that were Afanasy not endowed with the ability to reproduce wheezes in the people around him, no one would know his real character. He was an intelligent engineer and had been awarded many certificates of merit for excellent work.

I had long noticed that he couldn't smile. True, rather often he arched his lips prettily and wrinkled his eyes, but I wouldn't call it a smile. It was more like the expression on the face of a ball being squashed under a clown's foot.

One day I remarked to Igor, the boss of our lab, that Afanasy might be cooking up something in a Time segment of the past. For some reason I was convinced of it.

"Nonsense," replied Igor. "He's a coward. He wouldn't dare. Besides, there's the interlocking gear."

I didn't feel too secure about the interlocking gear.

Igor was a downright workaholic. Only once did he permit himself to be diverted from his work. That was when on purely scientific grounds and armed with instruments, protocols, and deductions, he studied my ability to elicit from others smiles drawn from my personal collection.

For two weeks Afanasy gnashed his teeth, threatening to write a report to the Institute's director about the improper use of laboratory equipment, but no one paid any attention to him.

At that point he said, "I detest smiles!" And slamming the door, he left work early. For the next five minutes, we all wheezed, sensing approaching death, hunger, pain, and debility.

Although Igor pursued his research to the bitter end, he did not send the results to the Academy, since the work on my unique gift in no way tied in with his; instead he sent it to a popular magazine. Consequently, journalists descended on me en masse, and for several days I was looked upon as a three-headed freak. Igor refused to have anything to do with this three-ring circus, so I had to cope with the press alone.

Several magazine articles about my ability to paste smiles from my collection on people's faces appeared. I was showered with all kinds of responses. I was called a charlatan. It didn't particularly bother me; in fact, I was even quite relieved when I was finally left in peace.

About five months later, smile shops began to open in almost every city. It turned out that the ability to elicit and collect smiles was present in every individual, to a greater or lesser degree, of course. There was nothing supernatural about it. But we've known that for a long time. Or if we weren't conscious of it, at least we sensed that that's the way it should be.

By this time, Afanasy Navagin had completed his research assignment on a specific Time segment well before the deadline. His efficient, erudite report with its quotations from the classics drew praise from the director of the Institute. He spent half a day strutting around the laboratory with a triumphant look on his face, making remarks and dealing out advice, and then he disappeared for several days. When Afanasy returned from this self-imposed leave, Igor grimly summoned him to his office, and we were sure there would be fireworks. For once in his life Afanasy had not toed the line. . . . But we were wrong. The conversation in the office of the lab chief lasted barely thirty seconds. Afanasy emerged glowing, while Igor didn't come out at all for hours.

"Well, it looks as if your waxworks of smiles is all washed up," announced Afanasy, sitting down at my table. "Kaput!"

We fell silent and waited expectantly, and Lyubochka, our academic secretary, sighed loudly.

"Do you know where I've been?" asked Afanasy.

"At the morgue," said shy Anatoly Krutikov, blushing.

"Correct. At the morgue. I went to a smile shop. It's more like a smile morgue. It's finished!"

Lyubochka sighed again. Andrew flopped into the seat of his mustang and disappeared. The others pretended that none of this particularly interested them.

"For three days I did nothing but browse through those shops," began Afanasy. The boss had probably intended to rake me over the coals for taking off without his OK. But he's a very scrupulous chap. After all, I was interested in smiles. Since it's beyond his comprehension, he won't do a damn thing to me. So, as I was saying, I was browsing in the shops and came to a conclusion . . ." He paused meaningfully, waiting for response.

No one spoke.

"No questions?" said Afanasy. "Then listen. All your smiles are washed up! You cooked your own goose. . . . Smiles can be bought on any street corner. Anyone can buy them. The selection is large but still limited. Some are a little worse, some a little better. And just you wait until some official style-setter comes along. You'll all have the same gorgeous, standard smile pasted on your faces. The whole smile business will be kaput. Ha, ha! Get it?!"

"Did you manage to come to that all by yourself?" asked Lyubochka.

"With my very own head," replied Afanasy triumphantly.

"No, you misunderstood me. I'm talking about *you*, your life, the way you look at things. Did you get there all by yourself, or did someone help you?"

Navagin was momentarily stunned.

"You, Ragozina, are an impudent woman!" he roared. "You can't even argue with me, because it's useless."

We all nodded in agreement.

"Oh, you're a cold fish. You've no soul, have you?" Lyubochka shouted back.

"Sure I do!" yelled Navagin. "I'm no different than anybody else! Get that through your head!"

"For God's sake, Afanasy, stop yelling." Krutikov stepped between the two of them.

"Listen here," Lyubochka brushed Anatoly aside, "even if smiles were selected like the size, style, and color of shoes, there would still be plenty of combinations. Think of all the different moods a person can have. . . . You can't do anything to smiles, they're here to stay."

"Oh, yes I can," muttered Afanasy.

I had the feeling that if it were possible to crush, burn, or destroy a smile, he would do it without a moment's hesitation.

Igor entered the lab and settled down at the other end of the room.

"Most likely there aren't any smiles to go with the size and color of your heart," said Anatoly.

"You're afraid I can't prove it! You're lying. There are!" Afanasy screeched and stamped his feet on the floor. "I paid a ruble for them. You can buy a hundred of them for no more than a kopeck, dirt cheap!"

"You wasted your dough," remarked Andrew, alighting from

his mustang. His face was pale, his expression impenetrable. From the way he glanced at me, I knew he had seen Ann; I felt and sensed her smile again. He always aged after such trips into the past. Now that Ann was dead, he shouldn't have made the journey. But who had the heart to stop him?

"Afanasy, show us at least one," asked technician Sveta. She was rather young and often defended him when the subject involved something more substantial than a smile.

"In a minute." Navagin was delighted with the opportunity to prove himself. After slapping his pockets for a few seconds, he realized that he was looking in the wrong place, and he turned green beneath the disapproving smirks of his audience. Then he said quietly, "Watch."

It was the smile of a scoundrel ready to sink a knife into the back of an unsuspecting victim.

Sveta began to cry hysterically, screaming through tears, "Please, oh, please stop!"

I grabbed Afanasy by the throat, but instead of tearing himself from my grip, he projected a whole range of cowardly, fiendish smiles. I don't know if it was a kopeck's or a ruble's worth.

"Such smiles don't exist," said Lyubochka, and Krutikov led her away.

"Let go," croaked Navagin, tearing my hand from his throat. Now he looked like a normal, slightly frightened young man. "I can still do another ten rubles' worth."

No one spoke. No one wanted to speak. Afanasy had probably finished his piece.

Igor rose abruptly and went over to Navagin. "Well, can you produce a simple, human smile for us?"

"What do you think those were, if not human?"

"So, you can't, can you?"

"Sure I can if I want to, but I turn them away, reject them," said Navagin with dignity. "The effect of a rejected smile. I discovered this effect. Thus, it will be called 'The Navagin Effect.'"

"You're wrong," said Igor. "You mean the effect of a rebounding smile. They bounced off you and you can't do a thing about it."

"The Rebounding Smile Effect," Igor hit it right on the head! For a long time I had been searching for a definition, for words that would describe Navagin's pathological traits. The rebounding smile effect! They really did bounce off him.

"Anyway, smiles are sold like potatoes. ha, ha!"

"That's better than selling machine guns!" Lyubochka's voice broke and she hurried out of the room.

"Goodness knows!" Navagin drawled meaningfully.

"Scram, Afanasy," said Andrew calmly, slapping him on the shoulder. "Come on, you'd better go."

"You can't do anything to me anyway!"

"We'll come up with something." Igor's tone left no doubts.

"You can't do a damn thing to me! I've done nothing illegal! You yourself asked me to show you some smiles." It was clear from his twitching lips and trembling hands that he was getting cold feet. He was beginning to regret that he had started this conversation. No one came to his defense.

"Get the hell out of here," I shouted. Glancing back and stammering, he headed for the door.

"Sashka," pleaded Igor when the door was carefully closed, "do me a favor, please! A little something from your collection. I need a lift."

I imagined one of Andrew's contemplative smiles.

"Oh, never mind," said Igor, smiling. "Let's go home."

4.

On the way home I dropped into a smile shop and browsed for a long time, hoping to find the one that Navagin had used from among an assortment of thousands of smiles. I didn't believe such smiles were sold.

But there it was, in the showcase, almost hidden beneath a pile of children's and women's smiles, beneath a selection of radiant, mysterious, happy, and bitter human smiles.

"Why that one?" I asked tersely, pointing to the object of my search.

"That one? Oh, well, not everyone's a genius," replied the sales-woman rather slyly. "This city has only six professional theaters, but more amateur groups than you can imagine. . . ."

"So, it's for untalented actors."

"Except that for some reason they never buy them, only rent them. Right after the show they return them," she shrugged her shoulders.

That meant Navagin had purchased this smile in another shop.

When I arrived at our apartment on the sixth floor of a typical residential building, I must have had a rather gloomy expression on my face, for try as I did to appear cheerful, Olga saw through it and forced me to tell her about Navagin.

Someday shops will sell happiness or simply give it away free to everyone," said Olga pensively. "Do you think even then there will still be people who can transform happiness into grief?"

What could I say to her? Possibly there would be. Everything depended solely on us.

Digging into the deepest recesses of my collection, I spent the entire evening trying to remember the smiles of Olga, Andrew, Igor, Krutikov, Lyubochka, my future son, friends, and people that passed me in the street; and I gave them to Olga. It lifted her spirits, making her laugh and sing.

Later I remembered Afanasy again, and Olga began to cry. It was then I first realized that a smile could be killed; that we must take good care of it, protect it, even fight for it.

5.

The following day Afanasy Navagin appeared in the lab as if nothing had happened, as if yesterday's conversation had never taken place. Even when Svetlanka, radiant with joy, burst into the room and scattered in all directions mischievous, impish smiles just purchased at a smile shop, Afanasy muttered, "Rather pretty, Mademoiselle." Svetka almost swooned with happiness and kissed Lyubochka. We all knew she had a crush on Navagin, the kind adolescents usually have on adults who are different, even for the worse, from others and have a mysterious air about them.

"Svetka, you're a doll," said Lyubochka.

Afanasy flopped into the seat of his mustang and shouted to Igor, "I have to check something out. I'll be back soon."

Igor waved his hand, and Navagin vanished.

"What's the matter with him?" Krutikov looked puzzled.

"I don't know." Svetka blushed.

"Could the guy actually have become human?" Igor asked himself.

"No," said Andrew, but no one except me heard him.

Two months of intensive activity passed at the Institute.

All of us had to defend our scientific reports. Using our reports, microfilm, photographs, tape recordings, and private conversations, one of the Institute's departments would spend a whole year analyzing why the course of events in a segment of Time flowed in a particular direction rather than in another and what factors determined the velocity and acceleration of civilization's development. Then a theoretical basis would be established for history's optimal path of development. Prognoses would be made about changes that could have occurred in human history if a past event in this segment had taken a different course. Hundreds of people and dozens of computers would be involved in this work.

It might be demonstrated that humanity could have become more civilized long ago and eliminated war; that people could have learned to understand each other, to moderate their desires in proportion to the desires of others, to respect each other and be people in the full sense of the word.

Time and time again history has marked time and rolled backward. Still, this didn't have to happen.

In about a year and a half we'll read a report telling us what humanity could be like, even now.

But all this is merely theory. For some reason, civilization doesn't always choose a shortcut toward progress.

We cannot influence the past or change it. Our sense of morality does not permit this. Would it be right to exclude the birth of millions of people so that millions of others could become better people? At what point, in which century, would we begin to change the course of history? In the process of changing history, how can we remain ordinary people and prevent ourselves from turning into omnipotent gods; from generating a new and terrifying religion? Besides, how reliable are the guarantees for our predictions?

We accumulate facts. We are history's unskilled laborers.

As usual, we had a breathing spell before starting to work on a new topic.

During the year, we couldn't always find the time to discuss certain elements of our work or we hadn't sufficiently digested the material to express our ideas about it. Now, at last, we had the time, and our opinions were well established. . . . So, there were lots of fierce debates, at times even too fierce and stormy. They covered everything, from "that's none of our business" to "we don't have the moral right" or "we shouldn't meddle." We would argue by the hour until someone would abruptly change the subject and we would suddenly realize that we were very tired and needed either a shot in the arm or something to unwind us. Then the conversation turned to soccer, fishing, and the smell of lilacs.

6.

Our daughter, yes, a daughter, was born in the middle of summer. I wanted to name her Helga because Helga and Olga have the same meaning, but my wife insisted on naming her Becky.

One day a rowdy bunch—all my lab co-workers—burst into our small apartment, bearing smile bouquets. By that time, the custom of presenting gifts of smile bouquets to friends and acquaintances was well established. Some people were past masters of the art. I even found two baskets of wine in the foyer, left unpretentiously by some shy guests.

The women immediately clustered around Olga and Becky, and it was impossible to make out a word of what they were saying.

The male visitors merely clicked their tongues as they hovered over the newborn infant with its inanely bulging eyes, and then they made a hasty, somewhat cowardly, exit to the other room. Andrew dragged a couple of bottles into the kitchen and began mixing cocktails. Afanasy diligently led the singing.

In the past few months Afanasy had changed markedly. It had been a long time since anyone had wheezed in the lab. But on several occasions I noticed Navagin jumping into his mustang, as if he were incapable of controlling certain overwhelming emotions. Fear and anger were evident in his every movement, but he tried not to show it. Afanasy vanished. For the past six months he had worked like a dynamo. His segment of history was processed so painstakingly, organized so well, that the assistant director of scientific research held it up as a model of creative work.

For a long time I had an urge to have a heart-to-heart talk with Afanasy, if only it were theoretically possible.

Our singing was rather uninspired. Now and then someone would begin speaking about our work. It was almost a sickness. Why hasn't the medical world paid any attention to this sort of ailment? I fail to understand it. After all, it's really an infectious disease. . . .

The women finally left Becky in peace, and she fell asleep. We were permitted to enter the room. I was the next to last one to leave the kitchen and caught a sentence uttered by Afanasy. Since he was running water noisily in the sink, he apparently didn't intend his remark for anyone's ears.

"Scarcely out of the womb, and they're beginning to smile. . . ."

I lingered, "Is that so awful?"

"I didn't say that. Anyway I'm not an expert on smiles. That's your territory. . . ."

"Say, can I have a nice quiet chat with you?" I asked.

He didn't reply or even look at me.

"Afanasy, why do you hate smiles?"

"Are you so sure I do?"

"Well, it looks that way to me."

"I could refuse to answer until you can prove you have the right to ask that question."

"OK, let's say I simply guessed it."

"All right, then you tell me why people smile, demanded Afanasy, leaning against the windowsill.

"Because they're happy, glad about something; because their hearts are singing."

"Their hearts? So, their hearts are singing, so what? That's on the inside. The external expression of the heart's song could just as well be anything else, like grinding your teeth or flapping your ears. What's the difference? Smiling is merely a custom, and that's all."

"An incontrovertible argument," I said. "Well, OK, but when people are happy they don't gnash their teeth, they smile, even if it's only the custom. Although you're actually wrong about that."

"But I don't accept that custom. Get it? There's no law that says you have to smile."

"OK, you don't have to smile. That's your business. But what do you have against it? Give me a straight answer. A smile is the external expression of a specific mood. The mood is the whole point. And that is what you dislike—happiness. If people were to wiggle their ears for joy, you would tear them off. That's so much easier than wiping a smile from someone's face. All right then, how about a straight answer?"

"Cut it out," said Afanasy, trying to push me away from the door. He was neither frightened nor worried. He was calm, and I realized that he had won this round: he would still not give me a straight answer, and I would not get anywhere with him. After the conversation in the laboratory he had become very cautious. I knew he might shout, although not too loudly, "Quit pestering me, Sashka, will you! Get off my back. All you yap about is smiles, smiles, smiles." The guys would hear him, open the kitchen door, yank me out by my sleeve, and tell me to cool it. Andrew and Igor would say, "Sashka, drop it. He won't understand this. He's a bird of another species." And I'd listen. And the others? They'd tell me this was not the time nor place to be arguing and that Afanasy had his little eccentricities like everybody else.

"Let me pass!" said Afanasy.

I stepped aside. He started to open the door, then changed his mind and returned.

"Well," he said, "suppose it's because I can't do it. I never learned to smile. Is that the kind of answer you expected?"

I shook my head and said nothing. He left the room. I was sure he would say exactly what he said. And I knew beforehand that it would be a lie. I didn't believe him.

If a person can't sing, does it follow that he or she hates music? Absolutely not. . . .

7.

The next day, the director summoned all of us to his office. When we arrived, ten important scientists and administrators were there. Smiling tensely, we took our seats. We had good reason to be nervous: it's not every day that the director of the Institute calls in the entire lab. In fact, I had never heard about anything like it before. This had to be something damn special.

The meeting, or chat, or whatever you'd call it opened with a question: "Do you know that rules and regulations forbid the transportation of anything into the past and that you are never to be visible to your ancestors?

The question was addressed to each of us individually, and we replied that we knew this because we were not permitted to make any changes in the past. And how we knew it! We learned that in our freshman year.

Then a man, whom we all knew from his portrait, took the floor. He was the president of the Academy of Sciences of Western Siberia.

"We," he said, "cannot continue studying the past indefinitely. Sooner or later we must close the feedback loop of Time." Glowering at us, he paused briefly. "We consider that now is the moment to begin."

Although stunned, we were rather delighted.

"First, we studied the reports submitted by all the Institute's laboratories. Naturally the most detailed report of a past Time segment interested us." All heads turned in Afanasy's direction. "That report is the work of Navagin."

Afanasy blushed.

A brief review of his report lasted about fifteen minutes. Actually Navagin had done a super piece of research. None of us had his meticulous approach, scrupulous technique, or capacity for work.

Then the following question was posed: What can be transported from the present into the past, taking into account the singularity of the experiment, the still unperfected method, and the complexity of prognostication (remember, human civilization is developing in Bergsonian, and not Newtonian, time)?

Of course we had been debating this question among ourselves for a long time, but we could never agree on what should be transported. Some opted for antibiotics; others, for bread; a third group, for knowledge accumulated by humankind to the present day; and a fourth group, like Afanasy, for machine guns.

Even now, we couldn't agree. Only Afanasy remained silent. He understood, as did everyone, that the experiment would be conducted within the Time segment that he had been studying.

We argued for a long time, then someone spoke up.

"For the time being, nothing of a material nature can be transported into the past."

Quieting down, we began to mutter complex questions among ourselves:

"Then what should we send?"

"What?"

"An absolute idea?"

"Why not a smile?" said Afanasy in bewilderment.

"Yes, a smile," the president of the Western Siberia Academy of Sciences replied calmly.

"Why?" I asked mechanically.

"Why?" said the president. "It can only have positive consequences, perhaps not very significant ones, but certainly positive consequences. People must smile. They must know how to smile. Must want to smile. And that's just a beginning. Afanasy Navagin and Alexsander Vetrov will conduct the experiment. We understand that Alexsander has a large collection of smiles. That will come in very handy." And, turning to Afanasy and myself, he asked, "Do you agree with my proposal?"

"I do," replied Afanasy, pale with excitement.

"I do," I replied, feeling the blood draining from my face too.

Our co-workers rushed to congratulate us. Igor tried to ask concrete technical questions. Everyone had something to say, but scarcely listened to anyone else. The room was noisy and charged with excitement. After all, this was an unusual occasion!

Preparations for the experiment proceeded rapidly. I studied Navagin's report and had a good idea of what I could expect to encounter in the past. Afanasy worked unceasingly on his mission in Time, polishing, honing, making the most minute details of events as precise as possible. Several times he asked me to show him my collection of smiles. "For the experiment, of course," he would say.

I doubt that he would ever have asked me about it were it not for the fact that we were slated to work together very soon.

"With this we can . . ." he remarked, looking through my collection and not once cracking a smile.

I assumed he meant to say, "We can begin with this one" and I was even flattered by it. Imagine Afanasy not censuring a smile.

8.

The experiment began at the end of the summer.

That day everyone was very attentive and considerate, offering us advice and assistance.

"Aren't you nervous?" asked the director of the Institute as we were about to begin.

I shook my head.

"It won't frighten me," said Afanasy.

The experiment was under way. . . .

We stood among a raging mob of men, women, and teenagers. Their distorted faces glittered in the crimson flickering light of thousands of torches. Here was a roaring mob, their feet stamping rhythmically; and hidden fear; and faces twisted with hate, savage anger, and fiendish delight. I had known what to expect; still, I was stunned.

The sight of these people was an entirely new experience for me. A huge bonfire blazed in the middle of a square surrounded by multistoried dwellings, whose balconies, windows, and roofs were jammed with people. Its flames were consuming piles of books being unloaded from vans and trucks. Howling with pleasure and fiendish delight, the people grabbed books and hurled them into the flames.

It was difficult to see what was happening from where we were standing, so Afanasy, grasping my hand, cut through the mob and pulled me closer to the fire.

Now we had a grandstand view.

To smile here would have been blasphemous. This, I felt, I could not do.

"My God, how can people do this?"

"Never mind. Something far more interesting is about to begin. Over there." Afanasy pointed past the fire and slightly to the right. "One chap over there who can't take what's going on won't hold out. And they'll kill him." Afanasy's voice was calm.

That very instant, from the spot to which Navagin had just pointed, a piercing scream tore through the roaring, raging mob. There, beyond the fire, the crowd began to surge forward. A man broke away from it, fell, jumped up, fell again, and began to crawl. Dozens of hands grabbed him by his clothes and tried to hold him back, but he continued to crawl, dragging the others with him. For a split second he managed to free himself; he reached the fire and snatched a badly burned book from it. Seconds later the crowd retreated one step from the fire. A motionless figure lay on the pavement.

"He's dead," said Afanasy. "Why the devil don't you show your collection?"

"I can't."

"You can't!" Afanasy shook me. "What do you mean you can't?! Get started, now!! What difference should it make to you whether you do it now or any other time? Start your show!"

I forced myself to remember Andrew's smile . . . a sad smile, but a vivid, pure, clever smile.

I thought that for a moment I detected a flicker of light on the faces of people who were casting their thoughts, life, hopes, and feelings into the fire. The rhythmic movement of their hands swinging books into the flames seemed to falter. But, no . . . the smile had rebounded from them. It was unnecessary, alien, disruptive, harmful. Carried away by their mission, they didn't even notice it. Suddenly one of them picked up a tommy-gun from the ground and released a random burst of fire. With a barely audible groan, the smile died.

"Did you see that?!" Navagin shouted to me.

I saw it all. They had killed a smile!

I could give them thousands of joys, big and little; and feelings and thoughts . . .

My God, they had killed a smile, killed it point-blank!

I remembered Andrew—his love, his hate, his music. And smiles fanned through the mob.

I saw them catch the smiles, only to dash them to the ground and trample them. They shot them, smothered them, dragged them to the fire, and tossed them into it. Defenseless human smiles. I saw that several smiles managed to cling to people's faces. Terrified, some tried to tear them off and fling them where they would not be seen. Others, bewildered, did not know what to do. Still others tried to hide them, timidly and clumsily. Anyone noticing a smile on the face of his neighbor ripped it off instantly, along with skin and blood from the sheared, shrieking mouth.

Now my bag of Andrew's smiles was gone. I refused to believe that people could behave this way, so I gave them other smiles:

Olga's, Lyubochka's, Svetka's, and Toly Krutikov's; the smiles of people I had once passed on the street; the smiles of friends; and even meaningless smiles, the utterly helpless smiles of my own little Becky.

Apparently it had some effect: it shook them up a bit. One chap hid a book under his jacket and vanished into the crowd. Many began to disperse hurriedly. Philistines, frightened to death, stamped their feet in helpless rage, still clutching their weapons.

I had only one smile left—Ann's. It was too bitter to give to them, but oh how desperately it yearned to live. So I gave them this last smile. I noticed the frightened expression on the face of a girl as she tucked something into her bosom. I am sure it was Ann's smile.

Once again they began to burn books.

After that, I remember nothing . . .

9.

When I came to, I was lying on some jackets on the laboratory floor.

"Where's Afanasy?" I asked.

"What Afanasy?" asked Igor in surprise. "What happened there?"

"Where's Afanasy Navagin?"

"Easy. Take it easy. Who is this Afanasy fellow?"

"You know . . . Afanasy, who did a super, too super job on his Time segment. Where is he?" I jumped to my feet.

"We never had any Afanasy here. You've got him mixed up with somebody else."

Many people had converged on the lab and everyone looked at me with a slightly bewildered and frightened expression.

"Afanasy hated a smile. Don't you remember that?"

"There was never anyone like that here."

"OK, we'll get to that later. But how the hell did I get out of there?"

"Andrew dragged you out," said Igor. His words were filled with pain. Svetka cried. Through her tears I heard, "He's dead. He's been taken away already."

"Dead!" I shouted. "Why?"

"He was shot in the back trying to save you."

10.

Several days have passed. I am trying to avoid people. I realize how difficult it is for people to be with me now. . . .

Subsequent experiments have been postponed indefinitely. No one remembers Afanasy Navagin. He never existed. He was never born. That means something had changed in the past, after all, to prevent Afanasy's birth.

Perhaps the girl that had hidden Ann's smile had rejected an ancestor of Afanasy's. Or maybe, having seen this smile, he hadn't the courage to approach her. In any case, Afanasy was not born.

Nevertheless, this experiment did change people just a little bit, and for the better.

After all, Afanasy isn't around.

But neither do we have our Andrew.

Why must our Andrews give their lives to keep the Afanasys out of this world?

All my smiles are gone. I cannot smile. Everyone understands my plight and tries somehow to help me, all except little Becky. I still can't explain anything to her. It's a terrible feeling—to stand over my daughter's bed and not have the strength to smile.

I read an article in the newspaper. Someone had discovered "The Law of Rebounding Smiles." Afanasy, too, had once discovered that law. So, he's not alone, far from it. And there's many more like him.

Friends drop in to see me. I see Olga often. They all give me the kind of cautious, brisk smiles reserved for the gravely ill.

Dear friends, don't be afraid!

I need your smiles, all kinds of smiles: smiles of children and grown-ups; smiles that are silly and serious, joyful and bitter, happy and sad. I need smiles coming from the bottom of your hearts, from the brightest, innermost recesses of your souls.

Dear people, I need smiles . . . because I plan to return to that blazing bonfire.

Hear ye, good people, I need your smiles!

Hermit's Swing

1.

Violet, a freight and passenger rocket, usually waited for the transstellar liner outside the oribit of Sevan system's fifth planet. This time, too, everything proceeded normally. Having beaten the timetable for escape into tri-dimensional space by one minute, transliner *Warsaw* materialized precisely at the designated spot. *Warsaw*'s captain instantly sent his coordinates through the ether. But *Violet*'s radar had already plotted the liner's appearance, and accelerating, *Violet* rushed toward the liner.

Excitement reigned in the captain's cabin on *Violet*. Ships from Earth rarely appeared in the region of Sevan. Now there would be new instruments and equipment, something Hermit's physicists, biologists, archeologists, and engineers always found in short supply. There would be new articles to read, new information, and those precious hours in the company of people who a short time ago had walked on Earth.

The events of those few hours would provide weeks of conversation on Hermit. *Violet*'s crew would have difficulty declining invitations: every cottage at Central Station would invite them to drop in for a cup of coffee. Each of the station's twenty bases would urgently request someone from the crew to help with some unforeseen work. And it was a small crew, only three members: *Violet*'s captain, Sven Tomson; his assistant and cybernetics specialist, Nikolai Traikov; and communications crewman, Henry Wirt.

Watching the sphere denoting *Warsaw* loom larger and larger, Sven Tomson said, "When I see that baby, I feel like making a beeline for Earth. On Hermit the feeling passes. But waiting here and watching *Warsaw* approach is different. I can barely keep myself from writing a request for leave."

"The Polar Star is beckoning him," sang Nikolai Traikov in a treble voice. "You're not going anywhere from Hermit. And Anita . . ."

"Shut up, Nik!" barked Sven.

"OK, OK. . . . Just don't send in any requests for leave, please."

"Hey, I left my fluorescent blue shirt on Hermit," said Henry. "Oza got everything mixed up again."

"Well, now, that is a catastrophe!" Nikolai smirked.

"You think it's very funny, but I don't. Everyone in the passenger lounge will be wearing fluorescent shirts, but I . . ."

"Take mine," offered Sven.

"Yours?" Henry asked in surprise, staring at the captain's tall, broad-shouldered figure. "What I don't need is a nightgown."

"As you wish," replied Tomson calmly. Suddenly he shouted, "Three minutes left! The hell with etiquette; we never gave a damn about it anyway. . . ."

"Welcome to the Hermit team!" *Warsaw's* captain greeted them through the loudspeaker. "How are you doing with that civilization puzzle there? Anything happening?"

"We're in great shape!" shouted Tomson. "But it's still one hell of a mystery. Is everything ready in the passenger lounge? Has the chef cooked up any surprises for us?"

"Attention *Violet's* crew!" a loud voice rang out. "Get ready!"

"We're ready," replied Tomson.

"Here's the countdown. Ten, nine . . . zero."

The transliner's enormous side filled *Violet's* scanner screen; then, maneuvering alongside *Violet*, *Warsaw's* metal and ceramic plates slid open and swallowed the rocket. The plates closed. *Violet* lay on a special platform in the transliner's cargo compartment.

Bright lights illuminated the area around the rocket. People, looking like ants in this enormous room, scurried toward the platform. The massive figures of robot longshoremen went into action.

Tomson pressed a key. Huge doors slid open and the robots began loading cargo into the rocket's capacious belly.

"You may exit," announced the loudspeaker.

All three crewmates rushed to the elevator and a minute later were standing on the platform, squinting in the glaring lights.

"How are things back on Earth?"

The Hermitians ignored the ramp, leaped from the two-meter-high platform, and embraced the people who had just arrived from Earth. It didn't matter that they were total strangers.

The Hermitians were deluged with questions, all kinds: simple, difficult, ridiculous, worried.

"Is it winter there now?"

"It is."

"Why's that? We're having summer."

"Aha, I see. Winter and summer at the same time. Say, that's great!"

Laughter. Friendly slaps on the back. Applause.

"How many microtanks did you bring?"

"When you sign the list you'll know."

"Fifty kilos of letters. A million and a half greetings."

Chatting about dozens of things at the same time, they left *Warsaw's* cargo compartment.

The liner's enormous elevator would not hold everyone at once, so they ascended in groups. Brightly lit tunnels led to somewhere in the distance and one could distinguish the figures of people and robots in them. As the elevator rose from floor to floor, the liner's passengers waved to the elevator's occupants although they could barely see them. All they knew was that *Violet's* crew was on their way up. The robots ignored everyone. They had no time to think about such nonsense: they had a job to do.

The endless ascent was over. Wirt, Tomson, and Traikov stepped onto the moving sidewalk, a bluish-gray ribbon of plastic that felt springy beneath their feet. Every one hundred meters, they encountered intersections leading into bright, spacious corridors. Huge, high-ceilinged rooms contained strange constructions: multicolored spheres, cones, parabolic spans, small suspension bridges, cylinders, and metal skeletons. Everywhere the liner's astronauts waved to the visiting Hermitians.

The liner was a huge laboratory, a complete research institute. *Warsaw* not only supplied vital equipment, food, specialists, consumer goods, and construction materials to exploratory planets, but also, almost one thousand scientific workers were doing research in four-dimensional space.

Warsaw made the rounds of twenty research planets in three Earth months. Then, following a brief stay on Earth, the cycle was repeated again.

Some twenty people were assembled in the passenger lounge. Tomson discussed the problems of cultivating new varieties of cacti in four-dimensional space with *Warsaw*'s captain, Anton Veresayev. Having gathered around him more than half the people in the lounge, Nikolai Traikov, rolling his eyes and gesturing wildly, told his listeners about Hermit's predators. Henry Wirt, hiccupping, chatted with two girls.

Then Veresayev introduced Early Kozales, journalist and physicist, to *Violet*'s crew. Early would return with them to Hermit.

Afterward, dinner was served. The variety of dishes would have fed all of Hermit's research workers for a week.

After dinner they went to the concert hall, then they watched newsreels; several hours were spent strolling from stateroom to stateroom, exchanging impressions and picking up information.

Leaving the liner, they rode in the spacious elevator again, past intersections, turns, tunnels, and halls. Everything earmarked for Hermit had been loaded. *Violet*'s cargo hatches were already secured. With slow, awkward movements, the robot loaders moved off to their hangars. Then came the final farewells and handshakes.

Early sat down in the cockpit. Wirt checked out radio communication; Nikolai Traikov, all the ship's cybernetic systems. Then Tomson announced into the microphone, "Ready!"

It seemed as if an invisible force had pushed *Violet* out of the transliner. The two-kilometer-long sphere gradually appeared smaller and smaller to *Violet*'s crew.

"Happy plasma!"

"Happy supercrossing!"

When *Violet* had moved off some thirty thousand kilometers from the liner, a faint bluish flare shone on its scanner screen. The transliner had entered four-dimensional space.

2.

For *Violet's* crew the seven-day journey to Hermit passed quickly. All the ship's systems worked perfectly, so the three astronauts retired to the small library to read books, magazines, and microfilmed newspapers, tearing themselves away only to eat, sleep, and check out the operations of the ship's systems.

Early was going to Hermit to gather material for a book about this strange planet. To save time, he studied the expedition's last report. It was very concise and factual; it appeared that the expedition's leaders could not offer a single theory to explain Hermit's countless riddles.

Hermit had been discovered eight years ago. The damp, hot climate of the equatorial zones gradually grew less humid as one moved toward the poles. But even at the poles the daytime temperature did not fall below fifteen degrees Celsius. Hermit had eternal summer and eternal spring. A rain forest, gloomy and ominous, extended for thousands of kilometers north and south of the equator. The rain forest's animal life was monotonous and loathsome: spineless creatures, like sacks covered with malodorous slime. Hopping and crawling, they spent all their time devouring the weaklings of their species.

The first spaceship had circled above Hermit for a long time, searching for a suitable landing spot and launching reconnaissance rockets. The terrain was the same everywhere, so the captain decided to burn out an area about one kilometer in diameter with the ship's planetaries. The ship landed. The explorers stepped outside. An hour later the last of the group returned to the ship, and two days later the recently burned-out landing area was completely overgrown again. Only the shaft of the ship, turned into the horizon, broke the gloomy monotony of the landscape.

The ship had lifted off and returned to Earth. The captain had been firmly convinced that the newly discovered planet was unsuitable for human life unless the rain forest were completely obliterated.

The speed with which the rain forest overran the area taken over by man was terrifying. Nevertheless, a second expedition was sent to this wild planet. It studied the planet from the air, using helicopters. The possibility that intelligent life existed on Hermit was out of the question; it had no mammals, or even reptiles.

On the fifth day, the expedition had stumbled upon a brown spot in the midst of the forest. A team of three came in closer in a helicopter and discovered several semispherical buildings with passages connecting them to twenty-meter-high white cylinders. This unexpected find thrilled the members of the expedition, but it was impossible for people to enter the buildings. They were unapproachable because a force field that held back the intrusion of the rain forest shielded the group of structures. The explorers organized round-the-clock surveillance of this small island of an unknown civilization, but it yielded no sign of life.

A day later, they discovered an area on the equator, which they immediately named Central Station. It occupied an area with a radius of ten kilometers. An enormous building in the center was also deserted. Soon they found nineteen more small clearings won from the rain forest; these were covered by strange buildings and carefully guarded by invisible sentries—the force fields. Twenty settlements left by the mysterious civilization were adopted by the explorers and called bases. Spaced at intervals of two thousand kilometers, they formed a ring around Hermit. There were no other signs of civilization—no cities, no roads, no rocketports.

The third expedition to Hermit learned the secret of shutting off the force fields; after this, systematic study of the planet and efforts to decipher its mysteries began.

For four months, cargo liners transported equipment, helicopters, half-tracks, instruments, complete laboratories, buildings, food, furniture, and people to Hermit. The expedition was superbly equipped. It had two hundred fourteen people: archeologists, zoologists, botanists, physicists, technicians, and engineers. Because the planet's history was such a mystery, it was necessary to send representatives of all the sciences.

Konrad Stakovsky, with whom Early had once studied, was the leader of the expedition. Stakovsky was upset when his favorite student, attracted to journalism, had left him. But Early had not abandoned physics completely; once he had become a full-fledged journalist, he specialized as a science writer. Now, at the invitation of his old teacher, he was on his way to Hermit. Konrad hadn't explained the reason for his choice, and Early couldn't figure out why he had been selected. Any journalist would have been flattered by an invitation to work on Hermit. Early knew this, and he was flattered, but there was one other factor. Among the group of archeologists working on Hermit was Early's ex-wife Lei. Was it possible that Stakovsky was interested in bringing about a reconciliation between two people he knew well? This possibility had occurred to Early, but he drove it out of his mind. Although Early dreamed of meeting Lei, he had done everything he could to prevent it. Now he had no choice. With only two hundred fifty people on this planet, it would be impossible to avoid meeting her.

Early tossed the report on the table. "It's useless," he thought to himself. "The zoologists and botanists had made some progress. But what kind of civilization had existed there? Where had it disappeared to? What are those amazing structures at Central Station? What had been the purpose of the settlements spaced at various distances from each other?"

Early left the library and walked through the brightly lit corridor, planning to stop in at the control room and have a chat with *Violet's* captain. Nikolai Traikov lounged in the library and had responded to all of Early's questions with either grimaces or curt statements: "Later. You'll find out everything."

And Sven had said, "It's a complete muddle. We're walking on a treadmill. *Violet* patrols the region near Hermit constantly as if we're expecting uninvited guests to drop in."

"Not guests, but the original occupants of this place," said Henry. "We're the guests and uninvited ones at that." Instantly he changed the topic. "Say, Early, what new names have they dreamed up on Earth? I'm expecting a kid . . . a daughter, of course. Oza wants to name her Seona. But I don't know, I haven't decided yet. . . ."

Two days had passed since *Violet* had left the liner. Now they were close enough to contact Central Station.

3.

Early had gone only a few steps along the corridor when he saw Henry coming toward him. Henry was obviously upset and when he reached Early he growled, "Lazy bastards!"

"Is anything wrong?"

"They won't communicate with us by radio before the scheduled time. I can't believe that Oza has nothing she wants to tell me. They're too damn lazy, and that's it. It happens when you're on regular patrol duty, but this is different. We're returning from our rendezvous with *Warsaw!* Right now they're counting the minutes till we get back."

"When are they scheduled for contact?"

"In two hours. But what difference should that make? I'm mad as hell. For the next two hours I'm going to relax and stay away from the transmitter. Nope, I won't go near the damn thing!"

Although Henry sounded mighty convincing, Early sensed that he wouldn't hold out even five minutes. Wirt headed for the library, and Early walked past the cabins to the control room. Sven was busy with some calculations. Continuing to press the computer's keys, he motioned to Early to sit down. Early did and fixed his gaze on the scanner screen, but against the background of the bright stars he could not find Hermit, no matter how hard he looked.

Early must have dozed off because he was suddenly aware of voices around him.

Henry was seated at the transmitter, his head turned toward the captain. He appeared very upset. "They don't answer," he said.

"What's the problem?" asked Sven, leaving the computer and going over to the radio operator.

All the while Early had been hoping, without admitting it to himself, that Lei might want to speak with him. Now, afraid that others might notice his feelings, he left the control room.

Two hours later the library door opened and *Violet's* captain and radio operator appeared on the threshold. Henry was pale; Sven, unnaturally calm.

"Hermit doesn't answer. Something's happened," announced Sven.

Traikov tore himself away from his reading. "What could have happened? Maybe a deviation in radio frequency? . . ."

"No, it's not that. The spaceport's signal tower would catch it. But remember, it's only a robot."

Early's heart sank.

"What should we do?" asked Nikolai.

"In ten minutes everyone must be ready. We're going to accelerate to 3 Gs, or . . ." Seven looked hesitantly at Early, wondering if he could tolerate the overload. "We're going to the limit, even if some of us can't take it."

Traikov switched on the cybernetic boosters and within a few minutes the entire ship and its systems were placed on emergency footing.

All four lay down on the recliners in the control room. Three of them, the crew, had special tasks to execute under super-G conditions.

Sven turned on the emergency engines. The ship tore ahead, and its occupants were pinned down by the mounting G-forces. For a few minutes longer, they tried to carry on a conversation discussing the possible fates of the people on Hermit. Maybe the transmitter had broken down? But in the time elapsed, it could have been repaired one hundred times over. Or could the rain forest have broken through the force fields and overwhelmed Central Station? Unlikely, but possible. They simply couldn't come up with any other explanations.

"It could be the rain forest," said Sven.

"Then help would have come from the bases," suggested Henry.

"They might have evacuated Central and gone to one of the bases," hypothesized Early.

"No," said Nikolai, barely opening his mouth. "The rain forest —that's nonsense. It's something else."

Powerful forces bore down on them. The slightest movement required tremendous effort, whether it was lifting one's finger or keeping one's jaw closed. Bags appeared under their eyes. Early suffered far more than the others. Before he lost consciousness, he marveled at the extraordinary endurance of *Violet's* astronauts.

Early came to eight hours later during a brief interval of weightlessness. Only Nikolai Traikov rose from the recliner, to drop a few spoonfuls of hot bouillon into the helpless journalist's mouth.

"What happened to me?" whispered Early.

"You blacked out. But it's better that way. It's easier to tolerate the G-forces when you're out. You'll be OK."

The crew didn't feel like eating or drinking. Then the braking stage began—eight hours more at 3 Gs.

For the duration of the journey they were unable to establish contact with Hermit.

When the acceleration ceased, Hermit's image occupied a quarter of the scanner screen and looked like an enormous watermelon.

Central Station was located right on the equator. The ship approached it from the northern hemisphere, which was clouded over by a semitransparent haze. This haze apparently consisted of artificial iridescent rings parallel to Hermit's latitudes. *Violet* was now about two thousand kilometers from the planet's surface and about four thousand from the base.

Suddenly something strange began to happen. Sven was the

first to notice it, sensing an almost imperceptible shift in the ship's movement. *Violet's* nose began to tilt slowly upward. G-forces began to increase immediately; then the ship braked sharply. *Violet* was out of control; it felt as if the ship had been forced into a layer of soft, spongy rubber.

Everything happened so suddenly and quickly that no one had a chance to do anything. Not even Sven had time to intervene. The ship was suspended in space at an altitude of fifteen hundred kilometers. Nothing held it there, because the engines had been shut down. It hung for an instant and then began to fall, not vertically but at about a forty-five-degree angle to Hermit's surface. It was a disorderly descent, as if *Violet* were tumbling down a mountain.

Sven managed finally to switch on the engines. Like a candle, the ship zoomed upward and began to slow down after moving about one hundred kilometers.

No one was injured, and even Early did not lose consciousness.

"What the hell did we hit?" shouted Sven.

"We didn't hit anything," Nikolai declared confidently. "At that altitude there can't be anything over Hermit."

"A meteor?" Henry suggested uncertainly.

"No, there are almost no meteor streams in the Sevan system."

"Almost? That means there are."

"There's no external damage to the ship," said Nikolai. "I checked it. The scanners found no evidence of damage."

"I think we ought to land," spoke up Early, silent until now. "We can work on this puzzler later."

"Damn it!" burst out Henry, turning away. I can't believe that anything happened to them down there."

Sven maneuvered the ship southward, toward the equator. Then, after hovering the ship directly over Central Station at an altitude of fifteen hundred kilometers, he began to bring it down very slowly.

They still could not make radio contact with Central. Henry Wirt tried the whole range of frequencies used for local communication on Hermit, but the ether remained silent.

Vibrating intensely, the ship dropped lower. Five hundred kilometers till touchdown. Three hundred . . . one hundred . . . Central was visible with the naked eye. Fifty . . . twenty . . . ten . . . three . . . individual structures on Central could gradually be distinguished. One kilometer . . . two hundred meters . . . from that altitude people should be visible. The ship shuddered faintly; the shock absorbers slid out, and the ship came to rest on the surface of the planet.

The spaceport was deserted; no one was there to welcome the ship.

4.

"We've landed," said Sven quietly. "Now what?"

No one answered him. Early touched one of the colored buttons on the armrest; the circular restraints parted and the chair sank gently. Feeling nauseous, and with his ears buzzing and temples pounding, Early rose. Awkwardly, on buckling legs, he walked to the door of the control room. Wirt followed.

"Nikolai!" shouted Sven. "See that everyone puts on space suits and takes blasters. . . ."

"Blasters?" Traikov swore. "The place is deserted. What in the hell do we need blasters for?"

"I just don't know. Does anyone know what happened here?" asked Sven. "Obviously not. I've locked the elevator in place. First let's take an air sample."

A minute later he announced, "It's OK. Now hear this! We go out together. No one does anything on his own. We don't know what happened here, so we must be very careful."

Henry Wirt and Nikolai Traikov were the first ones to jump out of the control compartment. Early knew enough to stay behind them: at least they were on familiar ground, but he had no idea what to expect. The floor was springy under their feet. A blur of lights rushed past them as they dashed through the corridor. Sven leaped into a cabin, searching for weapons, but they hadn't been used in so long that, after digging around the cabin for several minutes, Sven returned to the corridor empty-handed.

Henry was the first to drop to the launching pad.

Central Station's dome with its pretentious structures, turrets, passages, ramps, and open-worked towers was visible one kilometer from the ship. The colorful structures cast iridescent dappled spots in all directions and stood out boldly against the clear blue sky. Enormous energy storage cylinders stretched to the north and south of Central's dome. Still farther away, one could distinguish the silhouettes of warehouses, hangars, auxiliary structures, and cottages. Green parks dotted the landscape to the left and right, and from afar, Hermit's rain forest lay as a black strip along the entire horizon.

"On the surface nothing has changed," thought Sven, catching up to Early. Henry and Nikolai had rushed on ahead of them.

"What we need is a working hypothesis," panted Early.

"You're right. And Henry's beginning to show signs of cracking."

"Maybe whoever built Central has returned."

"Now? Right now? Why not one hundred years earlier or later? I suppose it's possible. If so, what should we do?"

Violet's return was usually welcomed by a parade of half-tracks jammed with laughing and shouting physicists, technicians, botanists, mathematicians, and biologists. The cargo ship's return was always a holiday for everyone. Today only dead silence greeted them. There wasn't a sign of life.

Two half-tracks stood near Central, and a third with open hatches stood midway between the ship and the station. Henry ran past it. Nikolai halted, scrambled onto the turret, and jumped inside the half-track. He switched on the lights and the dashboard lit up; then he quickly scanned the instruments and controls and found everything in order. The battery was fully charged. He glanced inside the passenger compartment, but no one was there.

"I wonder what they needed the half-tracks for!" shouted Sven, looking into the hatch.

"Maybe they were going somewhere."

"I can't see where they could go in them. They're awfully slow. You couldn't make it to the bases in them. For that, we use the helicopters."

Early also clambered onto the half-track's turret. Nikolai turned on the ignition; the engine roared and the vehicle lurched forward.

"Give us a hand!" shouted Early when he and Sven had caught up to Henry.

Central Station's entrance was wide open. Henry flew up the granite steps.

"The rain forest has nothing to do with it!" shouted Sven. "The rain forest didn't break through." Henry nodded in agreement. "Where are you going?"

"To the biologists."

"Wait for Nik and Early."

"I want to take a look at Oza's section!" shouted Henry, halting in the doorway.

"Take Nik with you."

"OK."

Wirt and Traikov disappeared into the corridor leading into the station's outer ring. The sound of their echoing footsteps died down around the corner. Sven gestured to Early to follow him. They rode the escalator to the very top of the station, to the expedition's staff room, the operations quarters of Konrad Stakovsky and his assistants, Ezra and Hume. The door of the room appeared to be locked. Sven and Early made several attempts to open it, but the door would not budge.

"No one here. The rain forest didn't break through. No sign of catastrophe," said Early. "Why did everyone disappear?"

"They could have flown to the bases; they often do. But someone must always remain behind; usually about five do. And they all assemble here to welcome *Violet's* arrival. Protection from the rain forest is a good deal weaker at the bases. But all twenty going off at one time? . . . No matter what, we must get into the staff room. Someone is always on duty there. The expedition's log must be in there. At least it will tell us something."

There was a long silence. Then Sven said, "I'll run and get something heavy." He dashed downstairs three steps at a time.

Slowly, Early walked through the circular corridor. On one side rose the staff room's wall; on the other, Central's dome, a transparent structure. The corridor's ceiling was transparent too, and the corridor was small, about fifty meters in circumference. Collecting his thoughts, Early walked through it several times. Sven was taking too long. Early was worried. Finally, unable to bear the suspense, he dashed down the escalator.

"Sven! Sven!"

No one answered. Early ran some thirty meters along the corridor of the third ring and shouted again. Rushing through a subterranean passage leading into the second ring, which housed administrative quarters, he realized that he could get lost in this maze of corridors, passages, and escalators. But he couldn't stay in one place. A series of lights stretched to the left; to the right it was dark. As he headed automatically for the lighted area, Early figured that it was Sven who had turned on the lights. So Sven must be there.

The series of lights suddenly shifted to the side, opposite some auxiliary rooms, and ended a dozen meters away by escalator number 5 of the third ring. Ascending on the escalator, Early found himself two hundred meters from the very spot his journey had started.

"Sven!" shouted Early.

"I'm over here," replied a voice very close by; and around the next corner was Sven, his ear pressed against a door.

"What happened?"

"Someone's crying in there."

"What?!"

"Hush!" whispered Sven. "Listen!"

Early tiptoed closer. Yes, someone was crying behind a frosted-glass partition. Gently Early turned the doorknob. The door was locked.

"When I heard it downstairs I rushed up here," said Sven. "Someone's crying in there and won't open up. We'll have to break down the door. We've no choice."

"Wait a minute!" Early rapped on the door.

The crying suddenly ceased.

"Open up!"

"No-o-o!" replied a sobbing, pitiful, hoarse voice.

"Break it down!" shouted Early.

Sven pressed his shoulder against the door, but it didn't yield immediately.

"Don't! Don't!" pleaded a terrified voice.

The door fell to the floor with a crash. Sven and Early flew into the room.

"Early, it's Eva!" shouted Sven.

"Eva?!"

"No. I don't know you. I don't know you," the girl whispered barely audibly. Slowly she moved backwards among the tables. She grabbed onto an instrument, and it crashed to the floor. In desperation she hugged the wall as if trying to squeeze through it.

"Eva, it's me, Sven, captain of the *Violet*. What's the matter with you?" His arms outstretched, Sven approached the girl slowly.

"No. It can't be you."

"Easy, Eva. Calm down."

"No . . . No . . ."

Sven touched the girl's shoulder and she looked at him with the terrified eyes of a hunted animal. Sven shook her.

"What happened?"

"Sven. Yes, it is you, Sven. Of course," suddenly she said softly. "It's dreadful here."

"Eva!"

"Hush, Sven. . . ." She pressed her face to his broad chest.

"Where's Stakovsky? Where's everybody?" asked Sven, trying to tear her away from him.

Suddenly the girl crumpled, and Sven barely kept her from falling.

"Early, she's fainted. We'll have to get her out of here. Do you know where her cottage is?"

Early shrugged his shoulders, then bent over the girl.

"She's out."

"First row, number seven. Do you need help?"

"I'll find it." Early lifted the girl gently into his arms and left the room.

Sven sat down at the nearest desk and dialed Henry Wirt on the intercom. Wirt didn't answer. Sven called Traikov.

"Hello," Traikov answered at once.

"Why doesn't Wirt answer?"

"He's sitting in Oza's laboratory. Leave him alone for a few minutes. He's hoping to find something, a note from Oza or something else. . . ."

"OK. Nik, we found Eva here!"

"What? Eva? . . . You mean there's someone here?"

"Only she for now."

"Eva!" Traikov was overjoyed. "Did she say anything?"

"No. She passed out. Get over to her cottage right away. Do you know where it is?"

"Of course I do."

"Then step on it."

"I'm on my way."

5.

Early carefully carried the girl out to the steps of Central Station. Sevan was almost at its zenith, and only now did Early notice how hot it was. The cottages were located about three hundred meters from the main entrance, and Early took a shortcut across the grass. Familiar Earth grass rustled softly beneath his feet; tree branches brushed his face and clothes. Their touch was surprisingly gentle and pleasant. Suddenly Early realized that everything occupying his thoughts until now had slipped into the background: his sole concern at this moment was the girl; he must not disturb her with careless movements.

Reality returned, and Early began to feel troubled. Time! How much time had elapsed since they had landed on Hermit? About thirty minutes. And still they knew nothing. Where was Lei? What had happened to everyone? All their hopes were pinned on Eva and the possibility of finding notes in the expedition's staff room. . . . They must find them!

He looked intently at Eva's face. What had happened to her? What had she experienced here?

Early found her cottage and kicked open the door. He passed through one room, then another. Where the hell was the bedroom? Damn those architects. He finally spotted a wide, low divan and placed the girl on it. She slept. Her heartbeat was regular, her breathing peaceful. Early looked out the window.

Leaping from Central's steps, Nikolai Traikov ran toward the cottage. Sven and Henry walked slowly. They halted several times. It was obvious that Tomson was telling Wirt something. Wirt merely shook his head in disagreement.

"What's wrong with her?" asked Nikolai.

"She's asleep now," replied Early.

"Didn't she say anything at all?"

"All she said was, 'It's dreadful here.'"

"What could that mean?"

"Well, it could refer to what everyone experienced, or what she alone went through, or both. We'll have to give her a shot to wake her up. We can't lose any time. She's got to come to. . . . Later she'll sleep a while."

"OK," replied Nikolai, and he went into the bathroom, where medications were usually kept.

Sven and Henry entered the cottage.

"Henry wants to use a helicopter," said Sven from the doorway.

"I'm just going to fly to Oza and come back. It won't take more than four hours," began Henry rapidly. "We'll have to get to the bases anway. And Oza is at the closest one. So, how about giving me a helicopter?"

"But you don't even know how to handle it," said Sven, turning away. Henry's pleading look was too much for him.

"It's really not that complicated."

"No, Henry, you can't go. There are only five of us. We've been here thirty-five minutes and we still don't know a damn thing! Nothing! Do you understand?" And he added softly, "Hold out a little longer. Eva will wake up any minute."

Henry sprang toward Sven and grabbed him by his jacket zipper.

"What right do you have to give orders?! We're not on *Violet* now, you know. Who the hell do you think you are? Stakovsky? There's two copters for each of us here! You can do what you damn please, but I'm going to Oza. I must know what's happened to her. And I have to know that right now. Do you understand? I'm not going to wait until you figure out what's going on!"

"Well, if that's the way you feel about it," said Sven calmly, "let everyone decide."

Nikolai returned with a hypodermic. He cleansed a spot above Eva's elbow with alcohol and gave her an injection. Henry suddenly sat down without a word, closed his eyes, leaned back in the chair, and clutching the armrests, slowly began to rock himself and the chair.

Eva opened her eyes, looked around the room distrustfully, and whispered almost inaudibly, "Boys . . ."

"Easy, Eva." Sven went over to her and helped raise her. He gestured in Early's direction. "This is Early Kozales, a journalist and physicist. He flew here with us. . . .

The girl sat down, tucking her legs under her and leaning on her right arm. "So, I haven't lost my mind, have I? . . ."

"Eva, what happened here?" asked Sven firmly.

"If I had only known this . . ."

"Eva, please tell us what happened here!" repeated Sven.

"I don't know what happened here. . . . But I'll tell you everything I know. Four days after you left Hermit, Stakovsky announced that everyone should get ready for departure to the bases. In the past this was done periodically. So no one was surprised. Preparations began. On the tenth only Ezra, Hume, and I were left here. The rest had gone to the bases in helicopters."

"All except the three of you?"

"Yes."

"Did Oza fly to her base?" asked Henry calmly.

"Yes. They tried to persuade her to stay here, but she insisted on going."

"When were they supposed to return?"

"On the twelfth, except for those who lived on the bases permanently."

"What did Stakovsky have in mind for this trip?" asked Sven.

"I don't know. I heard Ezra telling Hume that Stakovsky wanted to show them what the swings were."

"Swings?" Sven looked puzzled.

"What kind of swings?" asked Early.

"I don't know," Eva shrugged her shoulders. "Ezra and Hume were sitting in the main control room of staff headquarters. From there we can communicate with all the bases. It has a computer too. They sent me out for coffee . . . you know, as they usually do. I went downstairs. The coffee was in thermos bottles at the snack bar. I took one and went upstairs. The whole thing didn't take more than two minutes . . . it seemed to me. I entered the control room, and Ezra and Hume weren't there. Where they had been sitting were two skeletons and the remnants of decayed clothes. . . ." Eva covered her eyes with her hands and shook her head. "It's . . . it's so horrible. . . ."

Sven sat down on the edge of the divan and gently removed the girl's hands from her tearful face. "Then what happened?"

"I was terrified. I had no idea what had happened. That was the worst part. I called all the bases at once. No one answered. All their transmitters were out of order. I ran out of the dome and slammed the door. Maybe, I hoped, I could reach them with the external communications system. It serves as a dual system. No one answered there either. Then I imagined that I was all alone on this planet; I didn't know what had happened to everyone or what would happen to me now . . . any minute.

"I was the only one left. I was terrified. I forced myself to return to the main control room. 'I must get everything in order,' I thought to myself. You were due to return to Hermit! It was my duty to make your job easier, at least help you with something. But the computer's memory was blank—not a drop of information there! It was as if someone had deliberately erased it. The tapes of recording instruments had disappeared. Everything in the room had rusted and decayed. Not a single document remained that would help us learn what had transpired at the bases during those two hours before the catastrophe struck. You won't find anything there."

Eva grew silent.

"Please go on, Eva. There are five of us now," said Sven.

"Then I began to hallucinate. I thought I was going crazy. And that made me feel even worse, more terrified. Sometimes I saw Ezra and Hume. They walked through Central. They were always arguing. But they weren't really there. They were dead. Yet they were walking around. Had I gone crazy? A person can take only so much. What's today's date?"

"The twenty-third."

"That means my insanity lasted twelve days. Do I look crazy to you?"

"You're perfectly sane, Eva," Nikolai reassured her. "But you're very tired."

"I'm frightened."

"There's nothing to be afraid of now, Eva," Sven said, patting her on the shoulder. "Did you skip anything important? Think!"

"No. . . . I'm tired. I'm so tired from all of this."

"Eva, you'll fall asleep now. You must rest."

"You won't leave me alone, will you?"

"Eva, you will have to stay here alone for a little while. We must not lose time. You've got to understand that."

"All right, I'll sleep, but not more than two hours. That will be plenty for me."

"Go to sleep now, Eva."

The four men left the room. Full of hope, the girl watched them leave. Now there were five.

6.

Early went out onto the porch of the wooden cottage and looked around. What beautiful surroundings! Small houses were scattered here and there in the midst of a shady park. Central's enormous white hulk floated like a gigantic ship in a bottomless blue sky. And there was soft, green grass and wild flowers, as on Earth; and strange odors that made one giddy. There was so much that was unusual, new, unfamiliar.

He glanced around and cursed himself for getting so sentimental at a time like this: before him lay Hermit, its dense rain forest and thousands of unsolved problems. Two hundred ten people equipped with the most modern means of transportation, communication, and defense had not returned to Central Station.

Again, as before when he was carrying Eva, he began to grow terribly uneasy. If he had had time to analyze his anxiety, he would have realized that it was actually fear . . . fear that he would never see Lei again. There is no greater fear than not knowing what one fears.

"What should we do now?" asked Sven Tomson. "That's not going to get us anywhere," he said angrily, pointing to the others. "We must do something."

Henry Wirt was lying face down on the grass and crying. Nikolai Traikov was biting his lips nervously.

"Look," began Early, "we still don't know a damn thing. We've been here almost an hour. We've got to work out a plan of action. They couldn't have all disappeared at the same time. . . ."

"Why didn't you let me go to Oza!" shouted Henry. "Why?!" He banged his fist on the grass. Sven sprang to his side, yanked him off the ground, and shook him hard.

"Henry, for God's sake, get hold of yourself!"

"We're sorry, Henry," said Early. "You'll go to Oza. That's probably what we'll do. We'll go to Central right now and decide everything there."

Henry calmed down, rose, and headed toward Central with his companions.

"What are these swings Stakovsky was talking about?" Early asked Sven. "Do you know what he had in mind?"

"I haven't the vaguest notion," replied Sven.

"Had there ever been talk of it before?"

"I never heard anything of the sort."

They halted at the main communications console.

"How would one render swings?" asked Nikolai suddenly. The others looked at him surprised and puzzled.

"Well, to put it simply, can swings be rendered schematically?" Early drew a straight line across a sheet of paper, and at a small angle, he sliced through it with a short line.

"That's about how I would do it too," said Sven. "But what's the point of your question? Have you ever seen anything like it?"

"I have . . . very recently and more than once. Maybe a week ago, maybe more. But where and why? . . . I can't recall, but I'll try."

"Can't you do it now?" asked Sven.

"I'm afraid not."

"Well, for God's sake, try!" shouted Sven. "Maybe it's the key to the whole mystery. Meanwhile we'll work out a plan of action. We can't be together all the time, so we'll have to arrange to stay in contact with each other. We need a central point to receive all the information we collect. One of us must stay here at Central at all times. The best place is the main communications console. It will also be handy in case any of them should suddenly try to establish contact. . . . Who'll stay? Henry, of course, won't want to. . . ."

"No, I won't."

"Then who will? I have to go with Henry, although he could stay here alone."

"No," repeated Henry.

"Early hardly knows his way around here," said Sven.

"Eva," suggested Nikolai. "While she's asleep I'll stay here. When she wakes up, I can certainly find something better to do. . . ."

"OK." Sven rose and began to pace the room. "Now, everyone must stay in radio contact at all times. Everyone must carry at least a light blaster because we don't know what has happened here. Henry and I will take a helicopter to Oza's base. The whole trip should take four hours."

"The control tower isn't working there," said Henry. "I checked it with the transmitter."

"With the control tower operating it used to take only four hours. But without it . . . I don't know if we can locate it quickly on the map."

"I've been there many times," said Henry. "We'll find it quickly."

"Then let's go right away. Early, try to break down the door of the staff room."

"Eva said she had the key," said Nikolai.

"You're right. How could I have forgotten? All the better. OK, then, let's go. What we're going to do once we get there, I don't know."

"Let's not speculate," said Nikolai, and they went into the corridor.

"If the former occupants of this planet have returned . . . If they are hostile toward us, we'll have no choice but to take off on *Violet*. If I were convinced we were here alone, that all our people were gone, I would get the hell out of here on the double."

They needed about five minutes to find their pocket radios and blasters. Sven and Henry ran to the helicopter pad. Nikolai turned on all the receivers on the communications console. Early headed for Eva's cottage.

7.

Early decided not to waken Eva. He would manage without her for a few hours. Let her get the rest she needs. He rummaged through her bureau drawers but couldn't find the key. Together with a small medallion, it was on a chain around her neck. Trying not to waken her, he unhooked the chain and tugged gently at the key. The girl stirred slightly and gripped his hand but did not awake. Finally he slipped the key off the chain. Not wanting to waste time, he left the chain unfastened and tiptoed out of the room.

Reaching the door of the main control room, he paused, caught his breath, turned on his portable transmitter, and asked Traikov, "Nik, are they gone?"

"Yes. Everything's OK. I'll be talking with them every twenty minutes. I don't need you now. You can go about your own business."

"Great!"

"Where are you?"

"I'm opening the door of the main control room. I barely managed to find the key. . . ."

Early opened the door. The air smelled stale. That was strange. Had the ventilating system broken down? The automatic lighting system didn't work either. The wisps of light seeping into the room were not bright enough for him to distinguish anything.

Although he was unfamiliar with the room's arrangement, his eyes adjusted gradually to the semidarkness. He began to move about more confidently, but his confidence was shaken when the upholstery on the back of a chair crumbled to dust beneath his touch. Early started and halted. Too bad he didn't have a flashlight on him. But why didn't the lights work? He made his way to the door and groped for the light switch. He pressed it, but there was no click. The switch's components fell noisily to the floor.

"Early," Traikov radioed him.

Early started in surprise and whispered in reply, "Yes, Nik."

"What's cooking?"

"I can't figure it out. . . ."

"Need help?"

"No, Nik. But I'd appreciate it if you would tell me where I can locate a flashlight in a hurry."

"Flashlight? Where the hell are you, in the basement?"

"Don't think I've gone off my rocker, but the automation is on the blink, and the light switch crumbled in my hands."

"I doubt that you'll find a flashlight anyplace closer than the administration quarters. Want me to bring you one?"

"I'll get it myself. You shouldn't leave the transmitter."

"I have another thirteen minutes before the next contact. I'll get back in time."

"No, Nik. Someone should be at the transmitter every second."

Early dashed down the escalator, ran through the corridor of the third ring again, and dove into a subterranean passage. The butt of the blaster kept banging against his back. "A weapon is utterly useless here at Central Station," he thought to himself. The chain of lights along the passage moved along with him, even slightly outstripping him. Everything was working normally here.

In administration headquarters, he found the master control board. Early pressed the button for automatic lighting, remembered the sector number, and hurried on. By the time he arrived at the sector, the doors were already opening. There was no time to wonder about it; he grabbed a small pocket flashlight and put it into his coveralls' pocket. Spotting two large flashlights on the shelves, he took them; then, slowing down a bit, he grabbed two more.

Still running, he returned to the main control room, took a deep breath when he reached the door, and entered. Setting the flashlights on the floor, he turned one on, raised it above his head, and moved forward slowly.

It was a circular room, about forty meters in diameter. Emergency electronic equipment, computers, information banks, and automatic recorders stood in cabinets running along the walls. Operators' chairs were set near these pieces of equipment. Whenever Konrad Stakovsky began his periodic information processing operation, all the chairs were occupied.

The master console, a ten-meter-long horseshoe, stood in the center of the room. It had multicolored boards with keys for selecting programs, feedback apparatuses connecting with Hermit's twenty bases, the control board of the main computer, signal panels, and a video communication apparatus.

Several more chairs stood in the very center of the room. They were usually occupied by Konrad Stakovsky, Philipp Ezra, Edwin Hume, and some other members of the expedition.

Setting a flashlight on the control console, Early walked around it, touching nothing, and then went inside the horseshoe. The first two chairs were vacant. In the third and fourth lay two human skeletons covered in places with skin and remnants of clothing.

For a few seconds Early studied them, then inhaled the warm, stagnant air convulsively, and pressed his hands to his temples. A wave of fear swept over him, and he retreated to the exit, barely restraining a scream. Stumbling against a corner of the door, he started in surprise. The bright light in the corridor brought him to his senses. "Oh, Lord, what this must have done to Eva!" he thought. "A woman, alone. In spite of the shock, she still managed to tell us something."

"Early, what's going on there?" Traikov called to him on the transmitter.

"Now we have to find out what happened to the other two hundred eight . . ."

"That means . . . Eva told the truth?"

"And how!"

"Henry is calling me. I'm signing off."

"Yes," whispered Early, entering the room again, "we must find out what happened to the others."

8.

Almost a dozen helicopters stood on the pad. Sven started toward a small two-seater, but Henry stopped him.

"Suppose they are alive and we have to get them back here right away?"

Tomson didn't bother arguing; they ran to a large ten-passenger helicopter, tossed in their blasters, and scrambled inside. Sven glanced into the baggage compartment, hoping to find flame throwers. To fly to the rain forest without them would be sheer madness.

Sven banked the helicopter sharply. Central Station's dome rushed to the side; the energy-storage tanks whisked by like rows of white keys; the little frame cottages dotted the landscape like dark peas; and the last spots of bright-green parks quickly vanished. Below, stretched the rain forest.

"Henry," said Sven, "contact Central. We've got to check everything out."

"OK . . . Nik! Do you read me?" asked Henry, turning on his radio. "Come in."

"I read you," replied Traikov. "How's everything going? Everything OK?"

"Everything's OK," said Henry and he turned to Tomson: "Communication is OK, Sven . . . Nik! I'll be calling Central every twenty minutes, as arranged."

"Fine."

From above, the rain forest seemed monotonous, a gloomy conglomeration of muddy green vegetation. Here and there the eye might pick out patches of rivers or lakes. The terrain was flat: There were no tall mountains on Hermit.

"Rain forest, everywhere. No matter where you look!" Wirt wriggled his shoulders. "And what if it should break through any of the bases? Just the thought of it is frightening: the savage onslaught of those exceptionally hardy, disgusting creeper-plants and the animal world that exists only to devour its own kind. Blasters would be useless there. Ghastly! Of course, while the defense systems on the bases are working, the rain forest isn't so frightening. As far as I'm concerned, everything can go kaput except the defense systems."

Through the corner of his eye Wirt glanced at the speedometer. The luminescent line had reached the limit.

Sven and Henry were silent. Sven was diligently checking the map against the terrain unfolding before him. Henry was thinking about Oza: he didn't want to believe that anything had happened to her.

When twenty minutes had elapsed since their departure, Wirt called Central.

"Nik, how's the reception?"

"Excellent. But why are you talking so damn fast? Is anything wrong?"

"No, everything's OK. How are things there?"

"Early just spoke to me from the main control room." Nik's words came through slowly, in a painstaking drawl. His voice dropped a few octaves and grew hoarse. "Don't bother looking for Ezra and Hume. They're dead."

"What happened to them?"

"I don't know. That's all Early said."

"Nothing more?"

"Nothing, Henry."

"Your voice sounds awful, Nik, . . . hoarse and creepy."

Below stretched the murky green rain forest as far as the eye could see.

Sven turned to Wirt, "If everything goes OK we should spot base two in an hour. How many people were on it?"

"There *are* four on it!" replied Henry. Tomson realized that he shouldn't have used the past tense. "Oza, Vytchek, Jurgens, and Stap. There *are* four."

"I'm sorry, Henry. I'm not very good at cheering people up."

"Thanks. It's better that way. . . . I wonder if contact was broken with all bases simultaneously?"

"It's hard to say. Eva didn't get to the communications console right away. In those few minutes a lot could have happened."

"And the rain forest?"

"Breaking through at all bases at the same time? That's difficult to even imagine."

Another twenty minutes passed. Wirt called Central.

"Nik, how's the reception?"

His reply sounded like a low, hoarse growl. Something burbled and gurgled in Traikov's throat.

"Nikolai! What's wrong? What happened?"

The growling slowly subsided.

"Sven, what do you make of it?"

"We're heading back!"

"OK, but I'm asking you what you think it is?"

"Something happened there. We must go back."

"Something happened to everyone here, too. We're not turning back. Do you get me, Sven?"

"I'm taking this copter back!"

"It's less than an hour to base two, and we'll find out what happened there."

"Suppose the three back at Central are in trouble?"

"Do as you wish," Wirt leaned back in his seat apathetically.

The helicopter turned sharply.

"Damn it, get a grip on yourself!" shouted Sven. "And try to adjust the transmitter!"

"I'm trying," replied Wirt in a whisper.

Central did not answer Wirt's repeated calls. Roaring and dull rumbling sounds alternated with intervals of relative silence. Sven and Wirt listened intently to the incomprehensible sounds.

9.

Early entered the room again and, averting his eyes from the two chairs, arranged the two flashlights so that the entire area would be illuminated evenly. Then he developed a rough plan of action. First he decided to find out what had happened to the automation system; that he would look through the information bank, the computer's magnetic memory, and the automatic recorders. He would complete his investigation here with an examination of the two scientists' remains.

A very cursory inspection of the ventilation shafts told him that they were completely wrecked and that the compressors had turned into a pile of rubble. He couldn't examine the concealed electrical wiring, but all the switches and outlets were useless. The plastic was cracked and the contacts were covered with a thick layer of rust. There was no point in trying to turn anything on: a touch of the hand crumbled rubber hoses and cables. It was as if a plague or disease had attacked the materials composing the different instruments and mechanisms. Only the walls and floor, made of indestructible heat-resistant plastic, had survived in good condition.

Instrument knobs did not turn, keys did not depress, or they collapsed at the slightest contact and refused to rebound to their original position.

Nothing remained of the paper tapes in the automatic recording instruments. The computers' magnetic drums had buckled and their magnetic tapes had turned to dust. Not a bit of information was left in the memory-storage units.

Cautiously Early moved from one instrument to the next, trying not to touch anything, but now and then something would fall to the floor with a crash and crumble into a heap of gray dust or formless fragments of plastic and rusted metal.

Nevertheless, in this ghastly chaos of deformed, disfigured, dead instruments and objects, there seemed to be a kind of unifying thread. The planet's equator ran straight through the center of the room. Everything in direct proximity to this imaginary line had been reduced to dust at a greater frequency than objects located at the walls opposite them.

"Death began with the equator," Early said to himself.

Then he entered the large horseshoe-shaped control board and stopped next to the chair that Philipp Ezra had occupied. At the instant when death had overtaken him, he must have been seated. This was evident from the position of the skeleton. But time had not spared his skeleton either, and the skull's vacant sockets stared out from under the chair's rotted armrests. Early stood over it for about a minute. . . .

"What a horrible end!"

He tried to imagine what Philipp Ezra had been doing when death struck. Which keys of the program had he been pressing? What had he been thinking about? What had he wanted to do? What about Ezra Hume? What had they been discussing before they died? What was the significance of the word "swings"?

The results of his investigation did not lead Early to any conclusions. Ezra and Hume were no longer alive. Everything in the main control room had become useless, crumbled, collapsed. But the reason was a mystery. An epidemic? But why only here, in Central's dome? And where did the equatorial line fit into all of this?

How did he know that this had happened only in the main control room? Because the circular corridor was intact? But there were no instruments or anything else in the corridor. In fact, even in the control room the floor looked quite new.

Early stepped into the corridor and began to examine it carefully.

Sure enough, he found changes in the corridor's walls: the plastic veneer had cracked in several places. He opened a window in the corridor to examine the ground above the equator's imaginary line. But Central's roofs stretched a few hundred meters in all directions, and the ground beyond that was too distant for Early to distinguish anything. However, a dark strip seemed to pass along the roofs.

"There's some common element in all this, but I can't seem to put my finger on it," thought Early.

"Early," called Traikov on the radio, "I'm in contact with Wirt now. What else have you found out?"

"Everything is in ruins here. How long were you away on your flight?"

"Twelve days," said Traikov, surprised.

"What if I told you that you hadn't been on Hermit for some five hundred years? Well, why don't you answer?"

"In a certain sense, it could have been five hundred years."

"No, not in a certain sense. . . . I mean in the full and only sense! I'm in the main control room now. I can assure you that several hundred years have elapsed here. Maybe more. A few more or less . . . what's the difference. Suppose you were actually in flight for several hundred years?"

"Early, I'm coming over right away!"

"You don't have to, Nik. I haven't gone off my rocker. A few days elapsed on Hermit; even Eva confirms that. But a few hundred years here. Some sort of virus could have been responsible for it."

"Suppose the original inhabitants of this planet had returned and they . . ."

"Committed such wanton cruelty and destruction? Then we're in for trouble too. No, it's something else, something that eludes me. There's a regular pattern to it."

"What?"

"I'm going to verify it now."

"OK. I'm signing off."

Early went down to the third ring, having decided to go through it and establish what had happened in the laboratories located, like the main control room, on the equatorial line.

The communications switchboard was located in the right wing; Early went to the left wing. But he had gone only a few dozen steps when Traikov called him again.

Traikov was very upset about something although he tried to speak calmly, "Early, can you come over here now?"

"What's wrong?"

"Wirt and Tomson don't answer."

Early turned back immediately and went to the right wing.

"All I get is a whining sound. At first I couldn't get anything. Then I barely made out something, like ultrasound. Now all I get is a piercing whine."

What could have happened to them? Helicopters are indestructible. But so was everything else here, and much of it had turned to dust.

Early opened the door of the communications room.

Traikov was sitting with his back to him and shouting into the microphone, "Come in, Wirt! Come in, Wirt! Traikov calling! Come in, Wirt! Receiving!" Turning the knobs, he repeated his call on every frequency.

Early dropped wearily into a chair and covered his face with his hands.

"They don't answer," said Nikolai, turning to him.

"Keep trying!"

Nikolai began to call Wirt again.

"I didn't tell you this, but somehow it hadn't occurred to me before: You should record all frequencies on magnetic tape. True, we won't have time to listen to everything, but you can run the tapes through a computer. Let it process them. Maybe that way we'll get at least some information."

"I record everything and replay the tapes periodically. There's not a thing on the tapes. . . . Come in, Wirt! Traikov calling! Receiving."

"Two hours . . ."

"What did you say?"

"Almost two hours have passed since we landed on Hermit."

10.

They were flying toward Central base for about fifteen minutes. For an instant, the air in front of the helicopter became foggy, and the vehicle shot forward as if it were shot from a sling. They felt the streamlined fuselage vibrate from the air's violent resistance, and both of them were pinned to their seats. Sven decelerated, but the velocity suddenly dropped to half the maximum and they were thrown from their seats.

"What the hell!" muttered Sven. "Somewhere in this region, when we were on our way to base two, the velocity dropped sharply and I had to accelerate to the limit. Now everything is reversed, like some sort of threshold effect. I've never encountered such a phenomenon before. And the atmosphere is calm."

"And there was some sort of shroud, like a smoke screen."

"So I wasn't seeing things after all."

"Come in, Wirt! Traikov calling!" a hoarse and drawling voice suddenly came through their earphones.

"I hear you, Nik!" shouted Henry. "What happened to you? Why didn't you answer?"

"Everything's OK at this end. Why didn't *you* answer?"

"We tried calling you. You didn't answer. Then Sven concluded that something had happened to you, and we turned back. We're twenty minutes away from you now. Should we return or go to base two?"

"Early says it's OK for you to go to the base. . . . But why couldn't we reach you? And why are you jabbering?"

"Who's jabbering? I'm speaking normally. You've got the problem, not I: you sound like you're falling asleep."

Occasionally there were brief pauses between words and phrases, and each party thought the other was composing a reply.

"What the hell is going on?" muttered Sven again. "Don't break contact. Keep your line open all the time. Whatever it is that's coming between us bothers me."

"Nik," said Henry, "say something without pausing. Keep on talking. I wonder at what time interval the line will go dead?"

"Do you think it will break off again?"

"I don't know. Just keep talking. How's Early doing?"

"Early? Nothing definite yet. He has one hell of a theory: he claims we haven't been on Hermit for five hundred years!"

"Oh, ho! Not bad! Where is he now?"

"Sitting right next to me. I called him when communications broke off."

"For God's sake, Nik, will you please stop drawling!"

"Who's drawling?! I'm speaking normally. It's you guys who keep jabbering away. Where's the fire?!"

Their reply reached Traikov as a piercing whine interrupted by lengthy pauses. A dull, low roar coming through their earphones filled the cabin of the helicopter.

"Contact's broken, Sven," said Henry.

"There's that shroud again. The copter shoots through it like a rubber band. We've got to check it out, see what the devil's going on. I'll turn around."

"OK."

"Watch it closely. It's coming closer. Hold tight! Here comes the jolt!"

The helicopter shot forward, but Sven now handled the disobedient vehicle with far greater confidence than he had the last time. At that same instant, a voice came through their earphones, " . . . in Wirt! Come in, Wirt! Traikov calling!"

"Your voice sounds normal."

"What's going on there?"

"Let Early take a parallel channel."

"He's been on it all the time."

"I've been listening to everything, Henry. OK, shoot!"

"In this area some sort of shroud, like a semitransparent film, appears in the air. When we pass beyond it, radio contact breaks off. We go back and the radio works normally. It's probably some sort of screen."

"What other effect does this shroud have on you?"

"When we move away from you it acts like a tight spring or rubber band. Sven has to accelerate. When we return, it sort of pushes us forward."

"What's your velocity?"

"About two thousand kilometers an hour."

"Try approaching this shroud at about twenty or fifty kilometers per hour."

"OK, we'll try."

Turning the helicopter steeply, Sven decelerated. The speedometer dial crawled downward. The vibrating, blurred shroud was about five kilometers ahead, but the vehicle would not move closer, although the speedometer read almost twenty-five kilometers an hour.

"It won't let us move forward," said Sven. "The engines are working but we're standing in one place."

"Decelerate all the way, down to zero," suggested Early.

"I did," replied Sven. 'Now we're being pushed back slowly. The engines for horizontal flight are completely shut down."

"Fine. Move back about ten kilometers. Pick up speed and break through, as you did the first time."

"What do you think that was, Early?" asked Wirt.

"I don't know, Henry. Some kind of electrical barrier. Maybe we'll figure out what it is, but for now just break through it."

"What's the altitude of that thing?"

"I don't think it's very great. *Violet* also hit something when we were preparing to land on Hermit."

"Yes, that's right," said Sven. "We experienced almost the same sensation, except that we really got a good shaking up."

"Once radio contact breaks off, you'll be flying without any means of communication. You have about one hour before you reach base two. So, in a quarter of an hour we expect you to be on the air."

"OK, that's at sixteen hundred thirty-five hours," Henry ended the conversation. "Good luck."

"Same to you."

"I'm picking up speed," said Sven.

11.

"I'm free for the next few hours," said Traikov. "Eva will take my place here. What should I do?"

"It would be a good idea to examine the energy-storage tanks, Nik," said Early.

"I'll check them."

"I'd like to take a look at what's doing in the entire Central region. I'll need a half-track. Run over to Eva and leave a portable transmitter, also a note telling her not worry about us or to look for us. Call me more often, particularly if you notice something unusual or puzzling, even the smallest thing."

"I understand, Early. I'm on my way."

"Wait a minute. The planet's equator passes through Central, doesn't it?"

"That's right."

"Has it ever occurred to anyone to mark off this imaginary line? Can I find it anywhere on Central's territory?"

"It's marked off with pegs. Stap worked at it. He was a rather queer fish."

Together they left the building. Traikov turned toward Eva's cottage. Early clambered onto the half-track's roof, opened the hatch, and dropped down. He checked the controls. Everything was in order.

With a loud roar the half-track tore along a large arc, skirting Central's building. When he had gone a few hundred meters, Early stopped the vehicle and jumped onto the grass. Using the dome as a reference point, he walked a few dozen meters farther, examining the grass.

Finally he found what he was looking for: wooden pegs, several meters apart, had been driven into the ground. At one time they had been painted red so they would be visible against the grass. Now there was scarcely a trace of the paint. The pegs collapsed at the slightest touch.

Early collected several pegs and placed them carefully in the half-track's baggage compartment. Then he climbed back into the vehicle, raised the front panel for better visibility, and maneuvred the half-track slowly along this imaginary line. Soon he began to encounter enormous, half-decayed fallen trees. It wasn't possible for such gigantic trees to be on Central's territory. They simply could not have attained such growth: they had been brought here as seeds from Earth too recently.

He drove almost another kilometer, and by that time he was quite convinced that during the absence of *Violet's* crew at least several dozen years, and not just a few days, had elapsed in the strip along the equatorial line. He would learn the exact number of years only after he returned to Central and performed laboratory analyses.

He was about to return, when a dark strip of rain forest on the horizon caught his attention. It appeared unusually high to him.

He rushed forward at high speed, crushing grass and small shrubs, spraying fountains of water around the vehicle when he crossed small man-made rivers and lakes, soaring up mounds, dropping into flowering hollows. The appearance of the vegetation gradually changed: it looked wilder. But this did not surprise him: only the central part of the park had been cultivated, and the rest had been left to nature. True, the creeper-plants, Hermit's aborigines, were not allowed to breed here; only Earthly vegetation, cultured or wild, grew.

When he was no more than one hundred meters from the defense lines, he realized why the strip of rain forest on the horizon had looked so unnaturally high to him. Local vegetation grew no taller than five meters, but they could clamber on top of each other. Even here they reached several stories high and were so heavily intertwined that it was impossible to distinguish individual plants. They were an eerie jumble of roots, trunks, and branches.

Early climbed out of the half-track and went right up to the defense line. Only now did he realize that these were dead plants, piled in a huge semicircle along the defense line on the park's northern side. The barrier was no less than one hundred meters high. What force could have created this dead zone? Only a violent hurricane, a hurricane of unprecedented force, whose power it would be difficult to imagine. Evidently the hurricane had come from the north and, striking against the defense system's impregnable wall, lost its booty alongside it. But where could such a hurricane have originated? Hermit had such a moderate climate. And no fierce winds.

Then he wondered what had happened to the force field where it intersected the equatorial line. Again he climbed into the half-track and drove along the barrier, whose height shrank more and more significantly the closer it stood to the point of intersection. Noticing that everything was in order, he thought that the defense system here had probably extracted an enormous amount of energy from the storage tanks in order to close the breach, but it had not broken down.

Here, at Central, the energy reserves were practically inexhaustible. What had remained of the bases, if such a hurricane had swept through them? Collecting his thoughts he rested for about ten minutes on the grass in the shade of the half-track. What had he learned in the past three hours?

The following were now established facts: Ezra and Hume were gone; they were dead. Everything located along the equatorial line had aged by dozens or hundreds of years. But possibly it was the work of some microorganisms. Several hundred kilometers north of Central rose a mysterious force field, a force screen that repelled all material objects and blocked radio waves. During *Violet's* absence an unprecedented hurricane had struck Central. . . .

The problem was to put all these pieces together. . . .

"Early!" he heard Traikov's voice. "Do you hear me?"

"I do, Nik. What's the matter?"

"Hold your breath," began Traikov very calmly, "what should I do about people messing around near the energy tanks?"

"What people, Nik? What are you talking about?" Early sprang up and leaped onto the half-track.

"I think we had a private understanding not to consider each other crazy no matter what the circumstances. Early, there are a couple of people here. So far, they haven't spotted me, or they're pretending they haven't. I don't know them and we've never had anyone like them at Central."

"I'll be over right away, Nik."

"Fine. I'm on the fourth northern tank, the very top. The half-track is down below."

Early flung himself into the driver's seat. The engine let out a roar, and the vehicle, bearing due south, sped toward Central Station's dome, visible in the distance. Early didn't want to be seen by the strangers just yet. Who were they? Originally there were two hundred fourteen people on Hermit. Four of them were alive. Two were dead. Meanwhile nothing was known about the fate of the other two hundred eight. If these people were members of an expedition from Earth, Nik would surely have recognized them. Everyone knew each other by sight. Could they be representatives of the civilization that created the bases and Central? If so, the five remaining Earthlings would be helpless against them. They had returned to their domain. For what purpose? What should we say to them? How can we explain the Earthlings' mission here?

When he was no more than two kilometers from Central Station, he heard Eva calling, "Early! Do you exist? Are you real, Early! Oh, my God!"

"It's me, Early. Are you awake, Eva? Where are you?"

"Early! Take me away from here! Do what you like with me, but for God's sake, take me away from this place. I'm losing my mind!"

"Eva, where are you?"

"At the communications switchboard. Nik left a note asking me to stay here. I've been here half an hour. No one has called in. It's as if everyone has died or disappeared!"

"We thought you were asleep."

"Did you see them, Early?"

"Whom?"

"Ezra and Hume?"

"Yes, . . . I saw them. Of course, Eva."

"They just left the communications switchboard. Early, please, take me away from here! We still have the rocket and *Warsaw* will meet us in three months at our scheduled rendezvous. . . ."

"Eva, what's the matter with you? Calm down! I'll get over to you soon, but first I have to see Nik. Ezra and Hume are dead. They can't walk, Eva! They're dead!"

"Then I've really lost my mind. There's nothing left for me to do but end it all."

"Eva, don't you dare! Do you hear me, Eva? Don't you dare!"

12.

At high speed Sven's helicopter tore through the foggy shroud. Below, the rain forest stretched as far as the eye could see.

One thing disturbed Sven. He knew the area rather well, and besides, the map was right at hand. But now from time to time he noticed unfamiliar formations: lakes and burned-out spots that weren't on the map.

Henry grew quiet. Since the radio wasn't working, he had nothing to do. But sitting idly by and waiting, waiting . . . was becoming unbearable. Sven, too, was silent. He couldn't think of anything suitable to discuss with Henry. . . .

Several minutes after they had passed through the first force screen, they encountered another. Breaking through this one almost resulted in disaster: Sven blacked out for an instant and the helicopter began to fall. Fortunately he came to very quickly and regained control of the plane.

They overcame a third force screen a few dozen kilometers from the base.

Henry was almost desperate enough to jump without a parachute when the base's dome came into view. But a minute later it was quite obvious that the rain forest had overwhelmed the base. The defense system had failed.

The helicopter descended to the dome above the residential area. The roar of its engine probably resounded throughout the base, but no one appeared beneath the transparent dome. Moving slowly, they skirted the dome of the residential area. No one could meet them here: all around it were traces of destruction. The dome itself had burst in several places, leaving gaping meter-wide cracks. They could make out smashed girders and reinforced concrete walls, twisted furniture and broken equipment.

"What the . . ." Henry could barely speak.

"The rain forest. That's what," whispered Sven.

"Let me out!"

"I will, Henry. First let's work out a plan of action. Do you know how to use a flamethrower? Well, then take one with you. Our best bet is to drop through the cracks in the domes. There don't seem to be many of the creeper-plants inside."

Sven fastened a belt on him, handed him a flare, and slung a blaster over his shoulder.

"Stay near the cracks. It might be better to make a new opening. For now it's all right," he counseled Henry as he let him down on a cable from the helicopter's open cabin.

Wirt stood in a circular area on the second tier, around which were grouped the individual living quarters of base personnel. There were twelve rooms, but only four of them had been occupied very recently.

As soon as he opened the door of Oza's room, something rushed at him. A thunderous bang rang out over his head, and the intruder slumped at his feet, writhing weakly, quivering, and emitting a fetid odor. Sven had emptied his blaster in time.

The best approach now would be to clean the room out with a flamethrower before entering it. But that would destroy everything in the room associated with Oza. Rejecting the idea, Henry stepped over the slime and entered the room. All its furniture was overturned and disfigured. He didn't find a single object intact. The low divan was ripped apart and a built-in clothes closet was torn out and thrown on the floor. Henry turned it upright and carefully opened its shutters. The closet was empty. A night table stood upside down on a portable tape recorder whose wiring was gone—a useless object. For several minutes Henry stood there, looking around the room, until another shot rang out.

Sven was sitting on the helicopter floor with one foot hanging outside, leaning against the doorjamb. Now and then he pressed the flamethrower's trigger.

At that elevation he had a good view of what was happening under the disfigured dome. The dome wasn't worth worrying about, so he fired directly through the transparent plastic. The "bagees," as these creatures were called, somehow sensed the absence of human beings and now penetrated every corner of the living quarters. Although they had no legs, they usually attacked their prey by leaping at them. When a bagee's headless forepart touched a victim, it would, as it were, turn itself inside out, completely enclosing the victim; then, using its entire internal surface, it would begin to digest its victim. To take a new victim, the creature did not have to reverse itself. Now the inner surface became the outer one.

"Henry! Stick close!" shouted Sven. "I can hold them back for about five minutes, no more than that. Do you hear me?"

Wirt wandered silently through the deserted rooms.

"Do you hear me?" Sven shouted again between shots.

Henry waved his hand, signaling that he had heard Sven's warning. His heart pounded wildly. One of the rooms was empty, completely empty. On the room's outside wall he noticed several fused perforations next to a gap. Someone had been firing a blaster here. The gap itself had been made with a flamethrower.

"Henry, hook yourself up to the copter!" shouted Sven. "There's too many of them!"

Wirt glanced back. Clumsy-looking bagees were leaping toward him at a fast clip. He aimed a stream of flame ahead of him and kept squeezing the trigger until the weapon was empty. Then he abandoned the useless flamethrower, ran a few steps, and hooked onto the helicopter's rope. Still holding on to the flamethrower, Sven lifted the helicopter about five meters above the dome and only then pulled Wirt into the cabin. Sven didn't tell him anything, nor did he question him. "Let Henry decide when they should return," Sven thought to himself. "Maybe he wanted to go down once more. . . ."

"They tried to defend themselves," said Henry. There was a note of pride in his voice. "They even chose the right position for their blasters and flamethrowers."

"No, they couldn't surrender without putting up a good fight."

"Sven, some of them must be alive. They repelled their attackers at the entrance to the stairs leading from Vytchek's room. I saw the holes made by the blasters. One or two defended the entrance while the others escaped. To where could they have gone from this dome?"

A spark of hope appeared in Sven too. "Maybe Wirt was right!" he thought.

"We'll have to scour the base from above," said Sven.

Slowly the helicopter began to make its way between the disfigured domes.

"Sven, one room down there was absolutely empty, not a stick of furniture . . . no divan, no chairs, no tables . . . nothing, not even fragments. In the other rooms everything was topsy-turvy. But in Oza's room, all her clothes were gone. Where the devil could all this have disappeared to? Food stores, water, and the dining room should have been on the first floor. Too bad I didn't have a chance to have a look at it."

They flew around the base slowly.

The defense installations had been torn from their foundations. The remains of one were scattered over some fifty meters. Another wasn't even visible. That was why the rain forest had broken through to the base. The helicopter pads, the domes of the living quarters, and the communications and laboratory buildings stood out like islands against Hermit's murky-green, moving, crawling vegetation. The planet had recaptured the domain nearly won from it. Two smashed helicopters lay near the helicopter pad.

Sven dropped lower, almost to the level of two barely separated creeper-plants. In those few days, the growth had been so rapid that one could hardly believe it had ever been different here. The eye sockets of a human skull stared at them through the transparent bubble of one of the helicopters.

In a fury Wirt grabbed Sven's flamethrower and began spraying creeper-plants' sprouts. Although they were burned out instantly, others took their place immediately. There seemed to be no end to them.

"It's useless, Henry." Sven placed a hand on Henry's shoulder and with the other removed the flamethrower gently. "They still won't understand you. I wonder whose remains they are."

"All of them, except Oza, could pilot a helicopter. . . ."

"Which means that one of them we won't find alive. . . ."

"That's Jurgens. He was a pilot."

The second helicopter was empty.

The laboratory building was such a wreck that there was no point looking through it.

"Look!" shouted Sven suddenly. "That spot over there, like patches . . . on the communications dome. Someone sealed up the cracks and bullet holes!"

"I was right! I knew!"

The helicopter flew around the small dome.

"Where the devil is the entrance?"

"Everything's covered with plastic here. The spot where the entrance used to be is covered with plastic too. On the outside. Someone covered the entrance and stayed outside."

"What could there be in that tightly sealed dome? Documents? People? Who remained outside? And why?"

"Sven, there should be two more half-tracks here, parked next to the helicopters."

"But there aren't."

"That means that someone decided to break through to the base in the half-tracks. He went to certain death."

The helicopter made a few more trips around the sealed dome.

Suddenly the control stick slipped from Sven's hands.

"Oza!" shouted Henry.

A woman stared out at them, her arms and forehead leaning against the dome's inner wall.

"Oza!"

13.

A chain of energy-storage tanks stretched some two kilometers north and south of Central Station. They were enormous white cylinders with numerous annexes, masts, staircases, and elevators. Normally almost a dozen engineers kept them under constant observation to prevent the amount of energy stored in them from exceeding an established quantity. They supplied energy to the defense system that composed the force fields surrounding all of Central Station's territory. But the defense systems did not require that many cylinders for its source of energy. A trillionth of the energy stored in these cylinders was sufficient for the systems' operations.

Reaching one of the cylinders in his half-track, Nikolai jumped out and entered the elevator, which delivered him to a small, brightly lit control room. The sight of so many instruments demoralized him: How could he find his way through this maze? He soon realized that he could ignore most of the instruments. The control system was rather simple. He read the meter and jotted down its figures. He removed the tape from the automatic recorder that kept track of energy consumption by days, hours, and minutes, and then he went downstairs. He entered the half-track, shoved the tape into his back pocket, and sped to another cylinder. There he repeated the operation. Then he inspected a third, a fourth . . .

The elevator in the fifth cylinder had ascended to the top, and Nikolai tried in vain to bring it down. He thought that it might be out of order. Suddenly the lights on the indicator panel began blinking and the elevator descended from the tenth tier. Then it stopped at the fifth tier, where the control room was located. Nikolai tried again to bring the elevator down, but it was occupied. Suddenly the elevator rose again. Nikolai punched the button with his fist, but nothing happened. Then he ran to the side and noticed through the grating that the elevator was actually moving. Carefully, and as quietly as possible, he slipped into the half-track and drove it very slowly to the fourth cylinder. There he jumped into the elevator and rose to the top, to the twelfth tier. This was the cylinder's flat roof. Concealing himself behind the masts, he made his way to the roof's edge . . . and nearly fell off. The next cylinder was about one hundred fifty meters from him. Several figures were strolling on its flat roof. The truss-work of the fifth cylinder's elevator faced Traikov, and he noticed that the elevator itself was also at the twelfth tier. If they had been on the roof even two minutes, they must have seen his half-track. And he had tried so many times to get the elevator down.

At that distance, the half-naked figures of people seemed small. But, comparing himself to parts of the fifth cylinder's masts, he concluded that the strangers were about his height. Their skins were tanned, and they wore shorts and sandals, but no shirts. There was nothing on their heads. One of them appeared to be holding a very long sheet of paper. Each of them had a short rod, which closely resembled a blaster, slung over one shoulder.

At the very beginning of Earth's expeditions to Hermit, it had been firmly established that there were no people on the planet, nor any form of life capable of thought.

Who could these people be?

Nik called Early.

14.

Eva woke up immediately, refreshed by a peaceful, sound sleep. For a few seconds, she couldn't imagine what she was doing here, but then the most recent events slipped back into her

memory. If only all of it were a dream . . . but Traikov's note on
the night table fully convinced her that *Violet's* crew had really
arrived. A lightweight blaster stood by the night table. After so
many lonely days filled with uncertainty, fear, and grief, the
appearance of even one person would be a most joyous occasion
for her.

And those four . . . of course they would unravel the tangle of
strange and confusing events occurring on Hermit. If they didn't
. . . well, *Warsaw* with its incredible technology, with its huge
crew would come and . . .

With a familiar gesture she straightened her hairdo and stood
by the window for a while, inhaling the delicious fragrances
coming from the grass and surrounding woods. Then, slinging the
blaster over her shoulder, she walked leisurely toward Central.

She tripped lightly up the steps of the center and walked along
the ring to the communications switchboard. She was very anxious to call Early and Nik by radio, but she decided it might tear
them away from something important. After she had checked out
the receivers and transmitters, she walked over to the window to
enjoy the view of the park.

Something compelled her to glance back. There was no creak-
ing, no movement of air, no sound, but a sense of someone's presence. Before *Violet* had arrived, when she had been alone, she
had experienced the same sensation. . . . She was paralyzed with
fear. She knew she must turn around, but she was unable to
budge. "Turn, turn around, Eva. Look back," an inner voice whispered. She obeyed and saw . . .

Seated at the switchboard, his back to her, was a man.
Although she could see only the shaven back of his head, she
would have recognized it among thousands of others. It was the
head of Philipp Ezra. Then Hume entered, without opening the
door. The two were always together. It was clear from their lip
movements that they were discussing something, but there were
no sounds.

Eva clung to the windowsill. Ezra turned around but looked
right through her. He didn't see her. Holding rolls of drawings or

sketches, he walked to his chair, swung it around, and said something to Philipp. Philipp shook his head in disagreement. Then Ezra rose; both men walked to the side, unrolled a sheet of paper, and stood there for several minutes as if trying to demonstrate something to an invisible audience. The sheet was rolled up. Hume pointed to the door. Ezra raised his hand slightly and started for the window.

Eva let out a terrified scream and jumped aside, but they paid no attention to the noise. Philipp Ezra went up to the window, looked out at something, smacked his lips regretfully, and shook his head disapprovingly. Hume shifted impatiently from one foot to the other. Then both men walked toward the door. Hume made a movement as if he were opening it, but there was not even a squeak. They passed through the closed door.

For a few seconds Eva stood immobile, trying to collect her thoughts. "Are insane people aware that they have lost their minds? How do you know if you've gone crazy?" she asked herself. Then she called Early.

"Early! Do you exist? Are you real?!"

. . . No, he didn't believe that the two dead men could be wandering through Central. Would she herself believe it if she were in her right mind? Would anyone believe it?

She picked up the blaster and passed her cold, sweaty palm over it.

15.

The woman stared at them vacantly, expressing neither joy nor surprise at their appearance. Wirt opened the helicopter door, and sticking his head out, he shouted, "Oza! It's me, Henry! Oza! It's your Henry!"

They were separated by some ten centimeters of transparent plastic.

"Sven, we'll have to cut through the dome somewhere with a flamethrower. Otherwise we can't get in there."

Sven maneuvered the helicopter along the wall for several meters. Henry pulled out another flamethrower from the baggage compartment. But he couldn't use it: the figure of the woman followed them. Enormous blue eyes followed their movements attentively. But in no way did she indicate that she recognized Henry or Sven. Not a muscle in her face stirred. Moving like a puppet, she ran her fingers slowly over the wall.

"Sven, I'll hook up the belt and drop down on the rope with a flamethrower. You turn the helicopter around to the other side. She can't be in two places at once. One of us will have time to cut an opening."

Wirt slid down the smooth dome and stopped at floor level. The woman went over to him. Oza! Oza! How awfully thin she had become! Only her enormous eyes were still as lively. Why didn't she recognize him? Why didn't she give some sign that she was glad to see him?

Meanwhile, on the other side of the dome, Sven burned a hole through the plastic that was large enough for a person to fit through. Again the helicopter rose several meters and Sven pulled Wirt into the cabin.

A minute later Henry was inside the dome; Sven waited outside in the helicopter, holding the blaster in readiness because the slimy bagees had begun hopping their way upstairs.

"Oza!" exclaimed Henry, touching her face tenderly. "Why don't you say something? Aren't you happy to see me? Oza, darling, why don't you speak? What happened here?"

"I knew that someone would come," said the woman. "When Stap left, he promised that someone would come for me."

"Oza was pregnant," thought Sven. "Could Henry not have noticed that her figure is completely normal?"

But Henry had. He had noticed it earlier, when she was clinging to the wall of the dome.

"Oza, what happened to our child?"

"I don't understand," replied the woman.

"What's wrong with you?"

"With me? Nothing. I waited for you so long, alone. When Stap

left, he sealed the entrance from the outside to keep me from
going out and taking my life in a moment of desperation. But I
never had such thoughts. I kept an eye on the creeper-plants and
bagees."

"Oza, when did Stap leave? What did he get away in?"

"Five years ago. He was very good to me."

"What do you mean . . . five years?"

"I have kept a record of everything. We maintained radio contact for about one hour. Then he was silent. I think he's dead."

"Oza!"

"Please! I'm not Oza. She died eighteen years ago. I can't even
remember her. I'll show you where she's buried."

"Oza, what's the matter with you? Wake up!" Henry shook the
fragile figure by the shoulders, but she pushed his hands away
and said:

"Stap used to say that Oza was waiting for someone all the
time."

"Whom?"

"Henry Wirt. . . . He said that she waited so desperately for
him."

"I am Henry Wirt. I know how tired you've become, waiting all
these days. How terrible it must have been for you. But now it's
all over. Wake up, Oza! We're going to Central. Oza, don't look
at me like that!"

"I've told you that I am not Oza. My name is Seona."

"Seona? But that's the name we were planning to give our
daughter! Oza, you're not feeling very well. But it will pass soon.
We must hurry. The sun will be setting soon. What would you
like to take with you?"

"The sun? Oh, it will be quite some time before it sets . . . in
six months. I've read in books that the sun sets every twenty-four
hours. And then people go to sleep. But it's different here. A day
here is eighteen months long. Funny, isn't it? A day is longer than
a year. The night follows for a year and a half, and everything
here freezes . . . and there's continuous darkness. That's when I
take a liking to the creeper-plants and bagees; I even feel like

playing with them. Sometimes during the long night I'd get awfully depressed, especially the time when Stap left. Poor guy, he perished an hour later. At least I think so."

Henry turned to Sven with a pleading expression, as if asking for his understanding of Oza's temporary derangement. Sven nodded sympathetically.

"What would you like to take with you, Oza? We're leaving now."

"Seona . . ."

"All right . . . Seona. So . . .?"

"Oh, I'd like to take everything. I don't have anything at Central: I've never been there. But I've always wanted to go there. I won't take much. You're in a hurry, aren't you? Just a few dresses. No, I'd better not . . . they're awfully worn. I'll take this book and coveralls. It's still almost new. And Stap asked me to give you this," she said, removing a ring from her hand. In place of a stone was a small storage mechanism for one minute of conversation. At one time Henry had given it to Oza. "Stap said it was very important. Oh, and please pick up that box. It contains magnetic recordings and some paper. It's been standing here so many years; I don't believe it's ever been opened. But Stap said it would be of interest to the people who would come here."

Henry lifted the box, carried it to the wall, and handed it to Sven. Then he turned to Oza. God, how she'd changed since he had seen her last! She had grown so painfully thin. And her features seemed to have changed slightly; they looked sharper. What was she jabbering about to him? Poor woman . . . she must have lost her mind. . . . What she must have gone through for this to happen to her!

"Oza . . . Seona, don't be frightened," he pressed her to him. "Everything will be all right."

"I was never frightened. I always knew that someone would come. And now that you have come, I'm not afraid of anything at all."

They went to the opening in the dome. Henry supported fragile Oza-Seona with great care. He was overjoyed to have his Oza back again, but his heart was bursting with grief. . . .

"Sven, help her," he requested. But Sven's hands were already reaching out to receive the woman.

As the helicopter tore away from the dome, Henry grabbed a flamethrower and released its entire contents at the bagees and creeper-plants swarming below.

"That was unnecessary, Henry," said Sven.

"I know."

"That wasn't a very nice thing to do," said Oza. "They distracted me with their antics for so many years."

"H'm," muttered Henry, clasping his hands to his head.

Once more the loathsome rain forest stretched below them.

Sven piloted the aircraft at maximum velocity. He must reach Central as soon as possible. As it was, they were late for their radio contact, and Early and Nik would wonder what the hell had happened to them.

"Tell me exactly what happened here," said Henry. He couldn't get his tongue to say "Seona."

"I really don't know. It was before I was born. But Stap said there had been a storm, a terrible one. Then the rain forest broke through to us. There were four stationed at the base then. Pilot Jurgens perished immediately. They couldn't even drag his body from the helicopter. Then Oza died." Henry cringed. "There was one other person. His name was Vytchek, but I don't remember him either. He said that Oza would get a proper burial so the creepers couldn't get to her. They buried her. But after that Vytchek did not return. Stap couldn't hold back the creepers. The two of us were left. Then Stap went away. He wanted to get through to Central. He should have waited until winter. But he left at the peak of summer, when the sun hadn't set for six months."

"The sun business again," whispered Henry.

"Easy . . . get a grip on yourself," Sven said softly to Henry.

"Yes, the sun. . . ."

A minute later Sven said to Henry, "By the way, you know the sun hasn't budged an iota in the past four hours."

"Nor have you," muttered Henry wearily.

"Well, you can see for yourself."

But Henry only drew Oza closer to him.

"How good the warmth of a human body feels," she said.

The helicopter approached the semitransparent shroud.

16.

Early was running through the circular corridor when shots rang out ahead of him. They were coming from the communications section. Only Eva was there. "Oh, God," he thought, "what has she done? Couldn't she hold out?"

He leaped toward the door and stopped short. There was a gaping hole in it, and the corridor wall opposite it was shattered. Early turned the door knob cautiously. The room was quiet. Warily he took a step forward and whispered, "Eva, it's me, Early."

No one answered.

He took a few more steps. Before him stood Eva with a blaster in her hand. Slowly she released the weapon and it fell to the floor with a crash.

"Early, please, take me away from here! I can't take it anymore!"

"I don't have the right to, Eva."

"But if . . . if you wanted to? Lei talked about you all the time. But she doesn't love you. I know. We were close friends, and she told me everything, everything, Early. So much that I began thinking about you. I knew that you were coming here. And I waited for you. Maybe Lei did it deliberately, so that someone would love you. She was a kind woman and wanted nothing for herself."

"I always did what she wanted. But she didn't want anything for herself," said Early. "If it were possible, Eva, I would take you away from here."

She ran to him, clung to his shoulders, and looked into his face. "Would you? Really, Early?"

Early barely released her grip. "Eva, listen to me. There are some strangers at Central. Nik called me a few minutes ago and told me about it. He's observing their movements right now."

"You didn't believe me about Ezra and Hume, did you?"

He nodded.

"I just fired at them, but they vanished, like phantoms."

"All right, Eva . . . someday we'll figure out what it was. But for now, I want you to sit down at your post and get ready to listen. You'll be in communication with Wirt any minute now. I'm going to speak with Nik first."

Early called Nik. The response was immediate, as if he had been waiting for Early's call.

"Early! Where are you now?"

"At communications. Where are those people?"

"Some of them are on the fifth cylinder's roof. I can't figure out what they're up to. The rest rode to the sixth."

"Rode? In what?"

"They have something that looks like a half-track."

"I don't know what to do, Nik. To tell you to stay there or come back here. If only we knew what they were up to or who they were."

"Meanwhile I'll stay. I'll call you if anything comes up. . . . I can tell you one sure thing: They're not our people. I know all of ours."

"Well, OK. Be careful, Nik."

Early turned off the radio and said wearily, "My head is spinning. I can't figure out what happened. If that's at all possible. . ."

"I can sympathize with you, Early," said Eva.

At that moment Wirt called them.

"The base is destroyed," began Henry calmly. "Practically destroyed. Everything's ruined."

"Any people there?"

"One . . . Oza," whispered Henry.

"Why are you talking so softly?"

"She's next to me. Early, I've got to keep my voice down."

"What about the rest of them?"

"Evidently they're dead, Jurgens, in any case. We saw him."

"Henry, get back here as fast as you can. When you approach Central, come in from the south and skim over the trees for a landing right at Central's entrance."

"I have it," replied Sven.

"The problem is that some strangers have just popped up here. I don't know who they are. Nik is keeping an eye on them. It's better if they don't see us. OK?"

"Too many riddles for one day," said Sven.

"And the day's not over yet."

"OK, we'll be there in twenty minutes," said Henry. "I'm signing off."

Early gave Eva the microphone.

"Well, they found Oza. Something happened to her. Henry didn't want to discuss it in her presence. The other three are dead."

Looking in Early's direction, Eva rose slowly from her seat. Early stared at her in surprise. What was wrong? Eva lifted her right hand and covered her mouth, barely holding back a terrified scream. Early walked over to her, feeling an unpleasant chill behind his back. Turning slowly, he felt the hair on his head stirring. He was petrified.

The door of the room was closed, but from it protruded the figure of Philipp Ezra. He seemed to be standing on the threshold, pondering something. Then he strode into the room with a firm step and headed for the transmitter. Early shoved Eva behind a projection, but she clutched his shoulder with bloodless fingers. He too needed someone to hang on to at this terrifying moment.

Ezra made several changes on the transmitter's front panel; and not a knob or a switch moved. But Ezra manipulated them as if he were really shifting from channel to channel. Then he reached for the microphone and moved his hand close to his mouth, holding his fingers as if he were actually grasping a microphone. The microphone remained on the table. Evidently not receiving a response after having spoken several words into the imaginary microphone, Ezra tossed it onto the table. Resting his elbows on the back of the chair and drumming his fingers against the transmitter's panel, he stood there for a few seconds. Not a single sound accompanied any of his movements. Then he stroked his bald head with his palm and paced the room a few times as he glanced out the open windows.

Early stood there holding his breath. Yes, this was none other than Philipp Ezra himself: bald; large head; wearing, as usual, wrinkled trousers, a loose-fitting shirt, open at the neck, and green shoes, from which he never parted, even at the beach.

Ezra appeared to be waiting for someone. But whom? And how in the hell did he get here, wondered Early; both he and Eva had seen Ezra's remains.

Someone on the other side of the door seemed to call Ezra; he shouted something soundlessly and instantly left the room through the closed door.

"Early," whispered Eva. "This is the end! . . . I never in my life had hallucinations."

"That wasn't a hallucination, Eva. That was really Ezra. At first I thought I was finished . . . crazy. But now I think it really happened. I'm going to follow him."

"What should I do, Early?"

"Eva, you stay here. Sven and Henry will be arriving any minute. Have them come in here at once. Meanwhile say nothing about this to them or Nik. I'll be back very soon."

He opened the door and glanced into the corridor. The figure of Ezra flitted to the left side, in the direction of the exit. Trying not to make any noise, Early moved quickly to the other side and passed through several corridors and subterranean passages. A string of flashing lights accompanied Early everywhere, while Ezra walked easily through the darkness.

When they reached the escalator that led to the main control room, they rode upstairs. The door was still open, as Early had left it, but Ezra made a motion as if he were opening it. They entered, one behind the other. Early's guess that he would see Hume here was correct. Together, Ezra and Hume began to perform some calculations on the computer, pressing keys and interrupting each other; but Early could clearly see that the keys did not move.

Then they unfurled a roll of paper on which was drawn some sort of technical diagram.

Biting his lip, Early touched Philipp Ezra's elbow. His hand passed through a void, meeting no resistance.

From the south came the muffled sound of an approaching helicopter. Without turning around, Early backed out of the main control room.

17.

Sven practically landed the helicopter on Central Station's front steps. Oza looked around in amazement. Henry jumped onto the grass and helped her to the ground.

At the sight of the bright sunlight, the soft, green grass, colorful flowers, and shade trees, Oza whispered ecstatically, "I read about all this in books, but I never imagined it could be so beautiful."

With his arm around her shoulders, Henry led her up the steps. Sven slung two blasters on his back and followed them.

In the corridor leading to the communications room they met Early.

"Good to see you, Henry!" Early shook the woman's hand. "Hello, Oza!"

"I'm Seona. Oza is dead, you know."

A quick glance at Henry, and Early understood.

"Well then, we have very little time," said Early. "Let's go to the communications room. We must decide on our next step."

Sven entered the room before the others and warned Eva that the woman wanted to be called Seona. When they entered, Eva rose to greet them and said simply, "Hello, Seona!"

"Hello . . ."

"My name is Eva. This is Early. And of course you already know the others."

"Eva. What a pretty name."

"Seona," interrupted Henry, "take a look out the window. I know you'll enjoy the view." Gently he led her to the window and settled her comfortably in a chair. "See, darling, how beautiful it is! No creepers or bagees to worry about here."

Oza settled down in the chair and grew still.

Early called Traikov on the radio. Nothing of significance had occurred there in the meantime. Early asked him to stay put but to participate in their discussion by radio.

Each of them explained briefly what he or she had seen, what ideas or theories had come to mind; particular attention was devoted to the strangest and most puzzling incidents.

"Five hours have elapsed since we landed on Hermit," said Early. "Everything here is strange and incomprehensible. But I'm sure that each of us can contribute some sort of theory or hypothesis. Who wants to speak first?"

"Correction, please. Seven and a half hours," said Sven.

"Pardon me . . . five!" Early replied. "It's not difficult to establish the precise time. So, who's first?"

"Early, why don't you begin?"

"No, I'll be last. Henry, you begin."

Wirt paused for several seconds and then began:

"I don't know why Ezra and Hume died or what caused their death. But the rain forest broke through to the bases. There was some sort of hurricane, which destroyed the defense systems and buildings, and the rain forest finished the job. At any rate, that's what happened at base two. I'm sure that's what happened at the other bases too."

"All at the same time?" asked Early.

"I don't think so," replied Henry. "The hurricane hit one base after another."

"A hurricane hitting all of Hermit?" Sven was surprised. "Highly improbable. There's never even been a strong wind here."

"Not within our memory. Still, there was a hurricane," argued Early. "I saw the mess around Central's territory, debris a hundred meters high. The hurricane swept in from the north, and judging from the debris, the storm was a violent one and it could have rushed on southward for many thousands of kilometers. It could have originated several thousand kilometers from Central. Therefore, the assumption that the bases were destroyed by the hurricane appears to explain a lot of things. Otherwise people could have gotten through to Central in helicopters. But no one did. There was a hurricane. It's a fact. It's not clear why or how it originated. Would you like to add anything, Henry?"

"Nothing. A hurricane and the rain forest! No one was prepared for that."

"Sven?"

"I counted four energy barriers between Central and base two. Going through them on the return trip we bounced around like corks on water. Evidently the barrier screens out electromagnetic waves. That's why the bases couldn't communicate with Central."

"Communications broke down immediately after something happened in the main control room, where Ezra and Hume were," Eva joined in, "because when I came down here and tried to reach someone by radio, no one answered."

"Well, then it turns out that the energy barriers appeared with the beginning of the hurricane or slightly earlier," explained Sven.

"Very likely simultaneously," came Nikolai's voice through the loudspeaker. "Otherwise they would have had time to evacuate to Central. But something interfered. The hurricane?"

"Yes," said Eva, "I heard Ezra, when he was still alive, demanding that everyone return to Central immediately."

"So, there was an order for immediate evacuation!" exclaimed Nikolai. "Why didn't you tell us before? That means some people had already known there would be a catastrophe!"

"It happened when I left the main control room."

"So, they received the emergency evacuation order simultaneously," said Sven. "But the hurricane came from the north. Why, then, didn't the bases closest to Central, especially the southern ones, have time to evacuate? We can't assume that the hurricane struck everywhere at the very same time."

"You're right, Sven. I saw the debris only on the northern side. That means it came down from the north."

"Then we must assume that the hurricane swept through at a speed of several thousand, even tens of thousands of kilometers an hour. That I can't believe."

"I'm afraid you'll have to, Sven," said Early. "That's the only way we can explain their failure to fly out after they had received the emergency evacuation order."

"But then no one can explain the incredible speed of the hurricane."

"Agreed. But I'm inclined to stick to that version," said Early. "So, immediately after Ezra sent the signal to the bases for emergency evacuation, the energy screens popped up, the hurricane began, and the rain forest broke through to the bases almost instantly. Do you want to add anything, Sven?"

"There's one thing that puzzles me," said Sven, "and that relates to us. We were in flight almost six hours. I told you what we did at base two. It could not possibly have been accomplished in half an hour."

"Sometimes a person can do as much in an hour as it would take a whole day to do at another time," began Early, but Sven interrupted.

"OK, we'll put it down under the heading of inexplicable phenomena. And another thing: While we were there the sun didn't move a fraction of a degree for two whole hours."

"You wouldn't have noticed such a minute change."

"Well, that's the way it looked to me. It didn't budge."

"The sun doesn't set there for eighteen months," said Oza softly without turning her head and continuing to look out the window. Remember, I told you that?"

Everyone grew silent.

"Sven," said Henry, "let's hear more about it. What did you think it was? Maybe there's something to this."

"We'll take it into consideration," said Early, "but meanwhile it doesn't explain what had happened. Nor can the phenomenon itself be accounted for. Anything else, Sven?"

"That's all for now."

"Early, you'll admit it now, won't you, that you thought I was slightly daft when I told you about Ezra and Hume?" Eva broke in.

"Yes, I didn't believe it was possible."

"Then maybe there's something to what Sven and Seona are saying. Maybe they didn't imagine it."

"Please, I beg you not to . . ." Henry said softly, gesturing toward the window.

"Eva, let's hear from you now."

"After I saw Ezra's and Hume's remains and was all alone at Central, I met them several times. They're walking around Central. They appear very often here, in this room. . . . I even fired at them today. My nerves got the better of me. The shot went right through Ezra, smashed through the door and into the corridor wall. But he walked away calmly. Early saw it too."

"Yes, I saw them. But I can't offer any explanation for it. Are you finished, Eva?" She nodded. "Fine, it's your turn, Nik."

"I saw them next to the fifth energy cylinder. They are still there. I saw them distinctly. I am sure there is no connection between them and the planet's former occupants. They are dark-skinned and sunburned and each of them has a weapon slung over his back. They also have a half-track, but it doesn't look like ours. It has two turrets, with several barrels projecting from each of them."

"What do you make of it?"

"I assume they are strangers, newcomers. Hermit has no intelligent life, not even mammals. So, they came here from somewhere else. Maybe they are the planet's former occupants? They waited until all our people had gone to the bases, then created energy barriers to break radio communication. If they are capable of creating such powerful force fields, they can create hurricanes of unprecedented velocity . . . the kind that destroyed our bases. The rain forest did the rest of the job. The planet was deserted, our bases were wiped out, and suddenly we popped up when they figured they were the bosses. Now they're cooking up something again. Maybe they plan to blow up the energy tanks. Then the place will be a shambles for hundreds of kilometers around. That's my hypothesis. Far out, isn't it?"

"It's an interesting one. Why don't they destroy us in a much simpler way? All they have to do is shoot us."

"I don't know. Maybe there are so few of them and they are afraid. Maybe they can't stand the sight of blood. I was merely tossing off some ideas."

"Nik, your theory covers a lot of ground, but a couple of things are missing, like Ezra and Hume, the sun standing still, and the discrepancy in time."

"But Early, we can be dealing with two different events here, totally unrelated to each other," said Eva. "Something else could be causing the difference in the passage of time."

"And also, Nik, what about the main control room where everything turned to dust . . . about ten or twelve meters from each side of the imaginary equatorial line. It looks as if several centuries had elapsed in those few days. I checked everything right up to the boundary of the defense systems. None of this fits into your hypothesis."

"I'm not claiming that it explains absolutely everything."

"I realize that, Nik."

"Then maybe we should approach all this as two unrelated events," suggested Eva again.

"Yes. I suppose that's worth considering for now. But I'm still disturbed by the fact that they coincided in time. Somehow they must be related."

18.

Eva boiled water for some tea and made sandwiches in the communications room where everyone was assembled. They hadn't eaten in a long time. Oza remained by the window. Eva would occasionally speak with her, but the conversations ended very quickly. Several times Eva sat on the windowsill opposite Oza and tried to study her without being too obvious. She had known Oza before. A notion that had suddenly occurred to her bothered her, but she was afraid to express it aloud. Something held her back.

In the opposite corner of the room, Early was going through the contents of the box brought from base two. He rearranged pile after pile of charts. The paper often crumbled beneath his fingers, so he had to handle everything with great care. Even if the recording instruments on base two had worked around the clock, it would be utterly impossible to account for the huge quantity of documents that had accumulated. This caught Early's attention immediately. He continued arranging piles of charts, hoping to find something . . . a letter, a note, an explanation. The box was almost empty but he found nothing of the sort. . . . Then, as he began to tie up the piles, the first one slipped out of his hands. A date stood in the corner of each chart. But such strange dates! The first one read: "2195 days since the catastrophe". He began to sort through the pile until he reached the twentieth day. There were no earlier dates on the charts. One pile contained recordings of wind velocity; another, recordings of temperature; a third, recordings of pressure; then there was the program of time acceleration between two monitors ten meters apart. For this type of research, it was a meaningless distance.

The figures were incredible! Especially at the very beginning. Yes, at the beginning . . . Because it was obvious from the charts that from the moment the catastrophe occurred, no less than fifteen years had passed on base two. Then the recordings ceased for a time: apparently the people were too busy fighting for their lives against the invading rain forest. They survived, and their records were now helping Early to untangle the web of bewilder- ing events that had occurred here at Central.

Now many things fell into place. Now it was clear why Sven had insisted that the sun hadn't moved even a fraction of a degree during the time they had spent on base two. And it was also clear why they had insisted that they had been in flight six, and not four, hours. They could have spent several days on base two, and then learned upon their return that only four hours had elapsed at Central because for every twenty-four hours, for every revolution of Hermit around its own axis, eighteen months had elapsed at base two's latitude.

"Eva," Early called her over.

"Eva, everything that Seona said was correct. She really did spend twenty years there."

"I don't understand. But I can tell you this: That girl is not Oza."

Early stared at her in surprise.

"She resembles Oza strongly. It's an amazing resemblance. But she isn't Oza. Henry was too excited to notice anything when he first saw her. After all, it was a miracle that she had survived. Later he thought that Oza had lost her mind. I'm sure he will notice the difference himself very soon. . . . So, you say she lived there twenty years? When I realized that this wasn't Oza, I wondered if those strangers hadn't somehow reproduced Oza for their own purposes. I couldn't think of any other possible explanation. But if you say . . . well, that means she's Oza's daughter. And everything she's been saying is true."

"Well, we're making some progress. But there's still a great deal to be explained. Eva, take this data and the program on time acceleration at different latitudes on Hermit, and run them through the computer. I'm afraid the results will be shocking. Now I'm going to find out from Henry where they intersected the energy zones. It could turn out that these are neither energy thresholds nor barriers."

Early left communications headquarters and, after passing through several rooms, opened the door of the recording laboratory. Henry had been assigned to listen to the recorded conversations with Central of their crossings of the energy barriers.

Henry sat there with his head resting on the editing table. Around him were strewn memory crystals and magnetic tapes, and an empty cassette recorder was turning.

"Henry," Early touched him on the shoulder. "I have something to tell you. . . . Henry, listen carefully, it's not going to be easy for you to take. . . . Brace yourself. . . . That woman is not Oza!"

Raising his pale, worn face, he nodded several times. "I know, Early. It's my daughter, Seona. Oza's ring contained a storage crystal. Seona gave it to me. Oza told me everything."

"I'm sorry, Henry."

Early stood there for another instant and left the room in silence. Seconds later he returned. "Oh, Henry, I wanted to ask you something. At what latitudes did you intersect the energy barriers?"

Henry named the latitudes and added, "But those weren't energy barriers."

"I suspected as much."

"They were actually the boundaries of regions in which time flowed at different rates. The further the distance from the equator, the faster it flows. Listen to this."

He stopped the turning recorder, inserted a cassette, and turned the machine on again. A sharp, high whine tore through the laboratory.

That's Nik's voice at the very lowest frequency. Now listen. . . ."

He changed the speed.

"Come in, Wirt!" came a voice through the speaker. "Traikov calling. Come in, Wirt!" the voice repeated over and over. "What's wrong?"

'Beyond the first threshold, time flows twenty times faster than our time here. I don't know how many times faster it flows beyond the second one. At base two it's five hundred times faster."

"That's why you were pinned down at each threshold. Time flows faster, and therefore a tremendous surge of energy is needed to pass into it. That's why *Violet* turned over without apparent cause. Its energy thrust was insufficient," reasoned Early.

"What are we going to do now?" asked Wirt.

"I'll give this data to Eva and she'll run it through the computer. When we get results, I'll tell Sven and Nik about it. What about Seona . . . what will you tell her?"

"I'll let her listen to this." Henry opened the hand holding the special ring. With his other hand he picked up a small recording instrument, and he and Sven left the laboratory together.

Early gave Eva the data for the computer. Henry sat down next to Seona. She smiled at him. It was obvious that she felt uncomfortable among strangers, kind as they were.

"Seona," said Henry, "I'm not going to explain anything to you. My name is Henry Wirt. I want you to hear something very important. Listen carefully." He placed the ring in the recording device and turned on the instrument. A sad, soft voice began to speak:

"Hello, Henry darling."

Early took Eva's arm and they left the room.

"I'd like to determine the age of Ezra's and Hume's remains," said Early. "This must be done."

"I'll help you."

"No, I'll do it myself. It's not very difficult. But I don't know where the lab is."

"You'll have to take this corridor to the northern wing. You'll see a sign there."

"Eva, the computer's results should be ready very soon. Watch for them."

"I feel very awkward about going in there now. I'll walk you to the lab."

"Silly girl! I don't have that far to go."

"I'll walk you there anyway."

They had gone only a few dozen steps when a door opened and Henry shouted after them, "Hey, where did you disappear to?"

"Go on in, Eva. It's OK now. I'll be back soon."

Early walked hesitantly through the corridor, stumbling now and then from fatigue. When he reached the point where the equatorial line intersected the corridor, his curiosity got the better of him and he glanced into the engineering room. His expectations turned out to be correct. This room too was several hundred years old. Centuries of dust lay everywhere. Some two hundred meters down the corridor, he found the laboratory and borrowed a small instrument from it. Then, after taking the escalator to Central's uppermost tier, he stood for a few seconds next to the transparent dome, trying to make out the figures of Sven and Nik on the fourth energy tank, but he couldn't see anything.

In the main control room he encountered Ezra and Hume, who were forever arguing about something. But he no longer paid any attention to them. They lived in another time dimension.

Analysis of their remains indicated that they had died fifteen hundred years ago. Five minutes later Early was in the communications room. Henry wasn't there; Sven had summoned him. The strangers were up to something. Henry took the other half-track to the fourth cylinder.

Eva was in a dreadful state. "Early! I can't believe it. On base twenty, almost sixty years have passed! They've been dead a long time!"

19.

Sven and Nik jumped into the elevator and rode down. On the way, Sven filled in Early by radio.

"Early! Their half-track is waiting; they're coming down from the cylinder. I have a feeling they're headed for Central. We're going down to our half-tracks, too."

"Go back to Central. Don't let them see you!"

But they had already been spotted. The dual-turreted half-track with a dozen gun barrels aimed in different directions suddenly leaped out from behind the fourth cylinder. Henry swerved his vehicle across the road, blocking it, to give Sven and Nik a chance to duck behind the armor of their half-track. Evidently the strangers had not expected to meet anyone, and their half-track braked abruptly, rocking on its springs. Henry moved ahead. A heavy blaster lay alongside him on the seat, but he wouldn't be able to handle the weapon and the vehicle at the same time. His half-track was not a military vehicle.

For several minutes, the strangers did not expose themselves. It was so quiet, it seemed almost as if their vehicle were deserted. In that brief interval, Sven managed to pull up alongside Henry's vehicle. Then the strangers' half-track moved forward a short distance. Sven and Henry did the same. The distance between the vehicles shortened by a few meters. Nik remained in constant contact with Early.

"Go back! Go back to Central!" shouted Early.

"Then they'll follow us there," replied Nik.

"Let them! Here we outnumber them two to one."

"OK."

The strangers did not display any aggressive behavior. The barrels of an unfamiliar weapon disappeared one after another from the turrets. Then one of the half-track's hatches opened and a man with bronzed skin that shone like gold in the rays of the setting sun appeared. He shouted something unintelligible.

"Early, should we go out too?" asked Traikov.

"Wait! Has Henry told you yet what else we've learned?"

"Briefly."

"OK, then, listen. Those strangers have absolutely nothing to do with what's been going on here. It was already too late when Ezra sent out the signal for emergency evacuation. The acceleration of time at Hermit's poles jumped enormously at one bound. At base twenty, time flowed twenty times faster than here, at Central, and twenty times slower at the south pole. The gradient diminished gradually toward the equator. This was the cause of the unprecedented hurricane. The air from the zones of rapid time flow rushed into adjoining zones where time flowed more slowly. Almost instantaneously the hurricane engulfed the entire northern hemisphere. Then the smooth curve of time change acceleration altered step by step. Even now violent snowstorms are raging at the boundaries. All the bases were destroyed almost instantly. The rain forest finished the job. We don't know what caused the time jump.

"And now, the question of these strangers. They couldn't have gotten here from the bases, because if anyone there survived the hurricane, they would no longer be alive . . . not after several decades or centuries. These strangers have nothing to do with Hermit."

The man with bronzed skin was now standing in front of Henry's half-track and pointing to something.

"I think he wants us to let him into our half-track," said Henry. "Should we? He's unarmed. And they appear to be peacefully inclined."

"First find out what he wants," replied Early.

Henry stuck his head through the hatch and, using sign language, asked the stranger what he wanted. There was no response. Then Henry asked directly, "What do you want at Central?"

The bronze-skinned man walked right up to the half-track. Henry repeated his question.

"Kozales! We're looking for Kozales!"

For an instant Henry was dumbfounded. Recovering from the shock, he spoke into the microphone, "Early! They're asking for you."

"Me? Do they speak our language?"

"Whatever . . . I understood him," replied Henry and he motioned to the man to climb into his half-track.

In a few minutes they were at Central Station's main entrance.

Both men were silent. Henry led the stranger to the communications room.

Somewhat fearfully the stranger crossed the threshold and said, "How do you do! I would like to see Early Kozales."

"I am Kozales," replied Early, rising to meet him.

The stranger walked up to him briskly and extended his hand. Early shook it distrustfully.

"We've been traveling toward Central for nearly three hundred years," said the stranger. "At any rate three hundred years have passed in Bigee City. Konstak sent us. True, he's dead now. He died a very long time ago. But he left a program for us to carry out. There was another expedition before our time. Evidently they never reached their destination, since I see it still exists," he spread his hands.

"What still exists?" asked Early.

"This station. We'll have to blow it up. That's what is says in Konstak's program."

"Who is this Konstak, and what is Bigee City?"

"Konstak was a great scientist. You mean you've never heard of him?"

"If it's taken you three hundred years to get here, how the devil would I know him? I wasn't around then. And this Bigee place? Is it a planet?"

The stranger shook his head.

"Is it a solar system?"

"No. . . ."

"Then what is it? A galaxy?"

"No, . . . I can show you on a globe."

Unfortunately there was none nearby.

"You see, it's a former base. At one time it took only ten hours to get there from Central. Now it takes three hundred years. We aren't physicists. We're only executing Konstak's program. It states in the program that if we are unable to blow up the cylinders ourselves, we must find Kozales. We have a letter. It's a very old one. It must be handled very carefully. Konstak himself wrote it."

"How did you get here from Bigee City?"

"In half-tracks. We had five, but only one reached here. The others perished."

Early's head began to spin. So these chaps are from base twenty! But after three hundred years, all of them should be dead. Then where the devil could they have come from?

"Konstak! Why that's Konrad Stakovsky!" shouted Early.

"That's right. Konrad Stakovsky. He usually called himself Konstak."

"Sven!" shouted Early into the microphone. "Bring your half-track here, and the half-track with those people. They are ours! From base twenty!"

"What do you mean, from base twenty? Another new theory?"

"No, Sven, it's my old one! It all makes sense now. Get them over here right away!"

The bronze-skinned man looked around embarrassedly.

"How many people in your half-track?" Early asked him.

"Eleven. I'm the twelfth. Eight died en route."

"What is your name?"

"Enrico."

"You're probably starving. And so are we. Eva and Seona! I'd like to ask you to do something . . ."

Before he finished the sentence, the women had switched on the automation for a meal.

A few minutes later, a noisy band of bronze-skinned people with blasters slung over their shoulders, burst into Central. Sven and Nik followed them distrustfully.

"Dump those toys!" Early told them.

When everyone had quieted down, Enrico began his story.

"A hurricane of unprecedented force struck immediately after the evacuation order was received on the base. The base was destroyed. It was the most populated of the bases. It had fourteen people. One of them was missing in the very first minutes of the hurricane. . . . The others managed to take cover in the station's underground rooms. They could not leave their subterranean quarters for five years. And it took thirty years for them to manage, more or less, to clear the rain forest from the base's territory. Then they were faced by famine. Konrad Stakovsky was dead by that time. Gradually they found ways to process the creepers and bagees into something edible. Then the forty-year-long winter and night began."

"But wouldn't everyone who lived on the base have died eventually?"

"From the very beginning, Konrad Stakovsky knew what had happened on Hermit and he left instructions that someone must get through to Central. The people who lived on the base then couldn't even dream of undertaking such a mission. And children were born. By the time we left thirty years later, there were about sixty people on the base. And now there are probably many more. But Hermit is destined to perish. A time generator has developed on Hermit. Its radiant ring passes along the equator.

When the time at Hermit's pole coincides with the time that has elapsed in this ring, a saturation point will be reached and Hermit will explode. Stakovsky did not know when that would happen."

"In fifteen days," said Early, "the radiant ring will be fifteen hundred years old."

"We'll have to blow up the ring over quite a great distance, and that includes the energy-storage tanks and Central. We've calculated the energy reserves, and they are sufficient. But we don't know how the tanks are connected to each other. No one on the base knew. We had no engineers. But we can't wait fifteen days. Central must be blown up as soon as possible. Bigee City will barely make ends meet and will have hard times."

"We can airlift food to them by helicopter," suggested Sven.

"No, we can't," said Early. "The energy barrier there is too high."

"What about *Violet*?"

"*Violet* can land only at low velocity. Besides, Bigee hasn't a landing pad."

The work began after dinner. Under Early's guidance, *Violet* was loaded with valuable instruments, equipment, and research materials—everything needed by Hermit's colony after Central's destruction for its existence on *Violet* while awaiting its rendezvous with *Warsaw*.

Diagrams of the connections between the tanks could not be found. This complicated matters: weeks could be spent trying to unravel the puzzle.

Early suddenly remembered the drawings on the rolls of paper he had seen Ezra and Hume holding. Now he was sure they lived in a different time dimension where no one and nothing existed except Central and the two of them. They realized what had happened to them because they were conducting this experiment. And Early suspected that it was an experiment. When they lost control of the experiment, they both realized the consequences.

Ezra and Hume made their most frequent appearances in the main control room and the communications quarters, as if assuming that people would be present. Often they unrolled the diagram, now nonexistent for the living, as if inviting them to copy it. By sundown Sven had succeeded in doing this.

By midnight, everything had been prepared for the explosion.

Traikov was supposed to take *Violet* up and remain in orbit until a landing pad could be prepared somewhere. The rest would leave in helicopters: the aircraft would be needed in the future. Konrad Stakovsky had laid out the plan for blowing up the storage tanks in such a way that the acceleration or deceleration of time would proceed at a steady rate rather than by leaps. A second destructive hurricane had to be avoided.

Violet lifted off at the beginning of the first night. Before long Traikov's calm voice was heard down below, "Everything's OK."

Then two cargo helicopters with passengers followed. Early and Sven piloted them. The rest of the helicopters were programmed for pilotless flight. Eva and several people from base twenty flew with Early.

"Hey, I remember!" Suddenly they heard Traikov's voice. "Now I remember where I saw those swings! On the walls at Central . . . linear sketches! Right on the equator is a straight line parallel to the ground. The slope of the angle of those swings increases as you travel farther north or south. And the symbol for the angle varies. At the north pole it's positive, at the south, negative."

"Too bad it's too late to go back," said Early. "Strange, isn't it? Everyone saw them, but it made no impression."

The helicopters flew in close formation, moving eastward along the equator and turning slightly toward the north.

20.

They were about five hundred kilometers from Central when an explosion rang out. The evening sky was lit up by a brilliant flash.

One hour later a voice came through the ether, "Why an emergency evacuation! Ezra, what the hell is going on there?"

This had come from base twenty, located almost at the south pole. For them, only a few minutes had elapsed since the beginning of the catastrophe.

Early smiled nervously.

"Eva, tell everyone to stay in their seats. Henry will send them a message."

Then they headed toward base twenty.

Early put the aircraft on automatic pilot and took two letters from his pocket. One was from Konrad Stakovsky, the other from Lei.

"Dear Early," wrote Lei. "How much I wanted to see you again. . . ."

He folded the letter, started to tear it up, but changed his mind, and placed it in Eva's lap.

"You'll read it some day," he said.

She shook her head.

"Dear Early," wrote Konrad Stakovsky. "We achieved our goal after all. We can control time. I am certain that you will continue our work. I am envisioning a setup where on one pole, time will accelerate, and on the other, slow down. Now, in a matter of seconds, you will be able to perform experiments that once required years. I cannot even imagine how far humanity will progress now that time has been tamed and compelled to flow at its discretion.

". . . It's too bad that this discovery caused a catastrophe. But I am confident that you will continue the work and I shall try to help you. . . .

"If your passion for journalism has overpowered the physicist in you, then here's material for your book.

"We never did find out what kind of civilization had left its traces on Hermit. Maybe there never was another civilization? Maybe twenty years hence this system will be erected on Earth and, having been moved forward in time, will turn out to have been brought here, to Hermit. Indeed, research related to attempts to control time has been going on for years on Earth. Ezra and Hume lived for this idea. For a long time we could not understand the purpose of Central, its energy-storage tanks and

the bases. Then we discovered Hermit's radiant ring and gradually came to the conclusion that in this setting one could verify
experimentally the reciprocal transformation of space and time.
Basically, the expedition attempted to find out who Hermit's
former occupants were. Notes were found in one of Central's
many rooms, regular working notes from which you can't get
much, but we managed to get something. We realized that someone was trying to do experiments involving space and time. The
strangest thing was that the working notes were written in Earth
language. And your signature appeared in several places. I spoke
with Lei. She said that she didn't have any notes, documents, or
anything else of yours. I couldn't understand where you could
have worked on similar experiments. I, for one, had no knowledge
of them.

The preparations for our experiment were lengthy and meticulous. Four days after *Violet* lifted off from Hermit, Ezra insisted
that the experiment could begin.

"Only Ezra, Hume, and Eva remained on Hermit. The rest had
gone to the bases in helicopters. This was supposed to be a tremendous experiment and we didn't have enough people.

"On the eleventh at 0700, all twenty bases reported that they
were ready for the experiment to begin. It began at 0715. Ezra
issued the order on the transmitter and turned on the energy-storage tanks. Hume quickly processed the results of the experiment
on the computer and inserted a correction into the experiment's
program.

"At approximately 0800 everything proceeded as it had in the
preliminary small-scale tests. . . . The tanks expended seventy
percent of the energy, and no change was observed in the curva-
ture of space in Hermit's vicinity. Ezra began to get nervous. At
approximately 0803 the instruments registered a curving of space.
Time acceleration was equal to zero. Ezra decided to terminate
the experiment. Hume insisted on continuing it. A minute later
their argument was academic. The experiment had gone out of
control. Ezra turned off the energy source, but the curving of
space remained. All twenty bases confirmed this. Then the curva-

ture disappeared and time acceleration, particularly noticeable at the equator, began. There was no time acceleration at the poles. At 0810, time acceleration ceased, and the instruments registered a curving of space. The time acceleration was very slight, one second per hour.

"Ezra radioed everyone that the experiment had gone out of control, and he ordered immediate evacuation to Central.

"The rocking of the space–time system continued for another twenty-two minutes. . . . Then the acceleration of time began to increase at an incredible rate. Communications between the bases and Central broke off. Five years have passed and we still haven't emerged from our subterranean quarters. Early, what if these were *your* future working notes? Then we won't have to look for that other civilization; indeed, then we have done all this ourselves. Early, you must learn how to control time. . . ."

Base two was now visible ahead.

"Early," said Henry, "I'd like to linger here for a few minutes. . . . You understand, don't you?"

"Of course, Henry." Early turned off the microphone.

Fourteen helicopters hovered, and one, banking steeply, went in for a landing. In the rays of the setting sun it looked like a small golden beetle.